CONTENTS

CW01498413

Long Road Home - A Post-Apocalyptic Next-World Series

Volume 1

Lance K Ewing

COPYRIGHT

*L**ong Road Home A Post-Apocalyptic Next-World Book Series***

Book 1

Copyright © 2022 by Lance K. Ewing

The characters and events in this book are fictitious.

Any similarity to real persons, living or dead, is coincidental

and not intended by the author.

All rights reserved. The scanning, uploading and distribution of this book without permission is a theft of the author's intellectual property.

If you would like permission to use material from the book

lancekewingauthor@gmail.com.

Thank you for your support of authors' rights.

First Kindle edition: March 2022

ISBN: 978-0-9996765-6-1 (paperback)

Printed in the United States of America

DEDICATION

Dedication

To my wife, Hannah, our three awesome crazy boys, Hudson, Jax and Hendrix, and to my mom, Shareen, for her tireless editing.

Thank you to my brother, Kyle, who is always the most interested in my work.

To the readers who took a chance on a new author without knowing if there would be a second series.

Thank you to all readers who leave honest reviews on Amazon, Goodreads and Audible, making this continued series possible.

Chapter One Heading to Denver, Colorado

The flight into Denver took two and a half hours from Los Angeles, and I was happy for the break from school. Our official Winter Break didn't start until December 22nd, but nobody would miss a few third-year students for a week in November. Beth and I sat in the back of the plane with Shanan. Beth didn't like it, complaining that it took too long to wait when exiting.

"Why can't we be up front, in First Class, with our friends?" Beth asked. "I know your parents can afford it."

I looked at her with a that's-not-cool face; nodding towards our only friend without rich parents. Shanan just smiled.

Beth had flown with me before and knew I always sat in the back. I can't remember where I read it, but more than one credible source said the safest place during a plane crash is in the back. Plus, the one thing I hated most about traveling was the arrival.

"Please, no standing in the aisle" would come the call from the head Flight Attendant, and "Wait until the plane comes to a complete stop before gathering your belongings."

Not once, or a few times, but every single time the plane stopped at the exit ramp, every adult in aisle seats would stand, with a few jerks carrying bags in hand, trying to get a few rows up in front of me. Others pretended to get their bags from the overhead compartments, knowing full well they dumped their bag in a bin somewhere in front of them, further contributing to the traffic jam headed that way. Not me, though. I wait coolly in the back of the plane and still make it off less than five minutes behind the very first guy.

* * * *

"If you look out the left side of the aircraft, you will see the magnificent Grand Canyon," announced the Flight Attendant, "and soon you will see the fabulous Las Vegas strip, also on your left. We'll just make a quick stop if anyone wants to hit the blackja..."

Wham! It felt like something was pushing the plane down from above.

"Fasten your seatbelts!" I could hear the Captain saying over the loudspeaker.

My stomach dropped as we descended rapidly for a few seconds, which felt like hours. People around me were screaming and Beth grabbed my arm tightly. I looked across her to Shanan, who I knew wasn't a great flyer in the best of circumstances. She was glued to the window and in a fetal position. Drinks flew about the cabin, and pretzels were flying like ninja stars front to back. *Twenty years ago*, I thought, *TV dinners, peanuts and cigarettes from the smokers in the back of the plane would be added to the 30,000-foot buffet of flying objects.*

We sat in the very last row, just in front of the bathrooms, and I could hear banging on the wall behind me—presumably the woman and a small child she had taken in with her only moments before. As we leveled out again, the cabin was a mess and Shanan sat crying in the corner.

"Are you all right?" I asked her, reaching across to touch her shoulder.

"She will be fine!" snapped Beth, pulling my arm away.

"I'm okay, Alex," she replied. "Just scared is all."

"All right. I'll be back in a minute," I told her.

I stood and knocked on the bathroom door to check on the mother and child. There was no answer, so I knocked again.

"Ma'am, can I help you two with anything?" I said, trying not to sound like a weirdo outside the women's bathroom.

"They're fine," called out Beth. "Just sit down already."

"No," I stated. "I heard a loud bang, and I want to make sure they are all right."

Knocking again, I saw the slow slide of the "Occupied" lever going across and the zig-zag door folding in on itself.

"We're okay, I think," called the lady as she exited the bathroom slowly, with her daughter crying loudly.

I sat back in my seat, watching them head back towards the middle of the plane and wondering if there would be an explanation from the Pilot of what happened. As it turned out, we would get none.

"Look, there's Vegas," I pointed out thirty minutes later, with no response.

* * * *

We met up with our friends in the Denver International Airport Baggage Claim, happy that all of our luggage had come through. Considering there were six of us with atypical luggage, I wasn't all that confident it would happen. My dad hooked us up with a Suburban from an off-airport rental place, with a driver, and they were waiting just outside Baggage Claim.

"How was First Class?" Beth asked the others.

"Free drinks and plenty of legroom," replied Trey. "What's not to like?"

What a jerk, I thought, *leaving his girlfriend Shanan to sit back with us in Coach.* I watched as she kept cool and didn't react.

"All the cool people sit in back," I joked, "and we didn't die."

"Yeah, neither did we, but I had my own TV and six of those little Scotches," added Scott.

"Well, we know who's not driving!" I said, getting a smile out of Shanan and a look from Beth.

A middle-aged black man in a black three-piece suit stepped out of the driver's side of the van and introduced himself.

"Hello, everyone. My name is Grady Parker, but you can just call me 'Mr. Parker.'"

"Hi, I'm Alexander Kade," I said, reaching out my hand.

"But he prefers Alex," chimed in Shanan, getting a look from Beth.

"Alex is fine, and this is Shanan O'Sullivan, Beth Johns…"

"I think first names will do," chimed in Beth. "Let's get this show on the road!"

"Trey," I continued, "Scotland III, but we just call him Scott, whether he likes it or not; and finally, Jo, on the end," I pointed out.

"It's good to meet you all. And Alex, did you know your father was under my command in Desert Storm?"

"Yes, sir," I responded, "and he said you're the only reason he made it back home."

"Well, I don't know about that, but he was a fine soldier and a good man. He's hired me to help you all get to where you need to go."

"I wasn't expecting you to be driving us, but thank you," I replied.

"What's next, Grady?" asked Trey.

"It's 'Mr. Parker,' son," he responded, like a military man. "Are we clear on that?"

"Whatever," replied Trey.

"It's 'Yes, sir,' son, or I drive away right now and you're all on your own."

I was getting annoyed at Trey's self-righteous attitude and started to weigh in when Shanan took over.

"Trey, Mr. Parker and countless other men and women have fought for all our freedom. They are the only reason we get to go to some fancy film school and not worry about anything else. They fight over there," she added, pointing off to the east, "so we don't have to here. Have some common respect. You can be so obtuse sometimes."

That's the Shanan I remembered, and I was suddenly regretting breaking up with her last year.

"Would you like to know what's next, Trey?" Mr. Parker asked.

"Yes, sir," he replied quietly.

"Okay, everyone. As I've mentioned, Alex's father hired my business to escort you to and from your destination. I have helped him secure a cabin owned by the State and rarely lent out anymore. I typically run the office, but hell, it's good to get out and drive every once in a while. So, we are headed high up in the Rocky Mountains, with a stop for the night in Estes Park."

"Why can't we just go straight to the cabin tonight?" asked Trey.

"You can, as long as you don't mind hiking in the dark. In case you didn't already hear, you don't just drive up to this particular cabin; you have to hike in. By the time we made it up to the trailhead, it would be nearly dark already."

"I'm game," said Trey. "Who's with me?" None of us raised our hands, not even Shanan.

"Or we could hear Mr. Parker's plan," I interjected.

"Thank you, Alex. Your father has secured three rooms for you all, as he said you all are couples. I don't care who sleeps where but you have three rooms between the six of you."

"Where are we staying, sir," I asked, hoping it wasn't the place I was thinking of.

"It's called the Stanley Hotel," he responded.

"Crap!" I meant to say under my breath, but all apparently heard it.

"Is something wrong, Alex?" he asked.

"No, I'm just surprised is all."

I looked out of my peripheral vision to see Trey asking Shanan what was wrong. The moment was awkward for a few of us, for sure, with only Shanan and me knowing the real story.

"Alex, your dad reserved room 217 for you, the very same room horror author Stephen King stayed in and used as an inspiration for the book and eventually two movie versions of *The Shining*."

"I saw the first one," said Jo, "and I remember the room number being different. Number 237, I believe."

"Good memory," replied Mr. Parker. "The story says King stayed in room 217, but somebody asked the movie director to change it to 237. Now, I don't know why, but the whole place is kind of creepy, if you ask me. Except for the bar, that is," he added, laughing. "Did you know that the Stanley bar was used in the filming of the first *Dumb and Dumber* movie?"

Most replied no, with the exception of Shanan and me. We learned about it on our trip out here two years ago, where I had asked her to marry me just 90 feet outside the Cascades Restaurant and Bar, next to a running stream surrounded by rock formations.

"Sit back and relax. We will be in Estes Park in a couple of hours," announced Mr. Parker.

* * * *

I did as instructed and put my headphones on, hoping to drown out the conversation. Shanan got a call on her cell and ducked into the far corner of the SUV to take it. With my music on and classic Lynyrd Skynyrd's "Free Bird" playing, I couldn't hear a thing. Minutes later, she was waving at me, holding up her cell phone.

I took off my headphones as she said, "It's my dad and he wants to talk to you."

I'm smart enough to know you always talk to a Colonel on the phone when asked, even if you're not in the military. Her cell was passed down to me through several hands.

I put it to my ear, pausing for a moment before answering, "Yes, sir."

"Alex, listen closely. Can my daughter hear me over the phone?"

"No, sir," I replied. "Not right now."

"Okay. You know, I always liked you and even treated you like a son."

"Yes, sir."

"I was disappointed about what happened with you two, but you already know that. Listen, I need you to watch out for my daughter over the next week, and even a month or two beyond that. Now smile and nod your head, so your friends think we're just talking sports."

I did as instructed and didn't ask even one of the thousand questions I had in my head.

"Where exactly are you headed?" the Colonel asked. "And when will you arrive?"

"Near Fern Lake in Colorado, sir—above Estes Park."

"With arrival sometime tomorrow around 2 p.m.," called Mr. Parker from the front, as if he had heard my entire conversation.

"We are staying at the Stanley Hotel tonight, I'm told, and then up to the cabin for six days before heading back to school."

"Isn't that where you two kids stayed before?" he asked.

"Yes, sir," I replied, feeling uncomfortable both talking to him and with Beth staring at me.

I always hated when one person talked on their cell phone when surrounded by others, not caring about being rude, like in an elevator or on a plane before takeoff. Now I was that guy, but I didn't have much choice in it.

"Is Trey with you guys?"

"Yes, sir," I responded, hoping to keep the conversation one-sided.

"All right. I can't trust that guy, so listen closely, Alex. There is something big happening soon, and I can't discuss any details on this phone right..."

"Hello?" I said, hearing only static. "Hello, sir... Are you there?"

"Call him back," I told Shanan, passing the phone down to her.

"Hurry up, guys, and give her the phone." I said, getting a "Calm down!" out of Beth and a "What the hell?" out of Trey.

Shanan tried several times to reach him, with no luck, and gave me a worried look.

"What was all that about?" asked Beth.

"Nothing," I responded. "It was nothing."

"Bull!" replied Trey, turning back around and putting on his headphones.

"Is everything okay, Alex?" asked Mr. Parker.

"Yes, sir," I responded. "I'm sure it will be."

* * * * * * *

CHAPTER TWO HEADED TO ESTES PARK

"There are two main routes up to Estes Park," called out Mr. Parker as we drove north on Interstate 25 from the airport in Denver.

I could see the mountains out my left-side window and had forgotten how magnificent they truly are.

"The first route," he continued, "is a little shorter and cuts up through a town called Lyons, and the other route goes through the town of Loveland and up the Big Thompson Canyon. Both are scenic, and we should see a lot of wildlife either way."

"The canyon!" blurted out Shanan. "I want to go up the canyon, please."

"The canyon it is, then," I said aloud, remembering it was the way she and I had come last time.

We traveled another 45 minutes before entering the massive canyon carved into the mountain and winding like a snake to an elevation of 7,500 feet above sea level. The Big Thompson River rushed down the canyon over large boulders.

"Look for bighorn sheep!" called out Mr. Parker. "Also deer and elk, and maybe a few wild turkeys."

"What about grizzly bears?" asked Jo.

"Nope, none of those up here. There are a fair number of black bears around but not this time of year. They start to hibernate around late October and early November, so you likely just missed them."

"What about a moose and wolves?" she asked. "Do they live up here?"

"Yes, ma'am," he responded. "The moose do, but they are up in Rocky Mountain National Park. We may see one tomorrow. No wolves, but there are plenty of coyotes running around, and more than a few mountain lions as well."

"Don't forget about Big Foot!" I added.

"Well, that's comforting," said Beth sarcastically. "Did anyone bring a gun?"

No one spoke up.

"That's what I thought... I knew we should have just gone to Cancun instead. We would be on the beach right now," she added.

I caught Mr. Parker's eye in the rearview mirror, and he gave me the universal "I'm sorry" look that told me she wasn't just annoying me with her complaining.

"Does anyone know the history of this canyon from back in the 1970s?" asked Mr. Parker, changing the subject. With no hands raised, he continued. "Back on July 31, 1976, the Big Thompson Flood killed 144 people and injured nearly 150 more, and the flood happened at night. Unusual weather allowed a flash storm to stall over the canyon, dumping water and creating frequent lightning strikes. Fourteen inches of rain fell in the canyon in just four hours. A 20-foot wall of water careened down the canyon, taking stores, houses, cars, livestock, and people. Most of the reported 4,000 people in the canyon (mostly camping tourists) were able to evacuate or climb to safety. Others were swept away in their cars or homes, never to be heard from again. There were bodies recovered up to 25 miles downriver."

"That's crazy," I said aloud, not having heard that the last time we were here.

Rounding the last corner, the town of Estes Park came into view, first with the dam on the front side, and soon after, the quieted downtown.

"In the summer months, nearly four million people visit Rocky Mountain National Park, with many coming through this little town of only 5,000 full-time residents," added Mr. Parker.

"Up on your right—is that the Overlook Hotel?" blurted out Scott.

"Well, kind of," replied Mr. Parker. "You see, the Stanley Hotel bore the idea for the book and subsequent movies by Stephen King. Filming took place in multiple locations for the original movie, including studios in England and the Timberline Lodge on Mount Hood in Oregon. In the second adaptation, with Rebecca De Mornay, Steven Weber and Elliott Gould in 1997, the three-episode made-for-TV series, was shot right here at the Stanley. Both are worth a watch when you get the chance."

* * * *

Mr. Parker pulled up to the guard shack, flashing some sort of badge to be waved through.

"Here we are," he announced. "There's an outdoor pool, much more popular in the summer months. There is also a restaurant, bar, and gift shop."

"What's the nightlife like, sir?" asked Trey, being completely serious.

"The restaurants close early this time of year, and there are a few bars open late on the main drag."

"I say we go barhopping!" Trey exclaimed. "We've got our driver already."

"Two things just to keep in mind," said Mr. Parker. "I'm off duty in a few minutes, and my vehicle is staying here tonight. Tell me to take your luggage, and you will see firsthand how a United States Sergeant treats hostiles."

"Looks like you're on your own, Trey," I said, loud enough for all to hear.

"Not completely," he replied, making an obvious gesture of putting his arm around Shanan.

We unloaded our gear, and it seemed odd bringing backpacks into a four-star hotel. As promised, Beth and I had Room 217, with Shanan and Trey right next door, and Scott and Jo on a different floor.

"Can I buy you a drink, Mr. Parker?" I asked.

"Sure! I'll meet you in the bar in about ten," he replied.

* * * *

I informed Beth that I would be back in a few and she would have some time to get ready for dinner.

Sitting with my father's old friend and Commander, we talked about how he and my dad first met and had remained friends since, if only by telephone. He told me about his family and the luxury car rental business he started after the service, which had grown to six locations. And he asked me to call him Grady.

"All right. Your turn," he said. "You've got an interesting group you're traveling with. I've always been good at reading people, so let me see if I've got this straight. I know your father is in oil and gas, just like your grandfather was, but you're studying film in California, I hear."

"Yes, sir. I'm the one to break tradition, I guess, but my dad and I have an understanding that if I don't make it, I'll work with him."

"What are you gentlemen drinking?" asked the friendly bartender.

"Scotch on the rocks for me," said Grady. "The twelve-year up on the top," he continued, pointing to the bottle.

"Make that two, please," I added handing him my ID before being asked.

"Let's see," he started again. "Shanan—a little while back I heard you were engaged to a beautiful redhead who was level-headed and also well liked by your parents. I'm guessing by the way you two interact, that's her."

"Yes, sir. That's her—Shanan O'Sullivan. Doesn't get more Irish than that. She is a classically beautiful redhead who can drink me under the table, but only if challenged! We got engaged a little over a year ago right outside the bar here, and I just got cold feet, I guess, a few months later and called the whole thing off."

"I see," he responded, taking a sip of his drink, seemingly interested in the conversation.

"That's a good pour," he said, thanking the bartender. He paused, looking at me, and had my undivided attention. "When I was about your age, I thought maybe I could do better than the one I had. I was wrong, and it took me two more years to get mine back. When I did, I married her in three weeks. In all these years, I have never once regretted that decision. So, Shanan gets together with the Trey fella and you with Beth, but you're all friends?"

"Yeah, it's complicated, but the bottom line is those two are the only ones of our group not from Texas. Trey is from Los Angeles—for sure not my friend and, near as I can tell, is Shanan's rebound guy who could walk away tomorrow without her caring all that much. Beth is, well, you can see that she's like an 11 on a 1-10 hot scale, but that perk comes with a lot of baggage."

I paused, sipping my perfect drink with the ice just starting to melt.

Grady laughed. "I saw that...about Beth, that is."

"Scott, I continued, comes from a long line of family members who own like 1/8 of all the commercial real estate in Dallas. He has more money than he knows what to do with, but he's all right; we grew up together. His girlfriend, Jo, reminds me of that girl by the same name from those old *Facts of Life* reruns. The pretty girl next door, who can also fix your truck."

We both laughed. "And I got stuck with Blair, the hot blonde with all the problems," I added quietly.

"I think you are all in for an interesting week, cooped up in a small cabin together," Grady said, chuckling. "Beth was right about one thing, though," he said, handing me a soft-case tackle box.

"Take a look, but discreetly," he told me.

I opened it carefully to see a Ruger SR40C compact semiautomatic pistol, with two extra magazines and a box of ammo.

"I want this back when I pick you guys up next week," he added. "And don't forget, no target shooting in the Park. This is only for an emergency, understood?"

"Yes, sir, and thank you."

"I left something else up at the cabin. Just leave it there when you head back down."

He was gone before I could ask what it was. As it turned out, I would forget to ask him later.

* * * *

Trey took off for downtown without Shanan, who refused to leave the hotel. Beth was reluctant about her joining us for dinner but relaxed a bit when Scott and Jo asked to come along. We all had drinks, mindful of the hike we had tomorrow.

I sent a steak, medium rare, the best cut of Wagu beef the restaurant had to offer, up to Mr. Parker's room with a bottle of Glenlivet 18-year Scotch whiskey. I didn't have his room number, but discretely handed a $100 bill to a server, asking him to find out.

"I want to make sure it gets to the right room," I told him.

"How would I do that?" the young server asked.

"Ask him his rank," I told him.

Thirty minutes later he came back by, whispering, "Sarge says thank you, Alex."

* * * *

The five of us tabbed out around 11 p.m. and headed to our rooms, with no sign of Trey. Beth was taking off her makeup and listening to a podcast about the rise and fall of America's fascination with Jeffrey Epstein and his 2008 guilty plea.

"Did you know he had all kinds of famous people fly to his island called Little Saint James?" she asked.

"Yeah, I remember reading about that—politicians and celebrities, I think."

I had the inside of the bed, ironically facing the adjoining wall to Shanan's room. Saying goodnight, I turned out the lights, hoping Beth wouldn't want to mess around tonight. If there was one thing I knew about classic older hotels, it was that the walls were typically thin. I wasn't interested in making an awkward situation—even more so tonight. Luckily,

I fell asleep quickly, as it had been a particularly long day, waking up with yelling and banging on the wall closest to my side. A glance at the clock read 3:26 a.m.

I realized the walls were thin or Trey was out of control right next door.

Instinctively springing out of bed, I had put one leg into my jeans before tripping over a small end table, crashing to the floor. My right hand wiped the blood pouring from my nose, checking if it was straight. I had planned to grab a T-shirt from my opened backpack but skipped it, as the banging intensified. I walked barefoot into the hall.

"Come back here right now!" demanded Beth. "That's none of our business."

I ignored her, trying to hear what was being said. Sounds were muffled, and everything grew quiet as my nose bleed all but stopped. I waited for more than a minute, with nothing heard, before turning back towards our room.

A loud bang on the wall, followed by Shanan screaming, "Alex, help me!" stopped me in my tracks. I tried the door and found it locked. My first heel kick to the door didn't seem to do much, and I wished I had shoes on. A flashback of the *Karate Kid* movie, Part One—or was it Part Two?—stuck in my head. The second kick boomed through the typically quiet hotel hallway, causing a sharp pain in my heel.

Beth was now screaming at me to stop, and hotel room doors opened, one after the other, as guests peered out to view the commotion. I steadied for my third kick as the door flew open and Shanan ran out, crying hysterically. Running straight past her into the dimly lit room, I hit a stumbling Trey in the chest, driving him back into the far wall. With 40 pounds and 6 inches of height on him, I had the advantage but I didn't know if he could fight. He swung drunkenly at me, as I stepped aside with a turn and grabbed him from behind in a chokehold. While squeezing my right arm, I wrapped my legs around his, flattening him out. I gave one quick squeeze to his throat before loosening my grip.

"If you ever hurt her again," I whispered over both of our heavy breaths, "I'll kill you. Do you understand?"

"Let me go!" he demanded.

"That's not what I need to hear, giving another quick but decisive squeeze. Do you understand?"

"Yes, I understand. Now let me go!"

I released my hold, and he got up slowly, stumbling. The flashes of cameras and video in our faces from just outside the open door, and a few now inside the room, made me understand how celebrities could lose it sometimes when being bombarded with this, day in and day out. I was pretty sure of two things tonight. Shanan would be okay, and I would be on multiple social media platforms tomorrow. With only jeans on and blood covering my arms and chest, I must have looked like a crazed man.

Grady was just outside the room, talking with the hotel manager, who wanted Trey and me both kicked out of the hotel. Somehow, he convinced her to let us stay one night, with him taking responsibility for us both. Grady stayed outside Trey's room until he was sure he'd fallen asleep, and a calmed Shanan slept on the foldout in Scott and Jo's room on another floor. Beth was apparently not speaking to me, and I was too tired to worry about it tonight, opting for a quick shower. I had set the alarm for 6 a.m. and regretted that decision immediately.

* * * *

Forcing myself out of bed anyway, and with Beth still asleep, I decided to go for a walk. Approaching the hotel room door, there it was—the piece of paper facedown, as always was the case for the final bill. Typically, it would list the items purchased from the room charge and parking before adding in the incidentals of room service, movies, the minibar of course, and those couple of bottled waters you thought were complimentary. I had to laugh as I turned it over and saw that the final total was crossed out with bright red ink, reading "See Management." I stuffed it into my jean pocket and walked out the nearest side door for my morning walk.

Every vacation I had ever been on, even when I was just a kid, I would get up early every day and walk the area. It was something my grandfather said when I was just eight years old that stuck with me all these years.

He said, "Son, if you are lucky enough to visit a place you may never be back to, get up early before anyone else and walk the grounds. I call it the roundabout, just checking on what's around and remembering where you have been. You may forget everything else about the trip, but not that."

He was right, and I could recount the early mornings on every trip we took as a family since. Today would be no exception.

"I know this isn't what you meant, Grampa," I said aloud, looking up towards the sky, "but I'm walking the beat this morning, just like always." I could almost hear him say, "You're a good boy, Alex. You're a real good boy."

* * * *

Walking into the local coffee shop a quarter-mile away, downtown, with a large sign reading "Locals Always Welcome," the smile on my face was going to be obvious. I assumed they took this down during peak season, when the tourists descended like locusts on this small town, with nearly all needing their morning fix. I entered the crowded shop and was immediately asked where I was from and how long I would be staying in town.

I remembered from my last trip that Coloradoans, for the most part, don't mind Texans or Californians visiting, as long as they go home in a timely manner.

"I'm from Texas, but I'm just passing through is all. My family does not own any property in this state and we don't intend to do so," I stated, loud enough for most at the front bar to hear.

I was joking in my smart-ass way I had developed over the course of a lifetime, but today got several nods of approval from apparent locals.

They all started talking again until I answered the second question of where I was staying.

"The Stanley," I said in a normal voice, as the restaurant quieted.

"Did you see what happened last night?" asked a mother with two children in tow.

"Well...about that," I started to answer, as another man called out.

"I got the video from CNN right here!"

They all gathered around to view it, and more than a few looked back and forth from the video to me, like in the movies when somebody sees the face of the serial killer on TV as they are looking right at them.

"Wait," said another. "They have a statement from that Stephen King author fella who stayed in one of the rooms."

Are you kidding me? I thought—a statement from one of my favorite authors growing up about me fighting near his beloved room? *How is he even up this early?* I thought, remembering he lived in Bangor, Maine, and the time there was two hours ahead.

The phone in my pocket buzzed, and the screen said "Dad." I was relieved to have a distraction and ducked into a corner table to take the call.

"Hey, Dad. What's up?"

"Fox News, son. That's what's up, and apparently you're the lead story!"

"Dad, I can explain; it's all getting blown out of proportion."

"Just tell me what really happened, and we will get a plan together. I've already been in touch with an attorney up there, just in case."

I relayed the story to the one person who I could trust would understand.

"It sounds like you did the right thing, son," he acknowledged. "Keep an eye on Shanan around that guy."

"You really like her, don't you, Dad?"

"Yes, your mother and I always have."

"Why is it such a big deal—the scuffle, I mean? This kind of thing must happen often with all the eccentric celebrities and bands getting crazy in hotels all across the country."

"That's true, I'm sure," he said, adding, "They're saying it's the near 20th anniversary of the original movie *The Shining*. Any publicity from the Stanley Hotel to the author is good for ratings. And you just so happened to be staying in his famous room."

"I get the connection, Dad, and I'm sorry to drag you into this."

"Are you ready to come home?" he asked.

"No, father, we're good for the trip," I said, knowing he wouldn't want me to quit. He never quit, not at anything.

"You will be meeting Mr. Holman soon. He's a top-notch attorney, not just up there but across the country. I've known him by reputation for years, and we've hired him once or twice for the family business. I just didn't think he would show up on my lawyer search all the way up there in the Rockies. Anyway, do exactly what he tells you—nothing more and nothing less. Understood?"

"Yes, sir. I can do that."

"Okay. Stay safe, son, and give my best to Grady."

"Will do, Dad."

"I love you, Alex, and I think you're in for a hefty hotel bill. Put it on my card, and have a good trip."

"Thanks, Dad. I love you too!"

* * * *

I took my coffee to go and didn't answer any of the dozens of questions fired my way. The scene back at the Stanley was not the same as when I left. Fox News and CNN were not there, but outside there were a few crews up from Denver, talking with the manager I had seen up front last night.

"That's him! That's the guy!" they shouted, pointing to me as I walked up.

Crap, I thought. *I walked right into this one.*

"You're Alex, right?" asked a young reporter.

"Yes, that's right," I responded, trying to get past them, up the stairs and to the front door of the hotel.

"Can you confirm that there was a disturbance at or near Room 217, the one made famous by author Stephen King?"

"No, I cannot confirm anything like that."

"Then how would you explain this?" he asked, putting the scuffle last night on a 60-inch plasma mounted on a portable tripod.

I watched for a few seconds as it showed me putting a chokehold on Trey, with no one else in the shot. That was when I knew I would be doing some more explaining, but to people in uniforms.

The police were interviewing Trey, Shanan, Beth, and Mr. Parker just inside the lobby. Mr. Parker came over to me, pretending to hand me a coffee, and said, "Just tell them to talk to your lawyer and let your father handle it."

"Okay, I guess, but I didn't do anything wrong."

"I know, son. Just do what I tell you."

I was met by two officers out of earshot of anyone else.

"Do you want to tell us what happened last night?"

"No, officers," I responded as respectfully as possible. "I can get you in touch with my lawyer if you have any specific questions."

"Hello, officers," came a voice from behind me. "My name is Rick Holman, Attorney at Law. I've been retained on Alexander's behalf, and you can direct specific questions to me. Is my client under arrest?"

"Not at this time," one responded.

"That's good news. Officers, here's my card in case you need to get hold of me for any reason, day or night. Let's go, Alexander," he said, grabbing my shoulder.

"That's it?" I asked, walking with him.

"That's all for now, unless something changes."

"How did you get here so fast? I mean, I'm sure my dad hired you, right?"

"That's correct. And lucky for you, my office is right down the street. Plus, I know Grady here," reaching out to shake his hand as we approached, "from way back in the day. He actually filled me in on everything last night. I would have been here sooner, but I hit a bit of traffic."

"Traffic?" I asked, "in a sleepy mountain town in November?"

"We call anything up here that makes us late 'traffic.' Mine this morning was negotiating my hourly fee with your father. We're all good now, though, so don't worry about a thing and don't talk to anyone else about this outside of me, Grady, and your dad. Understood, Alexander?"

"Yes, sir. Can I still go camping?"

"Sure. We'll just need to meet when you come back down through here to see if there's anything else to do before you head home."

"That sounds promising, but like I'm also not out of the woods..."

"You made national news, Alexander—Fox, CNN, ABC—and probably every social media site in the country. Sure, it's great for my business but it makes it more complicated for you, and the Trey fellow also. I also need to speak with Shanan. Is she here?"

"Yes, sir. Right over there," I pointed. "The pretty one with red hair" just slipped out of my mouth, with a smile from Grady.

"Hold tight, and I'll be right back," said Mr. Holman.

"Is he her attorney now too?" I asked Grady.

"No. She doesn't need one, but she does need to be careful about what she says, for your and Trey's sake. Your father and I thought he should speak to her. Don't worry; she won't be getting a bill. There are a lot of eyes on this, and law enforcement up here is going to dot those i's and cross the t's—you can count on that."

"So, what now?" I asked.

"That's up to you," replied Grady. "What you have to do is run your father's credit card for the damage to the room, unless you are going to try to split it with Trey. After that, it's your call. I'm guessing your new attorney is going to ask you to stick around for a week or so, so you might as well enjoy your trip, but only if you're going to be okay with Trey."

"Nah, I'm not worried about it. Shanan won't let him get drunk enough up there to cause a scene. And I'm sure there's not a bar anywhere close."

"You're right about that!" Grady replied.

* * * *

Twenty minutes later, we were saying good-bye to Mr. Holman, and Grady promised to have me back in a week. The hotel tab, including dinner and drinks—along with a wall I knew we had put a hole in and a new door I was pretty sure I hadn't even dented—came to $12,596.19.

The hotel manager ran my credit card under the watchful eye of the officers on the scene.

"Sign right here, please."

I did as asked and walked back to the room.

"Let's get you all packed up. We leave out in 30 minutes," said Mr. Parker, "with a stop at the grocery store on the way up."

* * * * * * *

CHAPTER THREE ESTES PARK, COLORADO

We stopped at Safeway, the biggest grocery store in town, smack dab in the middle of an outdoor shopping center.

With the main dehydrated food already packed, and each with one water filter, we spread out on our own, breaking every rule about going into a grocery store hungry. Add in the fact that we would be in the deep woods for a week and most of us had our parents' credit cards, it was safe to say we went a bit overboard. Grady was engrossed in a conversation with his wife, who had seen the footage along with millions of other Americans. Even the President of the United States was caught off guard with a random question during a morning helicopter exit about what was now being called "The Rocky Mountain Wrestle."

"Well, I hope everything turned out okay, but all I can say is the kid's got good hands," the President remarked. Holding up his own hands, he was met with a round of applause and a soon-to-go-viral social media clip.

"These kids won't be getting too out of hand up there with 3.2 beer," Grady joked with his wife.

Colorado, as an apparent residual from the days of Prohibition, had a law that prohibited grocery and convenience stores across the state from selling full-strength beer and wine coolers. The alcohol by volume cap was 3.2 percent, certainly less than your average domestic beer and about half the alcohol as many microbrews. Coloradans knew you had to go to a liquor store to get the real stuff, but the tourists had no idea.

We all were caught up with our carts when Trey told Shanan his stomach was hurting and he needed to find a bathroom. Nobody noticed him skip out of the store and across a small parking lot to the liquor store, filling his small daypack with six bottles of hard liquor. Minutes later, he met back up with Shanan, as if nothing had happened.

Mr. Parker laughed as we loaded our grocery bags, one after another, in the back of the Suburban.

"This should be interesting," he said out loud. "Let's head out!" came the call.

* * * *

The drive high up into the Rocky Mountains was spectacular and, although I had seen it before, I felt like I was experiencing it for the very first time.

"This is incredible!" I said to Beth.

"It's just mountains," she replied. "What's the big deal?"

"You've got to be joking," chimed in Shanan. "It's just one of the biggest tourist destinations anywhere in the world, and we get to live in it for an entire week!"

The car was silent when I spoke up. "That's right."

"I hear you," added Scott, with a yes nod from Jo.

"Beth," said Mr. Parker. "I've been to a lot of places on this earth over the years, and I can tell you firsthand that this place here is in my top five...maybe even my top four!"

"What's your number one?" I asked, after she didn't respond.

"That's easy! Anywhere my wife is."

That comment got an "Awe" out of both Shanan and Jo.

"What about number two?" asked Shanan, joining in.

"Well, up until a few years ago, it was a fishing village in the far southwest corner of Mexico, called Zihuatanejo. You know, that town where that Andy guy and Morgan Freeman end up in *The Shawshank Redemption*."

"No way!" said Scott. "I thought that place was just made up."

"No. It's real, all right, and was really nice for a while. Now, its water is not what it used to be, so I would have to say my number two is called Saddle Ranch. We drove within about four miles of it when we first entered the canyon, coming up here. It's located in a lush valley, four miles from end to end, and backs right up to the foothills of these mountains."

"And number three?" I asked.

"Vegas, baby—old school, downtown at the Golden Nugget Resort!"

I laughed at that. "That's good to know," I replied.

"And this here is my number four spot in the world," added Mr. Parker.

"Up ahead, five miles or so, is the Bear Lake trailhead. From there, we will be hiking in with everything you want to take for a one-time trip.

"Just so there is no confusion," he continued, looking in the rearview. "Number one: I'll be hiking up with you, and in a week you will come down the same way and meet me where we start.

"Number two: I'll be wearing a light daypack with my water and a few personal snacks. Why is this important, you may ask? Because I won't be lugging any of your crap up the mountain. Everything you bought at the store goes up with you or back down the mountain to my refrigerator. We've got a 1.5- to 2-mile hike in, and we're lucky there's not much snow up here yet.

"Number three: there are dangers up here, from animals to accidents, with help being a long way off. A simple mishap with a kitchen knife, or maybe a misplaced fire, animal encounter, or even a fall while out hiking, can turn things from fun to serious in a hurry. So watch out for each other is all I'm saying.

"Last, I think—at least for now—I'll need to find us a new hotel to stay in on the way home, since a couple of you guys made the news!"

I looked two rows up at the back of Trey's head to see how he would respond, but he had his headphones on and didn't hear it. He didn't hear any of it...

* * * *

We pulled into a large parking lot, with only a few other cars occupying it.

"In the summer," said Mr. Parker, "this lot would be packed full with buses running back and forth from the lower lots all day long. Most people are just fair-weather fans, I guess," he added.

Packing the backpacks took more than 30 minutes, with Trey messing with his off to the side. We hadn't said one word to each other since last night, and I wondered how long it would last. *Maybe the whole trip*, I thought. As it turned out, I would be dead wrong.

"How much beer did we get?" asked Beth.

"One twelve-pack of cans," I told her, "and a bottle of Scotch I bought off the server last night."

"That's it?" she protested. "I hate Scotch—and not even one bottle of wine?"

"Nope, this is it," I told her, holding up two of her favorite bottles of wine I bought last night and had hidden in my pack. "Plus, we have to carry everything in on one trip. You heard him."

"Twelve beers and only two wines," she said, groaning and with that look of disgust that I saw more and more lately.

I thought I might end up single again when we got back, or "interested in women," as the social media sites would classify it. I got a nod from Grady and a smile out of Shanan so quick that nobody else caught it.

"Right this way," pointed Mr. Parker. "I'll take up the rear," he added, "so we don't lose anyone."

* * * *

It was early afternoon, right after lunch according to my watch, and the sun was shining.

"It's not too bad with the sun out," I said to Grady, as I fell back to talk.

"Colorado gets more than 300 days of sunshine each year," he replied.

"I didn't know that," I admitted, but it seemed plausible, given the weather today.

"I predict," he told me so no one could hear, "that all or at least some of you will come back down in a week with new hopes and dreams. I know it's none of my business, Alex, but Shanan adores you and I've known enough women in my life that I can tell you with confidence she is one to fight for."

"I know," I said, with a flash of her father telling me to watch out for her. Had she gotten hold of him again? With everything that happened, I forgot to ask.

"I broke her heart, and I don't want to do it again," I replied.

"Head left on that trail!" Grady called out, pointing up ahead.

"Remember what I told you, Alex. The right ones are easy to leave, but if you get the rare chance to get them back, you make it your mission to do so...

"All right, enough about that," he added. "Let's get back to the basics. What sort of outdoor skills do you have?"

"Not a lot, sir. Every time we were up in the mountains when I was growing up, we just asked the nanny for anything we needed. I took a weekend wilderness course with Shanan a few years ago but don't remember all that much... I mean, I can start a basic fire and build a lean-to if it comes down to it. I've been deep-sea fishing a few times with my dad, so I'm sure lake fishing can't be that hard."

He laughed. "Son, without a boat captain and sonar, you might swear there were no fish in these mountain lakes. What about hunting. Can you hunt?"

"I've been elk hunting up in Idaho," I said. "I killed a big male on my third day."

"That's good, but did you touch him?" Grady asked.

"I'm not sure what you mean."

"Did you skin him? Did you butcher him or pack him out?"

"Oh no. The guides did all that," I said robotically, just now realizing where he was going with this line of thinking.

"You're worried about us up here for a week?" I asked.

"Not exactly. I just always plan for the worst and hope for the best... Your cell phones won't work up there, you know."

"Oh, okay... Well, that's all right, I guess. The idea is to unplug some, so I guess it's fine. What about a TV?" I asked.

"Nope, nothing like that up there. Just good conversation...and the wind in the trees," he added.

For the first time I felt a bit uneasy. I knew I would be spending an entire week with that jerk Trey, but I had imagined him sitting in front of the television all day or playing on his phone.

"There's electricity, though—like to charge our electronic devices, right?"

"No, Alex. There is none of that up here."

"Oh, that's not great," I said, getting quiet.

* * * *

"Good job, everyone! We're about halfway now," Mr. Parker called out ahead.

Trey stopped, asking for a quick rest break. He grabbed a beer from the side of his pack and chugged it in about 30 seconds. Tossing the can sideways into the woods, he said, "Let's go."

We all froze, knowing that you can't litter in the woods and expecting Mr. Parker to say something.

"Trey," he called out without a response. "Trey!" he said louder, but he couldn't hear with his headphones back on and kept walking, getting farther up ahead.

"I'll get it," said Shanan, apologizing for him as she veered off the trail.

"You've got your hands full with that one, Alex," said Grady. "It's not too late to call this whole thing off and go home, you know."

"Thanks, but it will be okay. We're just hanging out in the mountains for a week."

"That's it—straight ahead," Grady called out. "I've got the key."

* * * *

We approached the weathered one-story cabin, with two windows facing us and a small front porch at the top of the outdoor stairs.

Trey waited right in front of the door, not taking his headphones off.

They were so loud I could hear Nirvana's front man, Kurt Cobain, belting out the chilling lyrics.

"Turn that off," said Shanan, pulling one headphone off.

He just shook his head and put it back on. As soon as Mr. Parker opened the front door, Trey disappeared inside, walking fast from one side to the other.

"Hey!" he called out, finally taking his headphones off long enough to ask, "Where are all the rooms?"

"This cabin," said Mr. Parker, not acknowledging Trey's outburst, "was built in 1925 and is known as The Fern Lake Patrol Cabin. This beauty is a one-story, one-room, no-bath studio with spectacular views from the front porch. She comes complete with central heat—when there's a fire built, of course—and could possibly also be home to several mice.

"It does not come with a stove, microwave, coffee pot, televisions or cable; no Wi-Fi or Internet of any kind, and no refrigerator. Wood is stacked under the porch, and I suggest you have a good fire going before bedtime if you don't want to freeze at night. Y'all know what a flue, or a flue damper, is?"

None of us raised our hands.

"How about you, Trey?" he called out, not being heard over the music.

"I'm done with that one!" Mr. Parker exclaimed. "Anyway, a flue is the part of the fireplace that needs to be closed when not in use to prevent animals and cold air from coming in. It needs to be open when there's a fire in there, to let the gasses and smoke out the top. This here chain will tell which way it goes. It's in the down position now, so closed; and the up position, like this, is open. Pretty simple, really. Just in case you forget which way the chain goes, you can always pop your head on in and look up. If you see the light up there, it's open."

"But only look if there's not a fire in there, right?" asked Scott, getting a look from the rest of us.

Mr. Parker, unfazed by the ludicrous question, simply answered, "That's right, Scott... I've saved the best for last," he continued, opening up the back door. "Your very own outhouse—to share, of course."

The door was opened, with a stale smell of a porta-potty, as you might find at a concert or sporting event, coupled with the scent of pine.

"Smells like gin and crap," said Scott, laughing at his own joke.

"That's about right," said Mr. Parker. "Now, which one of you packed in the toilet paper?"

All eyes went immediately to the wooden holder with the brown core on it, symbolizing the last sheet had been used. A quick scan revealed no more rolls inside.

"No way!" shouted Beth. "There's no way I'm using that thing without any paper. This place is disgusting!"

* * * * * * *

CHAPTER FOUR ABOVE FERN LAKE ROCKY MOUNTAIN NATIONAL PARK

"Oh, it's just a little joke, guys," Mr. Parker said. "There's a supplies closet in the cabin that's supposed to have some."

We followed him back inside to see a thick metal door with bars on the front, criss-crossed from top to bottom and left to right—the kind you could barely get one hand through—and a large padlock on the outside. Holding up the lit candle we could see clearly into the 5x5-foot room.

"This thing looks like Fort Knox," said Jo. "Why is it so...what I mean is...what's the word I'm looking for?"

"Reinforced?" asked Mr. Parker.

"Yes, that's it."

"It's the bears, especially in the summer months. They get into everything—trash cans, cars, and even cabins like this, looking for food."

He put the key into the heavy lock and sprung it open. I saw cleaning supplies, some pots and pans, one fire-starter log, a fire extinguisher, and seven rolls of toilet paper.

"Hey," I pointed to the corner shelf. "There are seven rolls of toilet paper. That's one each and one to spare."

"We'll see about that," said Mr. Parker, grabbing one and heading quickly out back.

"Don't forget to wash your hands," I whispered. Beth gave me a dirty look.

I took some time to look around the outside of the cabin, finding a few old rusted hand tools, a shovel, a metal rake, and an ax in the woodpile that was tucked up and behind the inside of the porch. Removing its casing, it appeared to be only a few years old and had a sharp blade, from what I could tell. I hid it farther back and out of sight, so one of my friends wouldn't get crazy trying to chop wood and get hurt. Feeling the top pieces of wood and finding them damp, I kept looking. I had always heard that damp wood could be near impossible to start a fire with. I checked down two layers and found some dry logs, easing my nerves a bit.

"You look pretty handy," came a voice from behind me.

I jumped, turning around to see Shanan standing there, smiling.

"You scared me," I told her. "I'm just glad I wasn't holding the ax..." I started to say, but trailed off.

"The what?" she asked.

"Oh, nothing. You just surprised me is all."

"Okay, I was only saying how handy you look, getting your hands dirty while everyone else is just hanging out." She smiled again, walking back up the stairs.

I followed her, meeting Mr. Parker coming in from the back. "Here you go, Alex," he said, handing me a ring with two keys on it. "This is the only set—one's to both the front and back door and the other is to the storage room."

"I checked the woodpile out front. The top is wet, but a couple of layers down is dry. So we should be good there," I told him, trying to sound like I knew what I was talking about.

"Thanks for checking that," said Shanan.

"All right," Mr. Parker said. "Listen up, everyone. There are a few last things to know before I head out. If someone gets really hurt, hike back down the way we came and flag down another hiker or sightseer. I'll be expecting you at the parking lot at noon on Saturday, November 23rd. Pack out everything you packed in, including your trash—there are bags in the closet. And last, Alex, don't forget to lock up... I almost forgot," he continued, opening his backpack. "I have six of these handy, one for each of you."

"Is this a radio?" asked Jo.

"Yes, and a flashlight and an electronics charger."

"Yes!" she said excitedly.

"Before you get too happy about it, there is one set of batteries in each. When they run out, it can be charged in the sun; it takes a while, though. And if you get desperate, it has a hand crank. Have fun, kids, and don't kill each other," he called out, waving a hand as he walked back down the trail.

* * * *

My watch read 3:16 p.m., and I called a quick meeting.

"Hey, guys. It's close to 3:30. Sunset is about six, and by 6:30 it's dark. We have a few things to think about getting done in the next few hours.

"First, we need to unpack, get all the food in one place, and figure out sleeping arrangements. Next, we need to get a fire going with enough wood to last the night. And I'm sure everyone is hungry, skipping lunch today. I'll get the fire going. Ladies, can you figure out where everyone is sleeping? And Scott and Trey, can you see what we can eat tonight?"

"Who put you in charge?" asked Trey. "We've been here 30 minutes, and you're already ordering everyone around."

"No, he's not," said a frustrated Shanan. "He's just trying to get things done. What are you doing besides listening to your music?"

"I'm just saying he doesn't have to give out jobs to everyone."

"Okay, Trey. What would you rather do?" I asked.

"I want to make the fire."

"Do you know how?" I asked, trying hard not to sound sarcastic.

"Of course," he said. "Where's the wood?"

We all pointed towards the front door.

"All right, Scott," I said. "You and I are on dinner."

We took inventory of the food and divided it into breakfast, lunch, and dinner. Most were freeze-dried, and one packet would feed two to four adults. We had used the oversized calculator at the camping store in LA to calculate the estimated amount of food for six adults, spanning six days.

"We're in the plus," I told Scott, "because we planned for a full day today but we missed two meals."

Each of us had 3 gallons of water we had carried up in canteens, a Sawyer camping water filter advertised to purify up to 100,000 gallons of water, and a LifeStraw for quick drinks. The ladies set up the sleeping arrangements, with Beth and Shanan only speaking when they had to. Trey, again oblivious to everyone around him, brought in wood, stacking full logs into the fireplace. I kept half an eye on him, hoping he knew what he was doing. I admittedly wasn't all that experienced at building a fire, but I had done it a few times before and knew the basic dos and don'ts.

"Trey!" I shouted until he took his headphones off.

"Yeah, what?" he grumbled.

"Do you know what you're doing?" I asked, watching him lay the base with dried pine needles from the ground.

"Yeah. I already told you I've got this."

"All right, but those needles are going to smoke. Don't forget the flue."

"Yeah," he replied, without turning around.

"Keep an eye on him?" I asked Scott. "I've got to hit the head."

I saw him digging around in his pack, looking for a lighter or matches, I assumed. "Let him use this if he can't find one," I told Scott, handing him a BIC lighter from my pocket.

In the outhouse, I noticed Grady had left only half a roll of paper. I left it on since it was extra anyway.

Scott was setting up the stove and didn't see Trey take a small white plastic bottle out of his pack. Trey didn't bother reading the warning label that included instructions about only using outdoors in a ventilated area. Dousing the logs and pine needles with nearly half the bottle, he turned to make sure nobody was looking.

"I'll show them how to start a fire," he said under his breath.

He pulled a single match from his pocket, the kitchen kind made of wood that could be struck on any rough surface.

I walked back in to the distinct smell of lighter fluid, just in time to hear him say, "Who says a rich boy from LA can't start a fire?" Quickly lighting the match on his oversized belt buckle, he reached towards the open fireplace.

I called "NO, Trey!" running towards him, somehow not moving my body as fast as my mind would like, as he flicked the match end over end.

The explosion was immediate, with flames leaping out towards him. The $1,500 jacket he wore caught fire. Scott and I got to him at the same time, knocking him to the floor and rolling him to stomp out the flames. The smell of singed hair overtook my nostrils as the thick black smoke poured out of the fireplace and into the compact cabin.

Shanan came running from the supply closet with the fire extinguisher, and I called out to Scott, who was closest, to open the flue. Violent coughing came from the back of the cabin, but I couldn't tell who it was.

Shanan started spraying the thick white foam into the fireplace and anywhere she saw flames. Scott, with a ski glove on, opened the damper flue. With the flames all but out, Shanan propped open the front and back doors with two small logs. Seeing more clearly now, we turned Trey over to see how badly he was hurt. Starting from top to bottom, his prized wavy blonde hair was no more than clumps here and there, and his eyebrows and lashes were no better. His jacket was burned through the chest area, as was his T-shirt. Red welts covered most of his chest and looked like a bad sunburn.

"Are you with us, Trey?" I asked.

"Yeah, that was crazy," he replied. "These old cabins have crappy ventilation."

"The flue was closed, and the lighter fluid didn't help," I told him, with no response.

"When's dinner?" he asked.

This time I didn't respond, asking Beth and Jo to look for the first-aid kit in my pack. The guy at the camping store said it was a good one, but we hadn't opened it.

Beth found it and brought it to me. "Can you take a look at him while I try to clean this fireplace mess up?"

"Ooh," Beth said, seeing the burns on his chest. "I'm not touching that!"

Shanan and Jo carefully cleaned the burns as best they could, with Trey wincing every few seconds and occasionally knocking their hands away. It was obvious to us all that he was in some kind of shock, as he didn't appear to be in the kind of pain anyone would expect, seeing his burns.

"It could have been much worse," said Shanan.

"How do you figure?" asked a snarky Trey.

"Well, Alex and Scott kept you from being burned much worse, and without the fire extinguisher we could have burned down the whole cabin."

"It's that driver's fault!" he shouted. "He should have told us about that old crappy fireplace."

"Mr. Parker did tell us about the flue, but you were too busy listening to your music to hear it, and it's just common sense not to put a bunch of lighter fluid on an indoor fire!" Shanan responded matter-of-factly.

"Whatever... I'm over it," he responded, now touching his head and face for the first time, as Shanan checked him for more burns.

"It just got your hair is all," she commented. "It will all grow back, but I'm not sure about the eyelashes."

He put his headphones on and sat in the corner, drowning out everyone around him.

* * * *

"Okay, everyone," called out Scott. "We've got Cheesy Chili Mac or Beef Stroganoff."

I voted for stroganoff with Shanan, but we lost three to two. I didn't bother with Trey to try for a tie.

"Chili Mac coming up," he announced.

I checked out the fireplace and it was a mess. The fire retardant would have to be cleaned out completely if we had any hope of building more fires in there. The sun set and we closed the doors, with the temperature dropping and most of the smoke gone.

"It's going to take a while to get the fireplace working properly again, so we'll have to bundle up tonight," I said. "Remember, the store owner told us we all have zero-degree bags, so nobody is going to freeze to death. It will be cold, though, so if you don't have to use the outhouse in the middle of the night, you will stay warm."

* * * *

Scott had the small stove set up on the front porch. I handed him a beer and asked if I could help.

"Thanks, I'm good."

"That's incredible," I remarked, pointing to the view.

I called inside for everyone to come outside and see the sunset. Shanan and Jo came out, taking pictures with their phones.

"Are you coming?" I called out to Beth, getting a "Nope, it's not my thing" back from inside the cabin.

"That's super cool," announced Jo, with Shanan agreeing.

For a split second, I wondered what it would have been like with just Scott, Jo, Shanan, and me up here. I quickly dismissed the idea.

* * * * * * *

CHAPTER FIVE ROCKY MOUNTAINS ESTES PARK, COLORADO

M r. Parker made it back to his vehicle in no time, being all downhill walking. He ran into some day hikers, saying the typical hello that passing hikers do without conversation. Once arriving back in town, he met with his old attorney friend Rick Holman, or the "Iron Fist," as they used to call him back in the day at their favorite restaurant—the Twin Owls Steak House at the Black Canyon Inn, tucked away into boulders just outside of Estes Park. They met for an early dinner and were among the first patrons at 5:30 p.m.

"It's hard to beat the 10-ounce prime rib or the 16-ounce bison cowboy steak—a bone-in ribeye that I get every time I come out here," he told his friend.

"Get whatever you want," replied Rick. "Dinner is on me tonight, and thanks for the referral."

"The big boys from Denver couldn't make it up here quick enough, so it was an easy decision," joked Grady.

"Ha, that's funny," said Rick, "but you know those guys don't have the Iron Fist!" he replied, holding up his right hand, balled into a tight fist.

Grady knew his friend had spent a former life in New York City as a top-notch attorney, leading high-profile cases, and was no stranger to the news outlets. He had disappeared for almost six years before resurfacing in this sleepy little mountain town, refusing any case that would take him back to the Big Apple—or any city, for that matter. Alexander's father knew him by reputation, as did most men and women in big business, but he had no idea he was still practicing or where. With Grady's referral, he would pay top dollar for his services.

Grady typically stayed over one night at his friend's sprawling 10,000-square-foot house on 20 pristine acres, only 5 miles out of Estes Park. With the peace and quiet paired with the breakfast his friend's wife always made them, he made the ritual several times a year, but usually with his wife.

"I'm going to have to skip staying over at your place this time," said Grady. "I've got to get back to Denver tonight."

"Yes, about that..." said Rick. "I hate to head back to the big city, as you know, but I need to consult with a couple of attorneys in Denver about the case."

"About Alex? I didn't think it would be that big of a deal."

"It wouldn't be, had there not been a dozen citizen reporters with their cell phones out. I think it could be bigger than anyone thought."

"There goes all your fee money, I guess," replied Grady.

"No. Your friend has deep pockets, and he's ready for a fight. Besides, I get paid by the hour, plus expenses, and your friend wants no surprises. I'm not trying to pad the bill, but I want to make sure your friend's son goes home after this and not somewhere else."

"Do you think it could be that serious?" asked Grady.

"There's a fine line between self-defense—of oneself or another person—and assault. The truth doesn't matter to anyone but those involved and what the jury is led to believe. So, it's me that would like to invite myself over to your place for a couple of nights, if that's okay?"

"Sure, old friend. I'll let my wife know you're coming. Do you need to stop at your place before we head out?"

"Nope. I'm already packed and I'll just follow you down the mountain."

"Sounds good," replied Grady. "We should be there by 10 tonight. By the way, I'll be back up here a day before picking up the kids, in case anything new has happened with the case."

Stopping for gas in Estes, both men agreed on the quickest way back to Denver, heading around some construction and a road closure.

"Lead the way," said Rick, as they left town.

* * * *

Heading out on Highway 36 towards Lyons, they skipped the Big Thompson Canyon that Grady had taken on the way up. With a nearly full moon lighting up the mountains, the Colorado drive was peaceful, majestic even, and did not go unnoticed by two residents.

"This is why I moved up here in the first place," said Rick, talking with Grady on the cell phone. "I've been a lot of places in my life, and I kept coming back here. I had to nearly disappear for a while to make a move from the city but I wouldn't change a thing. Do you think I did the right thing, Grady?"

"Do you mean leaving your wife behind?"

"Yes. I mean, we were separated, but I didn't stay to try and make it work; I just cut and ran. I think it was just the pressure of everything in my life at that time. The law firm was getting to be more work than I wanted, and after we lost our only son we just started to drift apart. She did want to go to counseling, I'll give her that. But I couldn't stay...I just couldn't."

"It's in the past now," replied Grady, having heard this confession before. "You gave her more than she asked for in the divorce and have never spoken badly of her. You moved on up here, remarried, and have a wonderful life. Your reputation as a top-notch attorney has apparently followed, and you work and live on your own terms. Your boy would be proud of what you've become. I know it."

"I hope you're right, my friend."

* * * *

"What the…" said Grady into his phone, as the brightest light he had ever seen shone above, violently lighting up the former quiet sky in an instant.

The lights inside his SUV went dark, as did his headlights. His foot was still on the gas pedal, but there was no power, no acceleration or brakes; the steering wheel felt stiff, like trying to turn an old rusty screw by hand.

He looked in his rearview in time to see his old friend slam his heavy Mercedes S550 into his back bumper with a crunch, sending him off course and heading for the trees.

"Hold steady," said Grady aloud, as his SUV squealed its tires and hit the embankment, careening into the ditch. A large tree branch smashed into his front windshield, splintering all the way across the glass surface. He braced for the airbags to deploy, but they did not. The vehicle came to rest in between two pine trees, and all was quiet.

He looked into the rearview to see if his friend was okay but couldn't see anything from this angle. The nearly full moon lit the otherwise dark surroundings, but he could see well enough. He instinctively reached his left arm out to open the driver's side door and yelled "Ahh!" as he looked down to see the large bump on his forearm. The pain was increasing by the second and he wondered why he hadn't felt it right away. The door opened from the outside as his friend said, "I'm sorry, Grady. I don't know what happened! Your arm, it doesn't look right…the angle, it's all wrong."

"Do you think it's broken?"

"Yep. I worked a few injury cases in my day. I'll bet an X-ray would show a clear break of one or both of the bones in your forearm."

"Both?"

"Yes, your radius bone here," replied Rick, pointing to the one from his elbow to his thumb. "That one's a given, and maybe also the ulna," pointing from his elbow down the pinky side of his wrist. "I need to get your watch off before it swells up and cuts off your circulation. This is going to hurt," he said, unclipping the tight watch from the already-swelling forearm. "There," he stated, pulling it gently off Grady's wrist. The outer ring glowed in the dark, and they both could clearly see that the second hand had stopped turning.

"I think you busted your watch," Rick announced.

"I wish I knew a good attorney," Grady joked, grimacing through the pain.

"Did you see that light?" asked Rick. "It was right after that when my car just turned off. All the electronics, lights, engine...everything. I just couldn't control it."

"Don't worry about it. I lost control of my car too," replied Grady, reaching for his glove box with his good arm. "Let me get my flashlight so we can see better... That's odd," he said, as he turned it on, with no light emitting. "Must be out of batteries," he declared.

"All right. I'll call a tow truck and we can get to Urgent Care to look at your arm, unless you want to go to the hospital."

"Awe, hell no. That will be an extra four hours waiting to get seen, unless you want to set it now and save me the visit."

"Absolutely, old friend. I've seen a YouTube video on that exact procedure—nothing to it," he added, pretending to reach for his arm.

"On second thought, I think I'll wait," said Grady.

"That's weird," announced Rick. "My cell won't come on."

"Try mine," offered Grady. "It flew out of my hands but it's somewhere on the passenger side, I think. Check the floorboard."

Rick went around the car, opening the passenger door and finding the cell under the seat.

"Got it!" he announced, handing it to Grady.

"It's not turning on either," Grady replied, staring at the blank screen. "What's going on here?" he asked his old friend.

"I don't know, but things aren't adding up, for sure," said Rick, shaking his head back and forth. "I'll flag down the next car we see for a ride to town... Hold on; I've got something for the pain," he added, handing Grady a large white pill and a bottle of water.

"What's this horse pill you're trying to feed me? Is it Oxy or Oxycontin? Where did you get this? Is there something I should know about here?"

"Nope. Nothing ominous—I just had some left over from my back surgery a couple years ago, and they work pretty good for pain."

"Okay, give me a couple of those."

"Just one to start, and we will see how it goes," cautioned Rick.

* * * *

Seconds turned to minutes...and into an hour, with no other vehicles passing by.

"Where are all the cars?" asked Grady. "I mean, I know this is a mountain road at night, but you would think at least one would be by here, Rick."

"This is a well traveled road, and there should have been 30 cars coming past here by now. Do you have anything," he continued, "like gear or a what-if worst-case scenario pack?"

"Yes, I have always carried one since I was in the military, because you can never predict anything nowadays."

"I've got one too. It might be a good time to see what we have, and we will need to take a look at your arm."

Rick got out his emergency suitcase and helped Grady with his pack. "Okay...we've got two sleeping bags, one 30-degrees, and one zero-degrees rating. We have one tent, a stove with a canister, some cookware and a water filter. There are a few other odds and ends, including a handheld can opener, cooking pots with plates, bowls and silverware, a few knives, some fishing gear... And what's this?" he asked, holding up a file box with silver pouches inside.

"That's my Farad... Oh, that's not good, but it makes sense now. How did I not figure that out an hour ago?"

"Hey, buddy. Are you okay?" asked Rick. "You're mumbling to yourself."

"Yes, I guess I was just distracted by the pain in my arm but now it's all coming into focus. Those silver bags are Faraday bags."

"Fara...what?"

"Faraday bags. They basically keep electronics from getting zapped if there is an electrical surge, like an EMP. It was first invented by an English scientist, Michael Faraday, in 1836."

"You, my friend, are still a walking, talking encyclopedia, but I'm not sure where you're going with this," stated Rick.

"Open the bags, but one at a time," suggested Grady.

Rick opened the first bag, containing two flashlights and a wristwatch.

"Try the flashlights; they should work. And then check the watch," said Grady.

Rick did as instructed and was amazed to see both flashlights turn on and shine brightly as he pointed them towards the woods. "That's amazing! And the watch works too!"

"Yes, it does."

"Do you have a phone in here?" asked Rick excitedly.

"No, that's one thing I don't have, but it probably wouldn't matter anyway. We're here for the night. It's going to get even colder, so let's get a few things together and we can sleep in your car while I tell you everything I know about EMPs."

Rick gathered everything of value from Grady's SUV and put it in his vehicle.

"I can't forget this," said Grady, reaching his right arm into the middle-seat compartment. "My trusty SR9," he announced, pulling it out.

"I've got one too, but it's a little .380," replied Rick.

"The seats won't recline," said Rick, trying them and realizing he never even gave it a second thought before.

"Nope, they're electric," replied Grady. "We will have to sleep sitting but it's better than being out on the ground. Grab that large Faraday bag, the one on the far end. It's got my shortwave radio inside. Maybe we can get some information on what's happening."

Both men got into their sleeping bags, as the temperature slowly dropped.

"I've got to admit, this is the last thing I thought I would be doing tonight," said Rick. They both laughed, with Grady grimacing through the pain.

"Okay, now to the fun stuff. An EMP stands for Electromagnetic Pulse."

"Where have I heard that before?" asked Rick.

"Probably on the news or in any one of the recent action movies involving military or superheroes. The concept has been around for decades and it has been used in warfare over the years. There are only two things I know of that can cause this chain of events, where it starts with a bright light and knocks out power to vehicles, cell phones, and pretty much anything electronic."

"Except for what's in those Faraday cages, right?"

"Exactly, and a few other things that are older, like cars built before the late 1970s," Grady explained.

"I wish I had my car in one of those cages, if they had one that big."

"Oh, they do! The military has a lot of their equipment protected—and did even back when I was in the service."

"So, they're protected and we're not?"

"Yes, that's about the gist of it. They are prepared, and when someone like me does it, I'm labeled a conspiracy nut. I know what you're thinking—class-action lawsuit, right?"

"You know me well, my friend," replied Rick. "With enough proof, I'll bet I could blow this thing wide open!"

"Well, unless I'm wrong, you will never get the chance," said Grady. "And this pill, man—it's doing the trick. Cut my pain in half already."

* * * * * *

Chapter Six South of Estes Park, Colorado

"Before we get off track again," said Grady, feeling a little loopy from the meds, "we have either had what's called a Coronal Mass Ejection from the sun or another country hit us with a high-altitude nuclear bomb, knocking out one or more of our power grids and every electronic not protected. I'm guessing we will find out which one it was, sooner or later. Best-case scenario, this is all temporary and can be corrected in days or weeks, but I think that is unlikely. Worst case scenario, if all grids are down, we are looking at survival of the fittest for the next months to years, and our country will likely never be the same again."

"I sure do wish we had stayed at my house tonight," said Rick, with the realization of the situation now sinking in. "The question is, do we head back up to Estes Park, continue to your place in Denver, or split up here? And what about the kids up on the mountain? They will probably have no idea what's going on until you miss the pickup."

"That's the easy part," said Grady. "My sons are at home with us until after Thanksgiving break, before they go back to school. They are home with my wife, and they will take care of her and head up here; at least that was always the plan for us all if things got really bad. We were all supposed to find our way here and meet at your place... I bet you didn't see that coming," said Grady, laughing out loud. "Besides, I don't want us splitting up, and I think things are about to get worse in the city."

"No, I didn't see that coming, but you know your family is always welcome at our house, for however long."

The long night was cold and lonely, with the wind howling down the desolate highway. Each took turns trying the shortwave radio from the Faraday bag, with neither finding a signal.

* * * *

"I want you to reduce it," was the first thing Grady said upon waking in the morning.

"What?" asked Rick.

"I said I want you to reduce my break as much as you can before we take off walking. The doctors can fix it later, but I want it as straight as possible now, and I think it might take the pain down some. I've seen it done out in the field more than once."

"Then you should know it's probably going to hurt like hell to try and set it."

"Yes, I do, but not for long."

"Okay. What do we need?" asked Rick.

"I'll need another pill, and we can get the rest ready while it kicks in. I've got some Gorilla Tape in my trunk and gauze wrapping in the medical kit. Once we start, it needs to be quick and finished, no matter the pain. We will both be sitting on the ground in case I pass out, but if I do, then finish it for sure."

"Are you sure about this?" asked Rick.

"Yes, and here's how it goes. First, check my pulse on my wrist, like this. We will do the same at the end and make sure it's the same. Next, we both are sitting on the ground, and you put a foot in my armpit like you're going to pop a dislocated shoulder back into place. My arm will be loosely wrapped in the gauze dressing. You will grab just above my wrist with one hand, and I'll brace my elbow with my other hand. You will slowly but strongly pull straight out until it looks straighter. Then with your other hand, place these two sticks—one on the top and the other on the bottom. You will wrap the tape, starting closest to my wrist, tight enough to hold it but keep an eye out for my fingers. I want to make sure I have circulation. There's no point in setting an arm, just to lose it later to tissue death. The gauze is there in case you have to cut the tape off quickly. It's easier for sure with more than one person and a bit more meds, but this will have to do."

Thirty minutes later, he was ready.

"It's kicking in—the med, I mean. Let's get this done."

With his arm carefully wrapped with the gauze. Rick did as instructed and put his right foot just under the armpit and began to pull.

"Aaah," groaned Grady, gritting his teeth as the pressure increased and his arm began to straighten. "Don't stop!" he commanded through the pain. "I guess I'm not going to pass out, after all," he continued, calling for Rick to start the tape. "I'll help as much as I can," he continued. "Just don't let off the pressure."

Wrapping the tape was slow but deliberate, with both men checking his fingers for signs of circulation. Grady rolled backward with a smile, panting at the completion.

"I'm sorry it had to be like that," said Rick.

"I'm not. It feels 50% better already," stated Grady. "Now, help me get my pack on; I've got one for you too."

* * * * * * *

Chapter Seven Above Fern Lake Rocky Mountains, Colorado

D inner was served on paper plates we found in the fortified storage closet. We agreed to store everything—food- and beverage-wise—inside and leave it unlocked. With me having the only key, I didn't want us to lose it and get locked out.

Dusk turned to dark, following an amazing sunset to the west. The cabin was dark without a fire, which I vowed to tend to in the morning. I put on my heavy jacket as the temperature dropped rapidly and sat on the front porch with a nearly full moon lighting up the mountains. Only Beth and Trey stayed inside, refusing to come out.

Scott, Joe, Shanan and I sat side by side in old lawn chairs on the deck, with me on the far right end, next to Shanan. We sipped the Scotch I had brought—and the girls did as well—minus the ice cubes I usually added.

As I felt for the lever to adjust my chair, my hand touched Shanan's. "Oh, sorry," I said, but not pulling my hand back.

"It's no problem," she replied softly, grabbing mine and not letting go.

"Oh," is all I could think to say. I guess it was good I was studying to shoot film and not act.

Shanan, Jo and I were all enrolled in the School of Theatre, Film and Television. Only Scott was enrolled in the Samueli School of Engineering. His parents had wanted him to go to their Alma Mater back East, but he wanted to stick with us—the rat pack that I split up last year. We talked, as we often did, about all the things we would buy when we made it big in film. It was kind of a running joke because we all knew Scott could buy anything he wanted, short of a country right now, whether he graduated from school or not. None of us ever asked him for anything, but he would do crazy things from time to time. A few months back, he kept hounding me about why I didn't wear a watch. I finally told him there's only one I've ever wanted and that when I can afford it, then I will wear a watch every day.

"What's the watch?" he asked.

"It's a Rolex Oyster Perpetual Submariner Date in white gold," I rattled off, sounding a bit like Ralphie in the movie *A Christmas Story* talking about his Daisy air rifle. "I want an official Red Ryder, carbine action, two-hundred-shot-range model air rifle!" he said in the classic line.

A week later Scott yells "Catch!" and tosses me the $38,000 watch across the living room, telling me to see his guy and get it sized.

"How do you know it's real, though?" I asked, not wanting to be rude but genuinely curious, having never seen one up close.

"Well," said Scott, "besides the receipt, it can be tough sometimes to spot a fake. Here's what I look for," he continued, showing me his.

"What do you notice?" he asked.

"It feels heavy and solid."

"What about the second timer? Is it ticking or sweeping?"

"Sweeping, I guess," I replied.

"Exactly! All true Rolexes have hands that sweep and don't tick. Although some think they just tick so fast that it looks like a sweep. The last thing is removing the bracket to view the serial numbers at either end."

There was no refusing a gift from him, I already knew, but I still tried before finally giving in and saying, "Thank you!" We all grew up together, and I think we were probably the only friends he had that didn't care about his money, especially Jo.

He came from money, not one generation or even two, but Kennedy- or Rockefeller-type multigenerational fortunes, with theirs being in real estate. His great-grandfather immigrated from Scotland by boat in 1898 with his wife and son and $2 between them. He worked in New York City sweeping floors, cutting meat and selling to customers in a popular butcher shop 14 hours a day to feed his family. Eight years later, the owner, a single man with no family, fell ill and gave him the business, free and clear. Within three years, he expanded to seven locations across New York City, and within ten years he was known far and wide for his real estate holdings. He spent his last 25 years in Dallas, Texas, buying distraught commercial real estate that would be repurposed and passed down to his son, and then to his. Scott's father continued to grow the business into one of Texas' largest landholder companies, with a net worth of $4.6 billion. His family was sure he had coined the famous phrase carved into his first Dallas skyscraper steps: *Luck is an equal combination of hard work and hard work.*

Jo came from money but more Beverly-Hillbillies style. Her family owned 100 acres of land in southwest Louisiana. They hunted it yearly but had no idea they were sitting on oil reserves, with their take at around $25 million. She never forgot her country roots, even after her family moved to Dallas and bought a 16-bedroom mansion on 50 acres. With her being an only child, her father converted one of the garages into a workshop where they could restore old Chevrolet Corvettes together. She didn't care about the money, not her family's or Scott's. She was all about family and friends.

Shanan's father, the high-ranking Colonel, hated her boyfriend Trey's liberal views but got him accepted to the school with a single phone call at the pleas of his daughter, who was the most important person in his life. Her mother divorced him when Shanan was just eight years old, due to his demanding job requirements. He didn't fight her for custody, knowing he would be halfway across the world most of the time.

He made a promise to Shanan that he would always be here for her birthday, as long as he drew breath. He kept that promise, more than once jumping on a red-eye cargo plane in the middle of the night to make it just in time for her party. He called her once a month like clockwork and truly felt part of her life from thousands of miles away.

Colonel O'Sullivan was both respected and feared by his colleagues and soldiers, with a sarcastic tone only his closest men ever saw. Shanan alone knew another side of him—a softer, caring side that never made it beyond her birthdays and monthly calls.

Sitting quietly with my three best friends in the world, I could hear Grady telling me to fight for her, get her back, and "Know you have the best of the best." I could only see the silhouette of her face but whispered to her, "I'm sorry."

* * * * * * *

Chapter Eight Above Fern Lake Rocky Mountain National Park

"I know," she replied, as the sky lit with the brightest light I had ever seen.

"Oh, my god! What was that?" asked Scott.

"I can't see!" said Jo. "Me neither!" I called out, trying to adjust my eyes to the dark once again.

"Was that the Northern Lights?" asked Shanan.

"No," I said. "I don't think so. That was something else—something different."

I had remembered hearing stories about UFOs in the Colorado Rockies and was familiar with NORAD, the command post in Colorado Springs that was literally dug into a mountain and, next to the White House and Pentagon, could be the next target of a hostile nuclear attack.

"Let's go inside," I told everyone, not sure if it would happen again.

"What the hell!" I heard, entering the cabin. "My headphones don't work and my phone won't turn on!" announced Trey.

"It's probably just out of batteries," said Shanan. "Try charging it with that hand-crank radio thing Mr. Parker left us."

"Yeah, okay," he said, frantically cranking the unit after trying the dead battery pack. "It's not doing crap; give me yours," he demanded. She did as asked but hers was dead as well.

"What time is it?" Trey asked, agitated, tapping his watch.

"I don't know. Mine's not working either," said Shanan, picking up her alarm clock and shaking it.

Normally I wouldn't have cared if I answered him, but I now had a new watch so I blurted out "9:23," watching the second-hand sweep, just as always.

"Yep. Mine too, just like always," announced Scott, looking at his wrist. "But these watches are different," he continued, staring now at his blank cell-phone screen. "They don't have batteries."

"What's going on?" asked Shanan.

"I don't know," I said. "But something is different; something has changed."

The candles, recommended by the camping store owner, lit the cabin enough to see and could be taken to the outhouse if there was no wind.

"I'll bring a candle outside right now if anyone needs to use the outhouse," I said.

"You can bring it inside with you, and I'll..."

"What are you, some kind of weirdo?" asked Trey in front of everyone.

"No, Trey. I'll wait outside with my trusty lighter, and anyone needing it can bring it inside with them. If it goes out, we will get it lit again. That's it—nothing ominous going on here right now."

"I'm going to sleep," he grumbled, slurring his words.

"Are you okay?" I asked him. "I mean the burns?"

"Good night," he said loudly, huffing without answering me.

* * * *

I lay down in my sleeping bag next to Beth but facing away. I saw Shanan across the dimly lit room doing the same. She winked at me and we both fell asleep, staring at each other. The temperature dropped into the teens, and my zero-degrees bag was taxed, with my feet freezing most of the night. At first light, I looked around to see others in fetal positions inside their sleeping bags and Scott outside of his, doing jumping jacks to stay warm.

"Well, that was a fun night. I don't want to do it again," he called out, noticing I was awake.

"Yeah, that pretty much sucked," I responded.

Twenty minutes later, everyone was up and about, and I started the stove for freeze-dried eggs with bacon bits. The electric starter wasn't working, but a flick of my lighter on the gas burner lit it right up. Over breakfast, we had a discussion of what may have happened last night and why none of our cell phones were even turning on. Nobody had an idea, except for Shanan.

"I don't know much about this stuff, but you all know my dad is a Colonel in the Army. Last year on my birthday, he told me about a small nuclear bomb that, if set off, maybe 300 miles above the U.S., could cause something... I can't remember the name, but he said it would basically fry all modern electric devices—like phones, radios, and even most cars. The aging U.S. power grids, not updated since the 1950s and not protected, would surely go down as well. There would be a bright light in the sky—like what we saw last night, I guess. I'm worried something like that has happened..." she trailed off.

"Something like *what* exactly?" asked Trey sarcastically.

"Something like we're not going home in a few days, or ever again," she replied soberly.

Scott and Jo weren't on board yet and looked skeptical. Trey and Beth both laughed out loud. I wasn't laughing or skeptical. I had spoken with her father on the phone—the United States Colonel, who was serious all the time.

"I believe you," I said aloud, getting "Unbelievable!" out of Beth and "Of course you do," from Trey.

"Thank you, Alex. I'm glad somebody does," Shanan replied.

"Hold on a minute. Remember the guy at the camping store? He said if we get into trouble to read this book," I said, holding up a copy of an apparently popular end-of-the-world novel.

"Anyone in?" I asked. Most raised their hands.

"Beth, how about you?" I asked.

"I guess," she replied.

"Okay. Trey, you're the last."

"All right," he said. "It's not like I can listen to my music anymore, so get to the reading."

* * * * * * *

CHAPTER NINE ABOVE FERN LAKE ROCKY MOUNTAIN NATIONAL PARK

I read the description on the back cover, talking about an Electromagnetic Pulse, or EMP.

"That's it!" yelled Shanan. "That's what I couldn't remember!"

"Is that what happened last night?" asked Scott.

"Yeah, I think so," I replied. "We've got nothing but time this morning. Let's see what this thing is really about."

After the first few chapters, my friends and I learned that almost all electronic devices were destroyed, including the ones in nearly all vehicles made after 1978, as well as all communications—including cell phones, televisions, computers, e-mail and radios.

We read about a family stranded a hundred miles from home, walking with everything they owned in a backpack through hostile territory.

"We're not a hundred miles from home," I said aloud. "We're more than 800! And you two," I continued, pointing to Trey and Beth, "are even farther than that."

Everyone got quiet in the small cabin, and as cold as it was inside with the simple window thermometer reading 21 degrees Fahrenheit, I felt flushed, and even warm.

"I knew we should have gone to Cancun!" cried out Beth.

"We would still be stuck," I told her—"only then in a foreign country!"

It was clear we needed a plan...and soon.

* * * *

"I need some air," I said, walking out the front door.

Shanan followed me out, no longer caring what Trey would say.

"You're brave following me out here in front of Trey and Beth," I said.

"Do you care about that, Alex?" she asked.

"No. No, I guess I don't anymore... You never got hold of your father again after I spoke with him, did you?"

"No," she replied. "I tried him a half dozen times, right up until we came up here, but it wouldn't go through. It happens sometimes, so I wasn't concerned about it."

"Yes. But Shanan, he was concerned about you. He told me something big was about to happen and that I should watch out for you for weeks, or even a few months. That's why I wanted you to get hold of him again, because he never told me exactly what was coming."

"Did he say anything about Trey?" she asked.

"Nah. I'm sure he likes him well enough."

"Alexander Bingham Kade, I know you better than anyone here—especially Beth. So, I'll ask you again, what did my father say about Trey?"

"Only that we couldn't trust him," I replied. "I'm not making that up—like a jaded ex, you know."

She laughed. "I know. He always told me that too. He liked you, though, like a son."

"I know," I sighed. "I messed up big time, and it took this trip for me to realize it."

"I'm sure he'll forgive you," she said.

"It's you I'm worried about," I told her.

* * * *

Back inside, coffee was the talk of the hour. I vowed to get the fireplace back in order and took a vote to make me the official fire guy from here on out. The decision was four out of six, if I was counting me in the yes group. Trey still didn't believe he had done anything wrong, but at least he didn't hurt anyone else in the process. I prayed for him, as my pastor back in Dallas would surely advise; I prayed for all of us. The temperature by noon was a nice crisp 35 degrees, and I had the fireplace cleaned out as best I could.

"Time to warm this place up!" I said, lighting the fire with small twigs under larger sticks, and finally logs. After a few blowing attempts, it held the flame. The opened flue did its job, and the smoke rose up high into the mountain sky.

"What if we can't get it started next time?" asked Scott.

"That's easy," I responded. "We just don't let it ever go out. We have enough wood to outlast our food supply," I said, without thinking. Everyone paused...frozen in place as they realized what I had just said.

We had five days of food left and were stranded miles away from the nearest town, without communication or any kind of transportation.

Jo and Scott got quiet, whispering to themselves. Beth started crying, complaining about why she ever came on this trip. Shanan held strong, and Trey pulled a bottle of something out of his backpack, taking a long drink.

"Take it easy over there, Trey," I called. "We need to be sharp, especially now for the next however long it takes to get past this."

"You mind your business, and I'll mind mine," he snapped back.

I ignored his last comment, not wanting to start something that would get us off track.

"I'm going to read some more of the book, if anyone is interested in listening."

Shanan sat beside me, and Scott came over with Jo. Beth joined Trey, taking drinks of whatever he had. Scott looked at me like I should stop her but I whispered, "It's all good, buddy."

We read on, changing readers with each chapter, and grew more hopeful and scared to death with every page.

* * * * * * *

CHAPTER TEN ABOVE FERN LAKE ROCKY MOUNTAIN NATIONAL PARK

"Alex, come out here quick!" called Scott, who had taken a break on the front porch.

"Look at that!" He pointed down the mountain, above the parking lot we had come up from only a day before.

Circling above the trees, I saw three hang gliders just before they disappeared, in for a landing.

"What are they doing up here?" asked Scott.

"I don't know," I replied. "But I do know they didn't walk all the way up here. Cars must still be working... I'll be back," I said, running inside to get my jacket.

"What's going on out there?" asked Shanan.

"A ride home or at least down the mountain, I hope." With that, I ran out the door and down the front stairs.

I went as fast as I could back down the trail, mindful of the trail changing directions and occasional splits. Halfway down the path, I caught a glimpse of something out of my right peripheral sight. It moved fast through the trees, 50 yards off to my right.

"What the..." I started to say when it happened.

My left hiking boot caught something hard, a rock maybe or a tree root—I couldn't be sure—but I was flying through the air and off the trail.

I was able to turn my head at the last second as I crashed into the low-hanging branches of a large pine tree. My head took the brunt of it, snapping small branches as I slammed into the tree with my head and right shoulder. Falling back to the ground, I lay with ringing in my ears and a wet feeling on my scalp. All was still except for my heavy breathing.

I opened my eyes, thankful to be alive. Newsflashes of several famous people—like Sonny Bono, one of the Kennedys, and probably many more average ones, I'm sure—being killed while skiing when they ran into a tree. I instinctively reached my hand to the top right side of my head and felt the warm, sticky blood now running down my cheek.

The high-pitched growl both startled me and brought me back to reality. I looked across the trail, still lying on the ground, and heard it again.

"Is it a bear?" I asked out loud. "Wait...no, it's too cold. They would be hibernating right now, Mr. Parker told us... That leaves dogs and cats," I said, still talking out loud to nobody. I heard it again, sounding like a screaming baby and cat mix. *That's no coyote,* I thought, as it came out of the trees, walking slowly towards me.

I had read a little bit about animal attacks in the woods, and all the well-meaning advice came back to me. "Fire a shot in the air" was one of the first suggestions. *Great, if I had remembered to bring Grady's pistol.* "Call out for help to another person nearby." *No luck there,* I thought, figuring I was about halfway between the cabin and parking lot. "Play dead" ran through my mind. *Wait, maybe that's just bears. Is that just bears?* I couldn't remember but knew if I got it wrong I would be dead in a matter of minutes.

Catching the first glimpse of him was terrifying as I gazed at the nearly three-foot-high, maybe seven-foot-long, one hundred and seventy-pound cat, I thought, just guessing. He closed in on me, zigzagging back and forth with that awful scream, each time coming a little closer and raising up on hind legs. I had already had enough fighting for the week, and this guy had teeth and claws. I decided not to play dead. If it was the wrong thing, as I thought it might be, I was done.

"If you're going to go down, do it fighting to the end!" I said aloud.

I slowly raised to a crouched position as he came closer still. Standing up, I noticed he stopped advancing. I wished I had my backpack to put on my chest for protection. I looked at him in the eyes, having heard that could keep me defiant and not be confused with easy prey. I crouched again, this time to pick up two sticks lying at the trunk of the tree that nearly killed me. They looked like natural walking sticks, maybe left by hikers during the summer months. He, or maybe she, again advanced slowly but in a straighter line now. As I stood up, the big cat stopped and growled.

"Get big!" I said aloud. "Get big!" In a flash, I remembered the words "Get big when dealing with a large cat, like a mountain lion," but I couldn't remember where I had read it, or maybe it was on a TV show. "Get big, and whatever happens, don't run!" I smiled nervously at the last part. My head was pounding, my right arm barely able to lift a stick, and I somehow twisted my left ankle. I wasn't running anywhere, and I knew it. Climbing up a tree was out as well—with a coyote for sure or maybe even a bear that didn't feel like trying—but not with a cat.

With me standing, he stood his ground but didn't advance. *Okay*, I thought, with my heart pounding in my ears. *Think! Think!*

"Get big! Get big! Get big!"

I lifted the stick in my left hand as high as I could and did my best with my right, not getting much above my mid-chest. I yelled out, not for help but angry, never leaving his gaze. He took one step back, and I took one step forward, then another. On the fourth step, I yelled at the top of my lungs, "Get out of here!" taking three more quickly in a row. The large cat turned and ran into the woods. Leaning up against the tree, I was breathing heavily. I was tired but couldn't risk sitting down. "Now that's an adrenaline dump," I said aloud to the birds and the trees.

Catching my breath, my choice should have been crystal clear, just to head back to the cabin and forget about what I saw down near the parking lot. Only I could not do that, not today. *They may be the only way out of here, and it surely would take some time to pack those gliders up*, I thought. Either way, I would be out here with the Colorado version of a hungry lion, so I might as well take the gamble.

I headed back down the path, more limping than walking, and I wasn't about to try and run. The last turn, where Trey had thrown his beer can, was just up ahead, and I knew I was close. A vehicle honked twice down below. I strained to see through the trees, hoping they were honking to get my attention.

"Hello!" I called out, not missing a step. "Hello!" I hollered louder, straining my ears for a response. Two more honks pierced the dense forest, but farther away maybe.

"No! No! No!" I yelled, trying to move faster still. My head was pounding and my shoulder felt off, dislocated. I wasn't sure, but something wasn't right. Every few steps I looked behind me, expecting to see my new friend chasing me down like a rabbit.

"Just make it to the parking lot," I said aloud, over and over. "They will help us. They have to."

I crested a small hill to see the sun shining off the blue metal of an old pickup truck, moving away slowly at the far end of the lot.

"Hey!" I yelled. "Hey, wait a minute!"

Waiving my good arm over my head, I watched as the vehicle and trailer slowly pulled away and disappeared in a puff of smoke. I walked just far enough ahead to see an empty parking lot and collapsed on the cold pavement, banging my fists on the asphalt. "No! No! No!" I screamed, watching my breath fog in front of me.

That's it, I thought. *We're stuck. Nobody's coming up here for a week, until Grady comes back. If he even makes it back. Wasn't he going back to Denver?*

* * * *

The walk back up the trail was slow and scary, if I was honest. There's a reason a child needs to learn to ride a bike while they are young and unafraid, I remember my dad telling me once. "When they get too old," he would say, "they get scared of falling off because they have seen it happen, and now they understand it." It's kind of the same thing, I always thought, with running in the street. It takes an adult, or at least an older kid, to know you will get smooshed, even though it's never happened to them.

Only an hour ago, I wasn't at all afraid to hike by myself without a weapon of any kind, but now I know what's out there, just beyond the tree line, and it's different somehow. I knew one thing for sure—I would never hike the same way again. I swore I heard the high-pitched scream carried through the steady mountain breeze several times but didn't spot him.

* * * * * * *

Chapter Eleven Above Fern Lake Rocky Mountain National Park

"Hey man, are you okay?" called out Scott from the front porch.

I couldn't see him and thought he must have been using binoculars to look for me.

"What the..." said Scott to Jo and Shanan. "He's got blood all over his face and shirt!"

"Let me see," said Shanan, grabbing his binoculars. Looking through the eyepiece, she had to adjust the center focus wheel to see clearly. As the image became clear, she gasped, tossing them back to Scott and running full speed down the staircase.

"Alex!" she screamed. "Alex, are you okay?"

"Yes," I called back. "Just a little banged up is all."

"What happened?" she asked, as she ran up and hugged me.

"Ow!" I said, startling her.

"I'm sorry," she said.

"No, it's all right. I just hurt my shoulder."

"You don't look okay. You look like you got attacked by a wild animal."

"Well, surprisingly, that's the one thing that didn't happen. I'll tell you all about it when we get back up to the cabin."

* * * *

I filled in Shanan, Scott and Jo on what happened, with Beth and Trey not bothering to come out and hear. To Beth's credit, she did look out the front door, briefly stating, "That's gross!" when she saw the blood on my face. Without another word, she disappeared back inside. Shanan and Jo checked my head and shoulder and got me cleaned up the best they could.

"The cut on your head looks like it may need stitches," said Shanan, "but I'm not sure how to do it."

"Check in the medical bag," I told her. "The guy at the camping store said they had some glue in there that's just as good as stitches. At least it sounds better than getting my head sewn back together."

"I've seen a dislocated shoulder before," said Scott. "It's crazy looking, I can tell you, and I think yours is okay. You probably tore some muscles or tendons, though, but it's going to be a week before we know, maybe longer. This should help." He handed me a Styrofoam cup of Scotch."

"Thank you, Dr. Scotland, the third," I said, in my best Scottish accent that even Shanan scoffed at. "You always know just the right medicine," I added.

Ninety minutes later, both Beth and Trey were talking louder and slurring their words. I could hear them talking about Shanan and me, citing some sort of conspiracy against them both, forcing them to come on this trip. Shanan overheard the same and started to weigh in. "It's okay," I told her. "They will both pass out soon, and it should be quiet—at least for a while.

* * * *

Two hours passed, with me occasionally adding to the fire and having to step around both Trey and Beth to do so. They glared at me with drunken disdain, and I heard Grady in my ear saying, "I think you are all in for an interesting week, cooped up in a small cabin together."

"Trey," I said. "Can we take a look at your burns?" I was trying to be civil and make sure he didn't get an infection.

"Nope. I don't need any help," he said. I noticed he or Beth had cut the rest of his hair off with scissors or a straight razor—I couldn't be sure.

"All right, but we're here to help is all I'm saying."

Beth looked like she would pass out or be sick at any minute, but Trey kept drinking, throwing an empty bottle, smashing into the fireplace.

"Come on, man," said Scott through the open cabin door. "We don't need broken glass in here."

"Mind your business, frat boy," Trey replied.

I quickly headed out to the porch and held Scott on the shoulder, telling him it was not worth it. He wasn't a frat boy, none of us were, but he easily could have been the lead with his dad writing fat checks for support. Most just saw the rich kid with the expensive clothes and the only one on campus I knew of with a Bugatti Veyron SuperSport. Sure, it was Los Angeles and there were some with Ferraris, Lamborghinis and McLarens, but at more than a two-million-dollar price tag, he was in the lead.

He wasn't spoiled, like they thought. The few of us he counted as real friends knew he spent most of every summer volunteering with his church to serve overseas. When the son of a billionaire spends more than half of his time off voluntarily digging wells in Africa and South America, it says something about his character. When the same man tells his parents he's in love with a country girl who accidentally just happened into wealth, it also says something about his character. What they didn't know, not even Trey, was that he had been a boxer since the age of five and a Brazilian Jujitsu Black Belt, with the best training money could buy. I told my friend again that it wasn't worth it.

"Let's hang outside, buddy," I suggested.

I grabbed two beers, and we sat back on the front porch. Everything was quiet for 15 minutes, with Jo calling out that she and Shanan were going to use the bathroom.

"That guy better watch his mouth," said Scott.

"I know, buddy," I told him. "I don't like him when he's sober, and even less now that he's on his second bottle."

"Where did he even get that?" he asked.

"I don't know, but I do know for sure that..."

The crash came from inside and a scream from Shanan. We ran in to see Trey throwing full logs across the cabin at her. I ran towards him in a flashback of the other night, preparing to hit him in the chest but drive him away from the fireplace.

I closed on him, not fifteen feet away, when I saw it. The silver pistol in his hand was unmistakable and familiar. I had seen it before. It was given to me on loan only two nights ago. I stopped as he clumsily racked the slide, and I thought about hitting him square first. It was too late now, and he waved the pistol back and forth wildly, demanding to know what was going on between Shanan and me.

"I see how she looks at you!" he screamed.

"Trey, please calm down," I said, noticing Scott was slowly edging to the side of him. "I'm not sure what you're talking about," I continued, trying not to lose his attention.

"I know you used to date and were engaged until you pussed out and left her without even an explanation."

It was true, and I realized the only two people in this world I told about getting cold feet were my dad and Grady. I hadn't even told Shanan. *Why didn't I do that?* I thought. *Who does that?*

"I understand you're upset, Trey, but we need to work together now more than ever to make sure we all get out of this in one piece."

"I don't need you," he snarled, as I saw Scott almost behind him now.

I resisted the urge to look behind me and see if the girls would be in the line of fire, worst-case scenario. I didn't want him doing the same. Scott was in position and only needed a distraction. I stepped forward, raising my right arm with a grimace of pain and pointing to the door, hoping I wouldn't get shot.

Trey's split-second look in that direction was just enough to give Scott the seconds he needed to grab him from behind and tweak his wrist enough to drop the pistol after firing a single shot into the floor of the cabin.

"Let's go, tough guy," said Scott, as he nearly carried him into the pantry with the metal bar door and locking the padlock.

"I hope you have the key," he called out to me.

Trey yelled and screamed, calling both Scott and me cowards and losers. I knew he didn't want to face Scott man-to-man, and he already had his chance with me. We ignored his continued slurred speech of hate and threats. I picked up the pistol, putting it back into my pack.

"You let him go through my stuff?" I asked Beth.

"No," she spat back. "He just did."

"But you didn't come to get me or say anything, did you?"

"No, you were too busy hanging out with your *real* friends."

And just like that, I was done with her. Almost an entire year of my life wasted on someone I had nothing in common with.

* * * * * * *

CHAPTER TWELVE ABOVE FERN LAKE ROCKY MOUNTAIN NATIONAL PARK

I remember my dad sitting me down as a young man, giving me "the talk." He covered the basic hardware differences between men and women, going right into the how-babies-are-made speech "but only when you're in love and married." Even then, I already knew the how-to part, as did most of my friends. And I had heard my older brother talking about the other things he did with his girlfriend, who he had not married yet. What I heard but didn't fully understand was the other part.

"Son," he told me, "there is a very good chance you're not going to marry your first girlfriend—or second, for that matter. But when you date a girl, make sure it's for the right reasons. Being attracted to her is certainly necessary, but it's not the most important part. You have to be compatible. You need to be able to have a conversation together and not just parade her around in front of your friends. And most of all, you need to be best friends."

"Sorry, Dad. You were right," I said under my breath.

Beth, now passed out on her sleeping bag, didn't seem concerned about Trey being locked up—or anything else, for that matter. I took the opportunity to move my pack and sleeping bag across the cabin. Not next to Shanan's, not yet at least, but away from the drunk girl I had nothing in common with anymore, if ever. The rest of us met outside after I put the logs back in place that had been thrown across the cabin and stoked the fire to keep it going all night, I hoped. Trey was still hollering inside but quieter now.

"I'm done with him," announced Shanan to nobody in particular.

Crack! came the sound from inside the cabin. *Crack! Crack!* Scott and I both jumped up, running in to see what was going on.

Did Beth get the pistol out of my backpack? I thought.

We stopped just inside the front door, as the next shot rang out.

"Get down on the floor, both of you!" called an agitated Trey, still inside the storage room but now holding a rifle.

"Where did he get that?" asked Scott, looking at me.

"I don't know," I responded, "but it doesn't look good."

"On the wall," I whispered to Scott. "Back up against it."

We moved quickly towards the same wall the storage door shared, flattening up against it.

"He can't shoot us from here," I said. "The small gap in the bars won't let him turn the gun this way."

"I see what you're doing," yelled Trey, slurring his words once again.

"You've got me locked in here, but I have the gun. I see I can't hit you, but I can fire every one of these 50 shells...oh, wait a minute...now it's 46, I believe. That's all there is. Trust me, I've looked. So, we're going to make a deal right here and now about who gets the guns and who gets the food."

"Give us a minute," I called out, nodding to Scott to come over out of earshot.

He got close, and I whispered as quietly as I could into his ear.

"I need Grady's pistol from my pack, but I can't get it without being in the line of fire, and I'm sure as hell not letting Trey out with a rifle, not now."

"I can get it," came the voice from right behind me. I jumped but didn't have to turn around to know it was Beth.

"Thanks, Beth, but I don't want you getting hurt," I told her.

"I'm not worried about that," she laughed. "I'm the last one here he should be upset with. Besides, I'm not suggesting it to be nice. There's a price for everything in this world, especially now."

"Okay, what do you want?" I asked now, talking normally since the cat was out of the bag already.

In a split second, my mind ran through all of the possibilities that she may come up with, from forbidding me to talk to Shanan to having her and me leave on our own, without my other friends, to me letting Trey walk out of here with whatever he wants.

"Now you two can give me a minute," she said, walking straight towards the storage closet without fear.

"Hey, Trey. How are you doing?" she asked.

"All right, I guess. Are you going to get me out of here?"

"I'm trying to do just that," she replied.

It was obvious to both Scott and me that they were both still intoxicated, and I wondered how that would play into the negotiations. I waved my hand, gesturing for Shanan and Jo to stay outside, the one safe place right now.

"What do you want?" Beth asked him, smiling flirtatiously.

"I want to go back home," he replied. "Back to Cali and as far away from these lunatics as possible."

"Me too," she said, quieter but still loud enough for Scott and me to hear.

* * * * * * *

CHAPTER THIRTEEN ABOVE FERN LAKE ROCKY MOUNTAIN NATIONAL PARK

"Just in case you weren't already sure," said Scott to me, as I nodded my head yes.

Scott and I waited for nearly ten more minutes as the two discussed their negotiation strategy. I thought about going outside and talking with the girls about what we knew so far, but I was concerned Beth would make a play for the pistol when I wasn't looking. Then he would have two weapons, and I would have the key to the padlock. I would still have the advantage, but it would be lessened, for sure.

"Okay," hollered Beth, heading towards us. "We have some terms to discuss. Number one, you let Trey out of that cell you have him in now. He and I are both headed in another direction from the rest of you. Number two, Trey and I keep one of the weapons, including all of its corresponding bullet things. Number three, assuming Grady is not coming back anytime soon, of course, we want to move as a group at least down the mountain before we split off and go our separate ways."

"Anything else?" I asked, not agreeing to the terms laid out so far.

"Did I miss something, Trey?" she shouted back over her shoulder.

"Just the food and the booze are all I can think of," he replied.

"An even split—the same amount for each person, I'm assuming?" I asked.

"Nope," replied Trey. "Half for your group and half for ours."

"That's not going to happen," interjected Scott for the first time in the exchange.

"Is that all?" I asked again, wanting everything out on the table for discussion.

"Yep," replied Trey—"nothing more and nothing less. Make your decision fast, though. I've got to piss bad."

"I'd say that gives us the advantage," whispered Scott in my ear.

"I would agree, but all of our food is in there, and I don't want him doing something stupid like peeing all over it, just to spite us."

"Yeah," replied Scott. "I didn't think about that, but he's crazy enough to try it."

"All right. Then give us about ten to discuss it and we'll figure out the next step," I replied.

"Ten minutes?" whined Trey.

Scott and I stood in the front doorway of the cabin with Jo and Shanan just outside. I still didn't trust Beth to leave the pistol in my pack if I stepped away for a minute. We reviewed the demands as Beth had told us and asked everyone's opinion. They all asked me to start the ball rolling and said they would jump in as needed.

"Okay," I said. "As I see it, we need to make a deal, one way or the other. That book we read said the EMP would knock out vehicles made after 1978 and render them inoperable. I'm pretty sure the hang-glider people had a truck older than that, but there are probably not too many others like it out on the roads. I know Mr. Parker's SUV won't fit that description, and most likely no vehicles in his fleet are that old. For that reason alone, I don't think he's coming back for us anytime soon. We can wait and see and be at the end of our food supply, or head down to Estes Park while we still have something to eat and at least get some more information about what's going on and how we plan to make it home."

"Agreed so far or not?"

All three nodded their heads yes.

"Okay. Let's move on to the negotiation part. It's clear that both Trey and Beth are looking to make their own way back to California once we all get down the mountain. Beth and I are done, as I assume you are with Trey," I said, looking at Shanan. "And I assume we are all wanting to head back to our homes in Texas."

"Done like a well-done steak," Shanan replied, "and I think we are all ready to go home," getting approval from the others.

"Then let's move on," I suggested. "We have to let Trey out of there sooner or later; I mean, we can't keep him locked up. I propose we let him out with the following conditions. First, we will give him and Beth the pistol with ammo, and we keep the rifle. That rifle is much more intimidating to anyone we may run into along the route with less than honorable intentions."

"Plus, it's better for hunting if it comes to that," added Scott.

"As far as food goes, we split everything six ways; we can't negotiate on those terms. Last, we can't exactly just ditch them and tell them not to follow us, so I am okay with getting down the mountain together, but then they are on their own. That's all I've got," I announced. "Any other ideas?"

"I'm good as long as Trey doesn't try anything with that pistol," said Scott.

"Me, too!" said all the girls.

Scott and I walked back into the cabin.

* * * * * * *

CHAPTER FOURTEEN ABOVE FERN LAKE ROCKY MOUNTAIN NATIONAL PARK

"Trey, we're going to come over to the door, but I want you to lay down the rifle on the floor and slide it out first," I said.

"The hell I will!" he said immediately.

"Listen, I'm trying to get you out of there so you can use the outhouse, but I'm not doing it with that rifle pointed in our direction."

"If I do that, then you've got two weapons, and I have none. No way!"

"Assuming we agree on the other terms," I continued, "I will give Beth the pistol, and we'll take the rifle—unless you don't trust her, that is."

"Right now, I trust her more than all of you put together," he replied, motioning to me, Scott and the girls outside.

"All right, then. We will agree to give you two the pistol and ammo. That, along with 2/6 of the food, and we will walk out of here together until we get down the mountain. At that point, you two are on your own."

"What about the alcohol?" asked Trey, with Beth nodding her head yes.

"That will be split when we head down the mountain. I can't risk another incident up here, and it will remain locked up from all of us until we leave." I looked at Scott, hoping I had his approval.

"It's going to be a long hike out of here, though," I added, "and I, for one, am not going to be packing heavy. So, minus my Scotch, I'm not taking any other spirits out of this place. So, what's your answer, Trey?"

I could tell he really needed to go out back, as he was squirming like a small boy trying to cross his legs when they had to go bad. I wasn't trying to use this as leverage, although I thought I could, but I had to get a deal before putting the key into the lock.

"Okay, okay. It's a deal. Now get me the hell out of here!"

"Beth," I called, you can get the pistol out of my pack and the box of shells, just as soon as Trey here slides out the rifle and ammo."

"Box of what?" she asked.

"The bullets, Beth," said Scott, frustrated. "Just get the box of bullets."

"You know I am trusting you to keep your word, Alex," said Trey.

"Yeah, I know. And you were the one I remember trying to shoot me. Try it again or hurt Shanan or any of us, and I'll keep the promise from the hotel. Understand?"

Without responding, he slid the rifle and ammunition under the door stock first, as Beth took the pistol awkwardly from my pack.

"Don't forget the alcohol from Trey's pack," I told her, as I held up my Scotch bottle. "It all goes in the closet."

I handed the rifle to Scott and unlocked the door, with Trey nearly running out the back door to the outhouse.

"So, we're done, you and me?" asked Beth aloud in front of everyone.

"I think we've both known it for a while," I replied.

I stepped into the storage room, keeping the padlock in my hand, and grabbed just enough food for tonight's dinner before locking it back up.

Jo and Shanan immediately reset the sleeping quarters, separating our group from theirs as much as possible in the small room.

"Looks like dinner minus the nightcap," I joked to Scott and the girls.

It was only around 7 p.m., I guessed, based on the sunset, and I was exhausted.

"How is your head?" asked Shanan. "It looks like the glue is holding."

"Better than my shoulder," I replied, rubbing it lightly. "I still can't raise my arm over my midline. But it has to get better to pack out of here, or I just deal with it."

"I'm sorry about you and Beth," she whispered.

"I'm not, but thanks. I'm sorry about you and Trey," I said, winking. There was a pause before we both started to laugh.

"What the heck were we thinking?" I asked.

"Hey, now, that was mostly you... I'm just kidding," she said.

"No, you're right. It was all me, and it took a trip like this for me to realize it. Can you forgive me? What I mean is, I'm so sorry for messing up your life, and will you forgive me sometime in the future?"

"I already have, a long time ago," Shanan replied.

"Can I kiss you?" I asked.

"You'd better!"

I kissed Shanan for the first time in more than a year, and it felt oddly comforting, like a favorite T-shirt but at the same time exciting and new.

"If we make it home, I'll be true to you for the rest of my life," I told her.

"Well then, we had better make it back alive," she responded, smiling.

"Hey, you two get a room!" joked Scott, walking out onto the deck with Jo.

"I did," I replied. "There just happen to be four other people sharing it. Kind of kills the mood, don't you think?"

"That's the Alex I've been missing the last couple of days," said Scott. "The smart-ass who always has a joke. Love you, brother."

* * * * * * *

Chapter Fifteen Above Fern Lake Rocky Mountain National Park

D arkness filled the valley, and the fire was doing its job, pushing heat into the cabin. It would need to be stoked several times throughout the night, but it had a good bed of coals now.

"You keep the rifle tonight," I told Scott. "Whichever one of us wakes up in the night can stoke the fire. I'm exhausted and need to get some sleep."

I slept right next to Shanan, with Scott and Jo nearby. I didn't bother checking on Trey and Beth, who hadn't left their side of the cabin since we let him out. Deep sleep with dreams of wild animals, gunslingers, and birds flying high over the forest trees invaded my brain. I remembered stoking the fire once but had no idea what time it was.

* * * *

"Crap! No! No! No!" came the sound that jarred me out of my slumber. I looked up to see the first light coming into the windows and Scott running around the cabin frantically.

"What's the matter?" I called out, as I looked towards where Trey and Beth had been sleeping.

"Oh..." I said, noticing their sleeping bags and packs were gone.

"The gun! Where's the gun?!" shouted Scott, looking in every corner.

I panicked, looking for the storage closet keys I had put in my pack right beside me. They weren't there, and I quickly unzipped compartment after compartment as I slowly realized what probably happened.

"Look!" said Shanan, calmly pointing towards the wide-open door to the storage closet.

I walked to the closet and slowly inside. The book we had been reading laid on the floor in the wet spot made by my opened bottle of Scotch with the contents poured onto the old wooden floor. One page was torn out and laid just under one Pop-Tart. It read "Screw you, guys," and underneath had a crude drawing of a Pop-Tart divided four ways.

"It's gone," I said, loud enough for everyone to hear. "It's all gone—they took all of the food." I sat down on the floor, putting my head in my hands.

"Sorry, man," said Scott. "I should have kept the rifle strapped to me. I never expected him to take it."

"I know. It's not your fault. I lost the keys, and I didn't expect it either. What I know for sure is we need to leave, and it has to be today."

"Can we follow them and get our stuff back?" asked Jo.

"It's tough," I replied, with all four of us now sitting cross-legged on the floor. "Criss-Cross-Applesauce," I joked at what we used to call Indian-style before the days of political correctness.

"Still have the jokes, I see," said Scott, smiling.

"Yep, and 1/4 of a pop tart, so I'm good," I replied, putting my arm around Shanan. "We do need to make a plan, though. Jo, I get what you're asking, but we don't know which way they are headed or how much of a head start they would have by the time we are packed up. We also don't have a weapon anymore. I suggest we get packed up quickly and follow the road back the way we came up here, down to Estes Park, and see what we are really dealing with. Maybe, if we're lucky, Mr. Parker is still there—or my new attorney, at least—so we can get some information."

"I wasn't paying attention to how we got up here," said Jo nervously, "and we don't have a map."

"It's okay, babe," said Scott. "There were only a couple of ways up here that I saw, and we should see the signs most tourists would follow to get back to town."

"Shanan, what do you say?" I asked.

"I don't think we have a choice but to leave right away. I mean...we're out of food and it's a long hike back," she replied.

"The trip is about 10 miles, I think, so we could make it today," added Scott.

Getting packed up was easier than expected, since we weren't packing the food out. Still, I took the time to clean the place up and make it presentable for whoever may need it in the future.

"Sorry, Grady," I said aloud, as if he were standing right in front of me. "I left it as you asked, even taking the trash, but I can't lock it up, not after what I've seen. This cabin may save somebody's life up here."

"Do you always talk to yourself?" joked Scott.

"No...only during an apocalypse," I said, laughing.

"How are you always so upbeat?" asked Jo. "I'm not trying to be critical—just curious is all."

"It's a fair question," I replied. "We lost our only weapon, our food, and we will likely have a heck of a trip home, if we even make it at all—and still, I'm cracking jokes. I wasn't always like this, you know. I mean, I was a serious kid growing up...like so serious my parents sent me to counseling to find out what was wrong with me. I wasn't a bad kid, or even messed up. I was too up tight, I guess, and always worried about getting good grades. Was my bed made straight enough? Did I get a hair out of place, combing it before school? All of it. I was scared to death to make a mistake and have someone look at me negatively. Then one sunny November day, it was a Sunday afternoon, I remember, and I was 10 years old when it all changed... We should get packing."

"What day?" asked Jo. "I mean, now I want to hear the story."

"Me too," added Scott.

Shanan was one of the few people I ever told besides my parents and brother, who of course was a witness, and she nodded to continue.

"Okay then. It's not a long story. Shanan already knows, but it has defined my life more than just about anything else. As I said, I was 10 and I was with my older brother, who would have been 12, and a few of our cousins up from Houston. There was a fast-moving river that always ran and never iced over completely, even in the dead of winter. We were fishing in one of our favorite spots when my brother Danny dropped one of his gloves into the water by accident. We watched it quickly be sucked downstream and under a large ice block without coming out the other side. 'Must have gotten stuck in there,' my brother said.

"I got close to the water and could see it just under the ice, flapping left and right. 'I can get it,' I told everyone in my serious voice, letting out my line to try and snag it with my favorite lure. I called out 'Almost there,' seeing it just beyond the ice edge and hooked on an underwater branch. 'Oh no!' I cried out when my favorite lure in the whole world got stuck on the same branch. Now, lake and river fisherman, and even kids, know that when you get snagged bad, and you can't just grab the lure, you have to pull the line in several directions, and if that doesn't work, you try to nudge it with the end of your pole, dislodging it.

"Anyway, I did just that from atop the ice block when it happened. The part I was standing on gave way—or broke off, I guess—and I plunged into the icy water with ten pounds of clothes on, plus my moon boots that are somewhat waterproof but not made to be completely submerged in water. In a second, I was on my back, grabbing hold of the ledge as my legs were swept under, entangling in the underwater brush and God-knows-what. I cried out to my brother and cousins to help me, and I could see they were doing their best, calling out instructions to me.

"'Alex!' they said. 'Hold on! Seriously...hold on!' My brother had hold of my collar but couldn't free my entangled legs. He was shouting, his face inches from mine and close enough to feel the spittle from his mouth, but I could no longer hear him. A calm came over me as I prayed to God to help me. I heard aloud, like a voice right next to me, 'I've got you. Fight and stop acting so serious all the time.' I thought it was my brother or one of my cousins, but it wasn't. I heard it again and snapped to focus and winked at Danny when I fought to get my legs free."

"You winked at him when you were about to die?" asked Scott.

"Yes, I did. It sounds weird, I know, and a minute later they had me pulled out of the water. Ever since then, I've never taken things too seriously, no matter the circumstance. Occasionally that backfires, though," I added, grabbing Shanan's hand. "But I'm learning. Got me out of counseling real quick, though, so that was good."

"I never heard that," admitted Scott, "but it makes some sense, I guess."

"All right, are we about ready to head out?" I asked.

Leaving the safety of the cabin felt odd and would have been a lot harder decision if we had plenty of food on hand.

* * * * * * *

Chapter Sixteen Above Fern Lake Rocky Mountain National Park

W e headed down the front staircase and walked single file down the trail. I was keeping half an eye out for the big cat I met earlier in the week but thought he wouldn't likely mess with the four of us.

"Hold up!" said Scott, in the lead, raising his right hand.

"What going on?" I asked, coming up front.

"Do you hear that?" he asked.

"Hear what?" asked Jo. Just then, we all heard it. "Sounds like someone arguing."

"You don't think it's them, do you?" asked Shanan.

"No way, not this close to the cabin...unless something happened," I replied. "Let's be really quiet, though, as we get closer. I don't want any surprises."

That was when I heard Beth's voice. It sounded like she was lecturing me, but this time it was someone else. I had to smile.

"What's so funny?" asked Shanan.

"It's just Beth. She's got a new guy to dump her crap on—and it feels good, if I'm honest."

"You're devious," she said, smiling.

"No, I'm just happy to be a free-wheeling bachelor with lots of girlfriends again."

"Yeah, right," said Scott, laughing. "Don't worry, Shanan. You're all he talks about when you're not around. It's annoying, really," he added, winking at me.

"In a good way, I hope?" she asked.

"Absolutely," I chimed in.

"So, how do you want to play this?" I asked Scott, "keeping in mind they have two guns to our none—and the food stealing, of course."

He sighed, thinking...

"We didn't catch up to them this quickly by chance," said Scott. "So, I'm guessing one had a change of heart or they got tired quickly from lugging out all the booze. Either way, we need to either steer clear or engage and try to get our stuff back."

"I, for one, want to bring Mr. Parker his guns back," I said, "so that's my vote. How about you, ladies?"

"Either way, I guess," said Shanan. "I don't really want to see Trey again, but I want to do right by Mr. Parker. So actually, I'm with engaging—carefully, though."

"Sure," added Jo, "with Scott taking the lead."

"I can walk up in the front spot," I told him.

"Nah, you're much more likely to get shot than I am... I mean, that guy really hates you. I'm joking...but not really," he added.

"Okay, I'll take the second position, then," I said, falling in behind him.

The yelling got louder as we crested the small hill, looking down the steep rocky path into the meadow we had come through on the hike up, but this time the yelling was from both of them.

"You're just lazy," I heard Beth say. "I don't have time for this."

"Are you frickin' kidding me right now?" Trey responded. "Look at my foot! Does it look like I can walk?"

"Well, I'm not carrying anything else, that's for sure," she responded sharply.

* * * *

"Hello!" called out Scott loudly.

I wasn't expecting that, but they knew we were here now.

"We need your help," said Trey, lying on the ground with his head on his pack.

"No, *you* need it!" said Beth.

"Are you still drinking?" asked Scott, looking squarely at the open vodka bottle in Trey's hands.

"Maybe, but I've got a good excuse," he said, pointing to his left ankle.

Instinctively we all looked at his left ankle as he raised his pant leg.

"That's bad," I said, looking at the grossly swollen ankle. "How did that happen in a field?"

"It happened on the steep part of the trail back there," said Beth, "and this was as far as he could hop on one leg with his pack."

I gave Scott a subtle nod to follow my lead.

"All right then. Good luck, guys," I said, walking around them and down the trail without another word.

Scott, Shanan and Jo followed close behind. I could hear Beth and Trey arguing about what to do next and slowed my pace just a bit, fully expecting to turn around. It was another dozen steps before I heard it.

"Please come back and help him!" called out Beth.

I stopped but didn't turn around.

"You have to help me; you just have to!" called Trey in a panicked voice I had never heard before.

"Your pack is too heavy," I called back, now turning around.

"It's just my ankle. I carried my pack just fine before."

"What I mean is, your pack is too heavy with everything you stole from us. Now you want our help?"

In a split second, I wondered if he would point one of the guns at us and demand it.

"You've got about 10 miles," added Scott, "if you're headed to Estes Park, that is. You'll never make it there on that leg, and even if you crawled to the parking lot, there are no cars around now to pick you up."

"What do you want?" asked Trey.

Scott looked at me, and I nodded, figuring we both didn't want to leave them here to probably die, even after what Trey did to us. But we weren't going to continue getting crapped on, either.

"We want everything," replied Scott. "Those guns you stole belong to Mr. Parker, even now, and the food was for all of us."

"What about the beer?" asked Trey.

"Really, that's what you're worried about right now?" asked Beth, as it even sounded strange to her.

"It stays," I said, "unless Beth is going to carry it, because I'm not."

"What about me? Do you carry me out of here?" asked Trey.

"No," I replied flatly. "When we get our things back, and only then, we'll make a drag sled and pull you down the mountain."

"So, what's it going to be?" asked Scott, clearly not wanting to spend any more time with this guy without a deal.

"Okay, okay. I'll take the deal."

"Don't you mean *we*?" asked Beth, sounding annoyed.

"Yeah, that's what I said," he responded.

"All right. Let's start with the guns and ammo," I told him, "and don't try anything you will regret."

Trey nodded to Beth to get the pistol and ammo out of his pack. And the rifle lying next to him he handed to me without a fight.

"Okay, now the food," said Scott. "We'll each carry our own share."

Shanan and Jo, with Beth's reluctant help, redistributed the food into each pack.

"We will need to fill the canteens with purified water at the creek, just down the trail a bit," I said. "But first, we have to get this sled made quickly if we are going to try to make it down there before tonight."

Keeping the rifle and handing the loaded pistol to Scott, we set out to find branches for the sled. I had never made one before, but Scott, who had formerly studied towards an Engineering degree, drew the schematics on the ground with a sharp stick and we gathered the materials.

"How much do you weigh?" he called out to Trey.

"Maybe 160," came the reply.

"We have paracord from the camping store, so that will make it a bit easier than the Native Americans had to figure out," I offered.

Two hefty sticks tied into a V and crisscrossed with smaller branches made up the sled's bottom. The thick leather rifle sling was secured to the front and would be used as a belt to pull both Trey and his pack. I was half waiting for an apology from him, but none came. Maybe he just considered his life in return for our stolen items a fair business transaction. It didn't matter much now, I supposed, and continued working.

"Let's give this a try," said Scott, having tied the last piece. "Help me get him in the middle of the sled, Alex... Now, Trey, it's important that you lie down like being on a stretcher to distribute your weight evenly. We'll put your pack crossways on the back, and you can lay your head on it and still see where we are heading."

* * * *

"I'll take the first drag shift," I said, fitting the sling belt around my waist.

It was tough going, as the trail carved out of the mountain wasn't made to be smooth for dragging; it was created for hikers who didn't mind stepping over rocks and tree roots. Switching off twice with Scott, we made it to the parking lot, and as far as we still had to go, I said a silent thank-you prayer for smooth dragging, at least.

"It's all downhill from here," I joked. "If we had some snow, I would have some fun and jump on that thing with you, Trey, and sled on down in no time."

"That doesn't sound like fun at all," he griped.

"I had forgotten how amazing the scenery is up here," I called out to no one in particular.

"I guess this is the best way to see it," added Shanan.

As Scott and I switched out the lead, my mind wandered to my old life—not the one with Beth but the one before that, growing up with my parents and brother, Shanan, and friends I hadn't seen for a while. *What would the country look like if this was all true?* I thought. *What would the world look like?*

"What if it's not true?" I said aloud. "What if it's all just some sort of coincidence—seeing a bright light and our phones not working... We don't even know about the cars working or not."

"There was a car or truck every few hundred feet on our way up here," said Jo. "I mean, I know it's winter and all, but we haven't seen any sign of one since...well...since that light thing happened."

"Except for the old truck with the gliders..." I replied, trailing off as I was coming to the realization that not only was it likely but nothing else would explain it.

"Anyone know how long it takes an ankle to heal up?" asked Trey. "I mean, I am going to have a lot of walking to do, sooner or later."

"My guess is later," Shanan commented, talking to Trey for the first time since the log-throwing incident. "But," she added, "it all depends on how bad it is."

"You guys are all going to stick around until I get better, right?" asked Trey.

No one replied, not even Beth.

"Nobody? Nobody is going to answer me?"

"I won't speak for anyone else, but I'll get you down to town, and then you're on your own," I finally replied.

"Me too," said both Scott and Jo.

"Shanan, what about you?" Trey asked. "I mean, I'm sorry about what happened. I was drunk, you know."

"Which time?"

"Huh?"

"I mean, which time when you were drunk and tried to hurt me are you sorry for?" she asked without any emotion.

The pause was awkward for everyone, I guessed, and all I could hear was the scraping of the sled as I dragged it down the center of the highway.

"So, it's like that, huh?" he asked. "After all we've been through."

I could see Beth out of the corner of my eye, shaking her head as her probable new man practically begged for his old girlfriend back.

"Yup. Just like that," Shanan responded.

"Time for a drag switch, Alex?" asked Scott, trying to break up the tension just a bit.

The awkward silence continued as we switched the belt and continued down the road. I was getting hungry and wanted to stop for a quick break but the conversation needed a pause.

"Let's take a break in 30," I called out, with everyone agreeing.

Nobody said a word for 10 minutes, and that was fine by me.

* * * * * * *

Chapter Seventeen Above Fern Lake Rocky Mountain National Park

"What is that?" asked Jo.

"What do you mean?" questioned Beth.

"I mean that sound, like a motor of some kind."

"I hear it too," I said, as the rest strained their ears and we all looked to the sky.

"It's a plane," shouted Shanan. "An old biplane, like a crop-duster. Look! It's heading towards us!"

We stopped and all raised our arms, shouting, "We need help!"

I put mine down, right after I started realizing there wasn't much danger to get to town; it just might take another few hours. But I wouldn't turn down a ride in the back of a truck, should the pilot's words get back to town. The plane flew right over us and circled once more, coming back over in the general direction.

"He saw us, right?" asked Shanan.

"How could he not?" snapped Trey. "You can be so stupid sometimes. If I wasn't sure before about why I left you, I am now."

I grabbed Shanan's hand lightly and shook my head.

"I know. It's not worth it," she whispered in my ear.

"Secrets now! You've got secrets, the two of you?" snarled Trey.

"Time for a drag dump," I said to Scott, stopping abruptly.

"Fine by me," he replied.

"Good luck, Trey," I said, as I left the sled on the road and continued walking. I didn't look behind me but figured the rest of the group was with me on this. Well, except for Beth, maybe. I got my answer as both she and him shouted cuss words at me as I kept pace.

"Are we really doing this?" asked Scott.

"We'll see; it's up to them really," I responded. "Let's stop here for a snack and water break."

I proceeded to unpack snacks and water, with others following suit. The yelling and swearing, only 50 yards back, continued for nearly 10 minutes before quieting down.

"Here she comes," said Jo quietly, nodding her head back towards Beth.

"If she had her pack on, I would say she wants to come with us; but since she doesn't, I'm guessing it's some sort of apology or negotiation attempt," I commented.

"Okay!" She finally spoke, stopping five yards out from us. "What do you want, Alex?"

I laughed, not meaning to be a jerk, but actually caught off guard with her question.

"Nothing," I responded. "I'm not asking for anything from you two."

"Well, Trey wants something," she said, with a completely straight face.

I didn't answer, as it didn't matter to me anymore, and all was quiet.

"What he wants," she continued without being asked, is an apology from all of you, but from mostly *you*," she added, pointing at me.

"Okay," I said, growing tired of the charade. "I'm done here. Tell him that I'm sorry it came down to this, and I really do wish you two good luck. Let's get packed up, guys."

We all started packing, with Beth just standing there, not sure how to respond. She huffed and walked back up the road.

"You might as well just shoot me then, you cowards," Trey yelled back.

Scott was getting nervous about the whole situation, I noticed, and he pulled me to the side.

"Hey man, what are we going to do here? I mean, we can't just leave him, right?"

"No, you're right. We can't, but I was hoping he would realize that. Apparently, he hasn't yet. Let me try to talk to him," I added, walking back up the road.

"Beth, can you please give us a minute?" I asked.

"She stays! She can hear anything you have to say to me!" commanded Trey.

"All right, Trey. I know we haven't gotten along well recently, but let's start a new slate of sorts right now. And once we get you to the hospital in town, we can go our own ways. For my part, I'll pull my weight, and with Scott's help we'll get you to town. And for your part, no more comments to me or anyone else. Your choice—you've got 10 seconds...9...8...7..."

"Yeah, yeah. Okay, let's go," Trey conceded.

* * * *

Picking up the sled, we proceeded, one step at a time.

"I'm quitting the gym when we get back home," I said to Scott, "and I'll just pull sleds around the house."

"Yeah, I'm right there with you!" he said, laughing.

It was nearly an hour later before Trey spoke of having to take a leak. Something had changed, as he politely asked us to take a break and help him over to the nearest tree.

"Thanks, guys," was all he said when done.

I gave Scott the what-the-heck look before quickly remembering that one respectful interaction with Trey didn't make up for all the rest before.

"There she is!" I called out minutes later, rounding the corner and looking a couple of miles down the valley at the picturesque town of Estes Park.

"We're on the home stretch!" called out Jo, with nobody responding and only the sound of heavy breathing from six college kids not used to the altitude yet. Only Trey didn't seem to be bothered by it.

"Maybe we should stick together after we get to town," suggested Trey. *Here we go*, I thought, without responding.

"Let's take a quick break," I told everyone, taking out my binoculars and looking out over the town. I could make out vehicles, with most seemingly stopped in the middle of the road. "They're all broke down," I said to Shanan, handing her the binoculars.

"I see that," she replied, scanning each street carefully. "Wait a minute... Look down there!" she pointed to Scott, who also had his out. "Look right by the church, just to the left. Do you see it?"

"Yeah!" said Scott, getting excited. "It's an old pickup, I think, and it's moving!"

"Hey," called out Beth, raising her arms over her head. "We're over here!"

I didn't say what we were all thinking, knowing they would not be able to hear or see her with the naked eye.

"Let's just keep moving," I suggested, picking the cart up again with a groan.

"I'll catch up in a minute," said Shanan, still scanning the town.

Minutes later, Shanan caught up to me, with a wink that she had some news.

"Scott, can we switch off for a minute?" I asked.

"Sure, buddy. I still have a little bit left in me."

I dropped back to talk with Shanan and hear the news.

"There is a hospital right over there," she pointed discretely, "even before you get into town. I can see the helipad on top," she added, still looking through the lens. "I don't want them coming with us past that point," she continued, matter-of-factly.

"Neither do I," my mouth whispered, squeezing her hand.

Scott would have to wait to hear the news, as I didn't want to give Trey or Beth the heads-up that we were only a mile or so from the departure point.

"The less time we all have to discuss it, the better," I whispered to Shanan, with her nodding in agreement.

"How's your ankle?" I asked Trey, before wondering why I even opened my mouth.

"The same, I guess," he responded.

We walked in silence, switching off on the cart until the turnoff I could see up ahead. "Estes Park Health Hospital entrance—555 Prospect Avenue" read the royal blue sign with white lettering.

"Here we are, in the homestretch now," announced Scott.

Closing in on the parking lot, people were milling about, with only a few even slightly paying attention to us.

"Get in a fight in Stephen King's room only a week ago, and everyone takes notice. Now six exhausted hikers walk down the middle of the highway, dragging a man towards the Emergency Room, and nobody even bats an eye," I told Shanan quietly.

"The times, they are changed," she whispered back, with a flirty smile.

* * * * * * *

Chapter Eighteen Kabul, Afghanistan

C olonel O'Sullivan ordered his men, like a fine Swiss clock, seamlessly into position for what was surely coming. He had trained months for this very scenario but only got the heads-up the day he phoned Shanan on her way up the mountain.

All at once, his tour in Afghanistan didn't seem like such a dangerous place. He quietly gathered a few of his top soldiers that he could trust for a secret mission. Each was given an opportunity to warn their families back home about what was to come.

Colonel O'Sullivan had only made two successful calls. One to Shanan and the other to her mother. His select group of six soldiers, including himself, were to head back to US soil in a matter of days, as the President ordered home more than half of the troops serving across the globe.

"Soldiers, as you have heard, we are headed back stateside in a matter of days. As you all know, my only priority, besides my work, is the safety of my daughter, Shanan. It's going to be every man, woman, and child on their own, starting right now. It will take a few days, or maybe even a few weeks, before things get really bad. But once it does, it's hard to come back from.

"I'm going to find my daughter and make sure she gets to a safe place, either on my own or with you fine soldiers. I've handpicked the lot of you for your flying and combat experience. At this point, I'm not sure what equipment will be at our disposal and want to cover all bases. Anyone who sticks with me has my word—we will not stop until all of your families are safe. My daughter is isolated and taken care of, I'm sure, so we will start with those of you having families in the city. If you lose track of them there, you may never find them. In addition to any of you who decide to carry out the mission with me, I'll have a Medic—you all know Kaitlin, I presume. I will get this done, even if it means breaking rank to do so. So, to be clear, if you're in, you are all in until we're done; and if you're out, I'll expect you to mind your tongue and speak of this no more. Hold up your hand if you're in."

Three men and one woman held up their hands, with two declining to do so. All four of his soldiers agreed to the rescue mission, rescuing their families one by one, starting with Private Bobby's wife and son in Washington Park, Chicago.

"You picked a hell of a place for us to start, Soldier. Washington Park in the 'Windy City' was a war zone before this ever started! It's the most dangerous neighborhood in the city, if I remember right."

"Well, sir, it's not so bad. It's number three on the danger list, I think," Bobby answered.

"Only number three, huh? That's where we will start, then," the Colonel replied.

* * * *

"Do you think she will like me—Shanan, that is?" Kaitlin asked the Colonel once they were alone.

"What's not to like? You're kind, tough, and feisty. If you had red hair instead of brown, you would fit right in with us Irish. Let's get packed up. We've got a few flights coming up."

Colonel O'Sullivan put in a request to transfer his group to the closest Army base to his daughter—in Fort Carson, Colorado. Fort Carson, situated just south of Colorado Springs and home to over 25,000 soldiers at any given time, would provide the best base, he thought. The plan to secure a helicopter that only two men in his group could fly and the firepower needed to keep everyone safe was conceived.

There was no doubt in his mind that he would be calling in a few favors he had saved up as he rose through the military ranks over the last 30 years. If he were honest, he would call in every single one and then owe some back if it would help him find his Shanan.

* * * * * * *

Chapter Nineteen Near Estes Park, Colorado

"Okay, Trey. Let's get you off of this sled and into the lobby," I said, as we stopped just in front of the hospital doors. "Shanan, can you please bring his pack in?" I asked. "I don't want to leave it outside so someone can walk off with it."

The formerly automatic doors were propped open with a cinder block on each side, lit inside by natural light. Checking him in was old-school, to say the least, with no computers working. Emergency lights flashed on and off down the hall.

"How long have these lights been flashing like this?" I asked the front-desk receptionist.

"A couple of days, I guess—ever since the power went out. I'm told we will have electricity again soon."

"All right, Trey. Your pack should be safe here inside, and I do wish you good luck on your journey home," I said, patting him on the shoulder as I walked towards the door.

"Now wait! Wait just a minute!" he said. "You guys aren't going to wait for me?"

Scott seemed nervous, as did Jo, but didn't speak.

"This was the deal," I spoke up. "You are in good hands here, and we fulfilled our end of the agreement."

I slung my pack over my shoulder with a grunt, now even more sore than two days ago, and walked out the door without looking back. Shanan followed closely, with Scott and Jo just behind her. I glanced back to see Beth pacing back and forth through the open door before disappearing inside.

* * * *

"Let's see if we can find my lawyer," I announced, as we headed down towards the center of town. "I just want to check in before we head home."

"Who's up for a coffee?" asked Shanan.

"Me—me, absolutely," I replied, still not shaking the headache from missing my fix this morning. "It's a drug, you know—caffeine—like coke and heroin," I told her, although I was sure I had told her the same thing before, in another life.

"First one's on me," she said, ducking into the same coffee shop I was in the last time I spoke to my dad on the phone. Even in the middle of the afternoon it was cold, and seeing her through the window with four large coffees was the most exciting thing I would see today. I went inside to help carry the cups when I saw the sign. It hung behind the register and read "CASH ONLY" in large black letters.

"I had to pay cash," said Shanan, seeing me walk in. "I saw the sign," I told her, as it sank in.

"No electricity...no credit cards," I mumbled. Once outside, I made the announcement. "All right, guys. It looks like we are cash-only, for a while at least, until they get the power back up. Let's see how much we have between us and use it sparingly."

I would have forgone the coffee and the $20 dollars it set us back if I realized this. My dad always had us kids carry cash when we were on a trip; I guessed so we would limit our spending. "Buy what you want," he would say, "and when you're out of money, you're done." Ever since my teen-aged years, I have always carried exactly $1,000 in small bills, with nothing over $20 in denomination. Even to this day, I felt a bit like I was trying to smuggle money onto a plane with my two-inch stack of 20s, 10s, and 5-dollar bills.

"I'll start. I have a grand," I said, digging into my pack and dropping the thick envelope onto the ground between us.

Scott, Jo, and Shanan dug into their packs and came up with $1820 between them, with most coming from Scott in $100 denominations.

"Okay, this is a good start," said Shanan, "We're going to need it."

"Let's split this four ways right now and agree on how we spend it going forward," I suggested. "All agreed?"

"Yep! Yes! Sure thing!" they all replied.

"Be back in a minute," I said, leaving my pack.

Walking back into the coffee shop, I inquired about the location of my attorney's office.

"You're the kid on the news," said the old-timer behind the counter.

"Yes, sir. I guess I am."

"You done the right thing as far as I can tell. I know Rick," he stated. "We're not too partial to city slickers coming up this way and building big houses on our mountain, just to let 'em sit. Do you understand?"

"No, not exactly," I responded.

"Well, your lawyer friend, he did just that—built a big house up on Devil's Gulch Road, but he and his wife stayed. They live up here full time, you know, and give back to the community. Hand me that there pen and a napkin," he told me.

* * * *

"I've got both addresses," I said, smiling as I exited the coffee shop. "His office is just a block down from here, and his house is a couple miles up the road. I'm not interested in sleeping out here on the street tonight, if we can help it."

"It looks like there will be plenty of time for that later," added Shanan. "I second the motion for a roof over our heads tonight, if it's even possible."

The sign on the door read "Rick Holman, Attorney-at-Law," with a smaller one hanging just below, reading "Closed."

"The house it is," I said, hoping we were given the right directions. "We can be there in an hour," I suggested, with all agreeing.

The walk across the mountainside, flanked by majestic boulders the size of houses lining several streams, was worth the wait. Cars and trucks were broken down apparently, every 200 yards, with most having been pushed to the side of the winding mountain road.

"I think that's it," I pointed out over an hour later.

"Yep, that must be right," added Scott, as we got close enough to see the sign reading "Holman" above the impressive twenty-foot double iron gate that secured the driveway from passersby.

"What now?" asked Jo, as we stood for several minutes in front of the gate.

"We can't just all walk right up to the front door," said Shanan.

"No," I added, "but I can. He knows my face. And besides, I was supposed to meet with him when we got back down the mountain."

I kept my pack with me and handed Scott the rifle, hoping not to look like a threat.

"Hand my pack over when I jump the fence," I told Scott. My shoulder still hurt badly, and I was now regretting not having it checked at the hospital. *Too late now*, I thought, as I grunted while climbing over the gate. I got lucky, and my pack was squeezed underneath.

"I wish I thought of that," I said, shaking my head back and forth.

"Well, it looks like you have an audience now," said Shanan, pointing down the long, paved road to the house while looking through her binoculars. "There's a woman standing at the front door."

"Is she armed?" I asked.

"Yes, and it looks like a shotgun. Be careful, Alex."

I walked the nearly quarter-mile towards the house with my arms raised as much as possible. My right shoulder felt restricted, and burned—like doing too many presses at the gym.

Calling out loudly and holding up my driver's license, I stopped in place.

"Hello, Mrs. Holman," not wanting to yell and appear hostile. It dawned on me that I wasn't sure if this was his wife, daughter, housemaid, or someone else. I just hoped I had the right house. Hearing no response, I kept walking. I was now close enough to see the rifle pointed towards me and I paused, stopping in my tracks.

* * * * * * *

CHAPTER TWENTY HOLMAN RANCH ESTES PARK, COLORADO

"Hello, Mrs. Hol..." I started to say again, when I heard the crack of the rifle. I ducked instinctively, falling onto the ground on my shoulder and yelling out in pain.

"First one's in the air," she called out, loud enough for me to hear. "But the second one won't be," she added.

I stopped, not daring to take another step.

"Mrs... I mean ma'am," I called back. "My Name is Alexander, and I'm...well...I'm a client of Mr. Holman. Is he home by chance?"

The woman paused, ducking back inside for a few seconds before returning to the front porch, with loud barking behind her but thankfully still in the house.

"Take off your hat," she called out, looking through her binoculars. "I can't read your driver's license from here, so we will do it another way. What was your dad's nickname in the service?"

I froze, racking my brain for a time he may have told me, but couldn't come up with anything. In a panic, I blurted out my, or our, last name.

"Kade, ma'am."

She paused for a few seconds before lowering the weapon.

"Come on up to the house," she called out.

"Thank you," I said cautiously, lowering my aching arms to my side.

"Have a seat, Alex," she said, as I approached the front porch.

"Do you want to see my driver's license?" I asked.

"No, son. Let's just talk for a minute, shall we?" she asked, handing me a glass of water.

"Thank you, ma'am. How did you know it was me?" I asked.

"When my husband lands the highest-profile case since his New York days, I like to hear about it. Plus, your face was on nearly every news station, and they even made a meme of your alleged altercation, with background music from the movie *Rocky*. Da, da da da da da da da da da," she hummed as she moved her arms in a boxing pose.

I couldn't help but laugh at her sense of humor.

"You and I have similar personalities," I pointed out.

"About your friends up at the gate. Are they the ones you came here with?"

"Yes, ma'am. All but two who decided to go a different way."

"The one you had trouble with?"

"Yes, and my girlfriend...well, the former one."

"Oh, I'm sorry to hear that."

"It's actually the best thing that's happened to me in a long time."

"Well, then, I guess I'm not." Now she was the one laughing. "I think we're going to get along just fine. Have your friends come on down, and we'll talk. I'll whip up some lemonade real quick," she added, as she disappeared inside the large log home.

I heard her say, "Oh, that's enough now," to the dog or dogs, it sounded like, coming from inside. "They have a big bark but only some bite," she added—talking to me, I guessed.

"Good to know," I called back, waving my good arm to my friends and motioning them to come down. I was sure the warning shot into the air was enough to keep them put for a bit.

They made it down the long driveway and onto the porch in time to meet Mrs. Holman exiting with a large pitcher of lemonade and five glasses.

"Hello, everyone. I'm Mrs. Holman, but you can all just call me Judy. Let me guess. With two of your group missing, you must be Scott, Jo...and Shanan, I presume."

"Yes, ma'am," they all said, as she passed out the lemonade.

"I've heard a little bit about you from my husband, and you're all welcome here until you either decide to move on or until Rick makes it back."

"Uh, ma'am?" I asked.

"Judy, please."

"Sure...uh...Judy. Is Mr. Holman going to be back soon? I was just wondering if he needed me to stick around, as far as the legal things go?"

"Well, I'm not sure that legal business means much with what's happened, but he and Grady were headed to Denver when it started. I'm guessing they either headed to his place or back up this way, depending on how close they were at the time. So, the short of it is that I expect him back in a day or two—up to a few weeks or even a month, I guess."

"We certainly don't want to impose." I said. "We would like to head back home to Texas as soon as possible and don't want to burden you."

"You mean, eat up all my food and lemonade?"

"Uh, yes, ma'am...I mean Judy. That's exactly what I mean."

"You may not know, but Grady and my husband have been friends for a very long time. And let's just say Grady is...I wouldn't say paranoid but let's just call him prepared. He talked us into putting a large basement under the house when we had it built, and I'll just say we have enough provisions to feed the town for a while, if it came down to it. That information stays right here, though."

"Oh yes, Judy. I can understand how you wouldn't want that floating around town, giving people any ideas," interjected Shanan.

"Let's get you kids settled in for a day or two, at least," she said, opening the front door to lead the way. "Oh, we didn't forget about you two—meet Scout and Daizy, our fearless ranch team. We've got a well out back and an outdoor shower if you want to get cleaned up. Sorry, it's not heated, but it will do the job. We also use the water to flush the toilets inside. So please bring a bucket with you when you use it, so the next person already has it filled. There are four bedrooms upstairs, so you can decide if you each want one or if you'll share."

"Share!" blurted out Shanan. "I mean...right, Alex?" she asked me hesitantly.

"Sure," I replied, trying not to look like a kid on his first date.

"Us too," said Scott.

"Okay, then just pick your rooms and get cleaned up for supper. Is everyone okay with freeze-dried chicken and dumplings? Don't worry; it tastes pretty good, considering it's survival food. With a few spices, it could almost pass for homemade!"

"That's what we've been eating for the last week," said Jo, "minus the good spices, of course," getting a "Hey!" out of Scott, who had prepared most of our meals.

"Won't be long before we're going to have to harvest one of the cows in our back pasture," added Judy. "My husband told me not to name them—for this reason, I guess—but I did. If Rick's not back before long, I'm going to need your help with that, Alex."

"Uh, yeah, I guess... I mean, of course! Whatever you need." *Hunting wild elk is a bit different from shooting someone's cow, especially already named*, I thought, but kept it to myself.

"Put your dirty clothes, all of them, in four piles outside in the garage, and we will get them washed in the morning. The garage door is hand-operated right now," she added. "Just lock it when you're done. I don't need any critters or anything else getting in that way."

* * * *

An hour later, we were cleaned up and sat down for supper, paired with a garden salad and all the fixings.

"How do you still have vegetables?" asked Scott.

"That's a good question. The Safeway got cleaned out on day one, as you can imagine, and I stocked up. I've got an old golf cart that somehow didn't get zapped when the cars did. Anyway, I took it up there with cash in hand and had to chain the cart right to the propane tank display to keep it from getting stolen. My shotgun made sure I made it back home in one piece. We're a tight community up here, especially in the winter months when there are only a few tourists. But there are still a few colorful characters, let's say, to watch out for, and it never hurts to be armed. After this week, we will have our first big greenhouse harvest of the season. We can grow year-round indoors, and I guess we will be bartering with the neighbors with the extras for as long as this thing lasts."

* * * * * * *

CHAPTER TWENTY-ONE HOLMAN RANCH ESTES PARK, COLORADO

"So, what do you think this thing is, Judy?" asked Shanan.

"I didn't know at first and just thought it was a power outage. I was actually asleep when the thing started, I guess. Anyway, the next morning, when I checked the breaker, I also tried to turn on my cell phone that I never turned off. When that didn't work, I decided to head into town, but my car wouldn't start. So, I bundled up and drove the cart down to the coffee shop.

There's an old-timer down there who goes by the name of Ray. Well, he told me a tale that I would have never believed just a day before. But he did explain why the power is out and phones and cars don't work. Everyone else around us was going about their business, but all were asking each other questions after checking their phones. That didn't last long, and either the word got around or people just knew something was off and immediately headed to the grocery store. Most were upset they couldn't use a credit card, but it wasn't long before they returned with cash. By that time, I was in line to check out with two full carts and my shotgun visible to all.

"So, it's either the sun or some country that has never liked us—like Iran, China, or North Korea. Either way, I think we are in for a long haul of not days or even weeks, but months or years before things start to look normal again...if that's even possible now. And we have to figure out how to get you all home. We can't solve the world's problems tonight—anyone up for a glass of red wine or Scotch?"

I raised my hand quicker than I should have, but it had been one trial of a day; and besides, I didn't want to be rude to our host.

"Follow me up to the third floor," she said.

"Third floor?" whispered Shanan to me as I shrugged my shoulders.

"Oh, wow!" I blurted out, echoed by Shanan and Jo.

The sun was setting over the mountains, and from the third-floor balcony our gaze rose above the trees and meadows to the tall mountains of Otis Peak, Hallett Peak and Flattop Mountain.

"It's just beautiful," remarked Shanan, squeezing my hand.

We watched, sipping our drinks until dark.

"Now, what do you notice?" asked Judy. "There are two things."

"Well," I replied first, "it's mostly pitch-dark except for the few lights on in town."

"Exactly," she replied. "It's pitch-dark since all the power is out, but not everything. Look there, there...and way over there," pointing across the land towards town. "Now look at that," she continued, pointing south. "That point is moving. It's got two headlights, and it's moving fast. It has to be a car or truck."

"I saw a truck, an old one, running after the light flashed. Maybe that's the same one, or another, I guess," I replied.

"A truck like that could get us home quick," I whispered to Scott.

"I wish they still took credit cards," he replied. "Back in Cali, my Bugatti is sitting in the garage, absolutely worthless, and here I can't even buy an old truck."

* * * *

Shanan and I shared a room this night, and I made a point to take whatever it was we were doing again slowly. The last thing I wanted to do was break her heart again. So, I just held her, and nothing more. It had been less than a week, but it felt good to sleep in a bed again. We awakened to the sunlight and a chilly house, with the extra blankets keeping us warm all night. I smelled smoke, not the kind like a house was on fire, but the sweet campfire smell of cherry wood...or was it hickory?

Bang! Bang! Bang! came a sound from downstairs, immediately following a frenzy of barking from the dogs, Scout and Daizy.

"What's that about?" asked Shanan.

"I'm not sure, but stay here and get dressed," I told her, jumping out of bed and dressing like I was in some kind of contest.

The banging came again, longer and louder, echoing through the house. I met Scott out in the hall, dressed only in boxers, when the yelling ensued. The unmistakable sound of a shotgun being racked from inside the house got our attention, followed by more loud barking.

"Judy, what's going on?" I asked, as she was now yelling to the people outside through the front door.

"Grab the rifle," I yelled to Shanan, as Judy called back to stay upstairs.

"Be right back," said Scott, darting back into his room.

Seconds later, he came out with jeans and a T-shirt on, carrying the pistol. Shanan handed me the rifle, and Scott and I headed quietly down the back stairs. The yelling on both sides of the door got louder, and banging turned into a thud that seemed to shake the house. *Bam! Bam! Bam!* The front door was being hit with some type of battering ram—maybe a log, I thought. *Smash!* I heard, stepping into the living room on the far side of Judy as the front picture window shattered, letting a cinderblock penetrate its center and careen into the middle of the room. The boom came as the first shot from Judy's rifle, followed by two more as fast as she could rack them, fired through the open window. Scott and I ran towards her across the long open room, diving to the floor when outside shots zinged over our heads.

"Stay down," I called to Judy, as she reached into a drawer, grabbing a box of shells and began reloading the shotgun. I shimmied closer to her, not wanting to have my head up any higher than I needed to. More shots came through the open window, with the formidable door stopping anyone from getting inside.

"I'm hit!" Judy screamed out...adding, "watch out for my dogs," as they ran back and forth across the front wall, like having a squirrel treed and not knowing what to do next.

"Fire!" I called out to Scott, who matched me round for round, at first out the window. I heard yelling and a few screams from outside but emptied 10 shells from my 15-round magazine, one after the other.

"I'm out," called out Scott, louder than I wanted.

"I've got five left," I replied, hoping my count was right.

I waited for return fire that didn't come. Judy was curled into a ball behind the large kitchen island, mumbling to herself.

"You're on notice, Mr. Holman!" came a loud call from outside.

"They're leaving," said Scott, cautiously looking out the open window. "I see maybe five or six down."

His words echoed like they were far off in the distance, as I crawled over to Judy.

"Judy!" I called. "Judy?" There was no response, as I reached out to touch her shoulder. When I did, she jumped, reaching for the rifle that lay on the ground just to her left.

* * * * * *

Chapter Twenty-two Holman Ranch Estes Park, Colorado

"Judy, it's okay. It's me, Alex. Those people are leaving. Where are you hit?" I asked, seeing blood on the rough hand-scraped wood you may see in a decorating magazine.

She didn't respond but breathed harder.

"Mrs. Holman, please. I need to see where you're hurt," I pleaded.

"Here," she said, pointing to her right arm.

"Is there anywhere else?" I asked.

"No. No, I don't think so," she said, as she started to cry.

"Let me take a look, okay?

"Scott!" I called out. "Make sure they are really gone, and then get Shanan and the medical bag from my pack."

"Will do, brother. Be right back."

I slowly removed her jacket, being careful of her shoulder. "I know it hurts, but don't worry. We're going to get you patched up like new."

"It's not even that," she replied. "It's this whole thing. What if my husband doesn't make it back? What if something already happened to him? If they are shooting at me in my own home, I can't even imagine how bad it is on the highways."

I didn't have an answer. None of us did. And I wasn't about to patronize her with predictions of her husband making it home.

"My dogs... Check on my dogs first," she said, as Daizy came up and kissed her on the head. "Where's Scout?" she asked, concerned. "I hear something bellowing across the house. Alex, check on it before you do anything else—please!"

I heard it too across the house but couldn't see from here—a bellowing sound mixed with high-pitched barking. I ran towards the sound, fearing the worst for Scout but happy he was still barking.

"Are you okay, big boy?" I asked, nearly sliding around the corner of the smooth hardwood floors in my socks. Rounding the corner, I saw him looking out the window and back at me. "It's okay, Scout; let me check you out." He stopped barking, but the bellowing continued, only I realized it was coming from outside. I scanned the field with my binoculars, half expecting one of the bad guys to be down and moaning. But it wasn't. It was instead one of Judy's cows down on its side, bellowing and repeatedly trying to lift its head.

I reported the news to Judy, who just shook her head from side to side and said, "Hold on, girl... We're coming to help."

"Scout is fine but won't move from the window," I told her.

"It's Ms. Bossy, for sure. She's a handful with the others, but Scout loves her to pieces. I hope she will be okay. Don't let Scout outside until we know it's clear," she added.

"Now, Judy, we need to get you looked at," I told her, seeing Scott had already started.

"I'll be very careful," I told her, "but I need to see what we are dealing with here."

The wound was deep and would undoubtedly require staples or at least stitches, but it appeared to miss the humerus bone in the upper arm, I thought, bringing me back to my anatomy class in high school. Still, it bled profusely and I put a dishtowel from the sink on for direct pressure. I had a million and one questions about what just happened but decided to save them, at least for now.

Shanan came bounding down the stairs with the medical kit, asking who was hurt.

"It's just me, sweetie," said Judy, regaining her composure but still breathing moderately loud.

"We need to get you to the hospital," I said. "Didn't you say you had a golf cart that still worked?"

"Yes, that's right, but it's not safe to leave here right now. We can't just take a drive up to the hospital, not yet. Do the best you can with it," she added, now fully aware of her surroundings and with confidence back in her voice. "Stitch it if you have the supplies for it," she ordered.

"Sorry, I don't have that, but we have something a lot less painful, I think. We can glue it," replied Shanan.

"Glue it?" she asked curiously.

"Yes, last year my cousin cut his head open pretty bad, and they just glued it at the hospital. This glue here says hospital grade, and it dries in three minutes. That's the easy part, but we need to get this wound clean," added Shanan, "and it's going to hurt, I'm sorry to say. I'll hit it with some cold spray first, and it should dull the pain. Take these also," she said, handing her two pills that Judy took without a question.

The cleaning process took nearly ten minutes, with her screaming out occasionally but instructing Shanan to continue. We controlled the bleeding, and fifteen minutes later we were gluing the wound shut, lining the edges, and holding them together. We held her arm completely still for more than five additional minutes as the glue dried, just as advertised on the container.

"Help me up, Alex, and fetch my binoculars over there," she pointed across the room. "I want to make sure they are gone for sure before I tell you what I know... Follow me and bring your rifle, Alex," she told me, leading the way to the third-floor balcony. "The rest of you, please stay down here for a few minutes," she called back over her shoulder.

I wouldn't have bet all of my money on it, not that I had much anymore, but I was pretty sure this was going to be about her cow, Ms. Bossy.

Quickly looking with her binoculars, she reported, "That's what I thought. I'm sorry, old girl. Scout is going to miss you, and so am I. Alex, I need you to focus and send her home with one shot. One-shot to the head, and hopefully no more."

Judy didn't ask me if I would or even could, just telling me to use the top rail to steady my rifle. It took a few seconds to find her in my scope, but her head moving caught my eye.

"I know you don't want to do this, Alex, but she's suffering and I'm not sure if any other bad guys are still out there or I would do it myself, up close after saying good-bye."

"No, I understand, Judy. It's just different from shooting an elk, and that's the only experience I have with it...well, before what happened downstairs, I guess. Anyway, I don't want her to suffer either."

I said a quick prayer, silent but mouthing the words, asking for a clean shot and only one. Judy was silent, composed as I couldn't imagine someone who had just been shot in her own home.

Beef doesn't originate at the grocery store, and animals should not suffer, I told myself. She was in my crosshairs and I steadied my breath. *Just breathe,* I told myself, slowly squeezing the trigger.

In a moment, it was over, and both a view from my scope and Judy's binoculars told us Ms. Bossy would suffer no more. I wondered what my friends downstairs would think about the seemingly random gunshot, but it was Scout who drew our attention. He came from the front of the house, *probably out the shot-out window since the door was never penetrated,* I thought. Judy yelled at him to come back, but he didn't stop, not even for a look. He sniffed his old friend before curling up next to her, nose-to-nose.

"Breaks my heart," said Judy, "but it had to be done. That no-good Mayor shot my cow, and it wasn't a stray bullet towards the house. Thank you, Alex, for making her suffering short."

Sure. Anytime, I almost said, as if I had done it a thousand times over before catching myself. "I'm sorry about her, too," I said, "and you're welcome."

* * * *

She took a full twenty more minutes to scan the property, both front, back and sides, using her left arm and checking the balconies off each floor before officially declaring them gone from the property. I was eager to hear the story of what she thought this might be about; we all were but didn't ask...not yet.

"What a mess," Judy said, as I followed her back downstairs, looking at the window glass strewn about the floor. She pointed to the back wall littered with small holes, which protected them from the bullets that penetrated the heavy logs.

"Be dears, boys, and help me clean up this glass. We don't need anyone getting cut by it."

Scott and I did as asked, picking up large and small pieces while Shanan and Jo swept the rest into the trashcan.

"Just set those bigger pieces right outside the front door, boys. But watch your heads—just in case they left a shooter I can't see."

"Yes, ma'am," we both replied, carefully unlocking the three front-door deadbolts and cautiously opening it with a creaking sound I hadn't heard before now.

"Look at that," said Scott, pointing to the outside of the heavy wooden door, littered with bullet holes and impressions from the log laying on the ground that they had apparently tried to ram it with.

"The door!" I called back inside. "It held all of the bullets—amazing!"

"It's wood on the outside," she said, but the middle is lined with a quarter-inch steel plate. That's why they had to shoot through the window."

"Who are they?" I started to ask, when I saw Scott looking at the ground.

"The blood..." he said. "It's everywhere!"

I stepped out, hoping I wasn't in a sniper's line of sight, and saw the same.

"How many?"

"What?" asked Scott.

"How many people did you see them drag away?"

"Oh, that... Two or three, I guess... I don't feel so good," he added, kneeling on the ground. "We killed them," Scott continued. "I mean, one of us—maybe all of us—killed those people."

"We don't know for sure if they are dead," I replied, feeling sick to my stomach too.

I had seen blood before—my own after a bike accident and some drunk guy cliff-diving who shouldn't have, but never anything like this.

"Let's get back inside," I told Scott, helping him to his feet.

All at once, it hit me that my scuffle with Trey in the hotel paled in comparison to what just happened here.

* * * *

Once back inside, I deadbolted the door, even though it felt strange with a wide-open ground-level hole opened up where a picture window used to be.

"Those men," began Judy..."they work for the Mayor."

"What?" I asked, shocked. "I thought you were all friendly with each other around here! And since when does a small-town mayor send a goon squad to a constituent's home, anyway?"

"Oh, we are friendly—most of us, that is. But Mayor Haskins is not one of us. I don't mean like being born here, because Rick and I are new around here as well; but he doesn't fit in, is all. He got into office a few years back when the last mayor died suddenly and there was nobody to fill the spot. He was new in town and seemed to have good ideas. They tried to get my husband to run, but he wasn't interested at the time, so Haskins ran unopposed. It didn't take long to realize that we as a town had made a big mistake.

"I can tell you he's here for our supplies and my husband's loyalty, and not necessarily in that order. It all started innocently enough when the Mayor wanted to make changes to established rules and by-laws of the town that had stood for nearly 100 years—since its incorporation in 1917. It was like trying to change the Constitution of the United States. We all voted no, and it was done, we thought.

"Only a few months later, there was money missing from the Town Fund and businesses were being pressured to gouge tourists and pay an unwritten 'Mayor's Town Tax.' Those who refused were welcomed with slashed tires on their vehicles, threatening notes left on their business doors by a masked person, and some even said they were missing house pets found shot with arrows. It got worse and worse, and repeated complaints to the State fell on deaf ears. I guess nobody really cares about a small town way up in the mountains, except when it comes to tax time.

"Well," Judy continued, "fast forward to about six months ago. My husband was asked by many in town to run against that thief of a mayor in the next election this coming April. He told them he didn't really want the job but would consider it if enough people wanted him to.

"Three weeks later, we found this tied to our front gate." She reached into a drawer and pulled out a notebook with page after page of written names, addresses, and signatures. "Look here," she said, turning to the last page, with the number 2755 filled in. "We only have about 5,500 full-time residents, and a fair number of those are children. So maybe 3,000 or a few more are actual voters, and I've got a book with almost 3,000 adult signatures, asking Rick to run for mayor.

"Well, we prayed on it, and the next day he declared he was running for the seat. No helpers, no ads on the radio or in the local paper, no fliers or speeches, just handshakes and talking to people about what they want, like how it used to be. Now the current Mayor's got a few men with him, I guess, and he's trying to rig the election by force, or maybe to not have one at all.

"The town Sheriff isn't bad; he grew up here and initially backed the town against the Mayor but eventually backed down. I get it, I guess. He's got a family to feed, and it's not like we're handing out jobs up here left and right—well, except for the summer retail ones, mostly taken by the kids nowadays.

"Anyway, as I said, he's not a bad man; he just needs the work. We don't mind sharing what we have stored up with townsfolk, but I'll be dead before anyone is just going to take it without asking. So that out there was the Mayor's doing. He was the one doing all the hollering outside, backed up by a few police and some low-life residents just looking for part of the handouts."

"It sounds like they don't know Mr. Holman is not here," I said aloud, "since they addressed him by name at the end."

"I must have missed that in all the confusion," said Judy. "What did they say exactly?"

"Well," I started, "one man at the end yelled, 'You're on notice, Mr. Holman!' I'm guessing that was the Mayor."

"I just hope Rick makes it back, and soon!" she replied.

* * * * * * *

Chapter Twenty-three Holman Ranch Estes Park, Colorado

*B*ang! *Bang!* was the knock on the front door. "Everybody down!" I called out, reaching for the rifle.

"Who's there?" I called out, staying close to the center of the formidable door, away from the window.

"Dan, from down the road. You two all right, Mr. Holman?"

"He's okay. You can let him in," Judy said.

I slowly opened the door to see a burly man—maybe six feet, six inches—with a large gray beard and a double-barrel shotgun pointed to the ground. He saw me with my rifle and took a step back, raising his.

"Whoa! Whoa!" I said, not raising my rifle barrel but not pointing the weapon to the floor either.

"Dan, it's all right. These folks are friends of mine," said Judy, walking up from the back room.

"Yes, ma'am," he said, lowering the weapon. "Sorry about that," he told me. "I heard a lot of gunfire, and then I see you, who I don't know, with a gun."

"I get it and understand," I told him. "I would have thought the same thing."

"How long are you all staying?" he asked.

"Um...I don't really know yet," I responded.

* * * *

Judy made the introductions and informed him of what the Mayor had done.

"I wish that weasel had come over to my place first. You would still have that window intact, just like new."

"Thank you, Dan. You've always been a good neighbor and friend. Rick's out of town, but I hope he will be back soon. Thanks for checking up on us."

"Sure thing, Judy. I'll be back by in a bit with a couple of my handymen to get this window boarded up. Can't have it wide open like it is now, especially after dark. Anything else you need, I'm your man," he added, walking out the door.

"He seems sweet," said Jo.

"Yes, he does," replied Judy. "He's a good man, but he's always had feelings for me and doesn't hesitate to tell me every now and then—when Rick's not around, of course! He's harmless, though."

"You didn't tell him you were shot," said Shanan.

"Nope, don't need anyone else knowing that right now," she stated bluntly. "Plus, you guys already fixed me right up anyway."

She sat on the couch quietly, talking with Shanan. "I bet you miss him. I can see it in your eyes," said Shanan. "I miss my mom and dad too. Do you think we will ever see them again?" she asked, with tears rolling down her cheeks.

"Oh, yes, sweetie," Judy replied, putting her good arm around Shanan. "We will see them again—in this life or the next, I'm sure of it."

* * * * * * *

CHAPTER TWENTY-FOUR NEAR ESTES PARK, COLORADO

G rady and Rick walked back up the mountain, looking for a stream or river to filter water for their canteens.

"It's uphill for most of it," said Rick, "except for the very last part dropping down into Estes."

"I know," replied Grady. "You don't notice it driving a 5,000-pound hunk of metal through the mountains, but ride a bicycle or walk the same roads and you find out in a hurry what the terrain is really like!"

"Finding a freshwater stream in the Rocky Mountains is like finding a coffee shop in New York City," joked Rick. "There is one every block."

"This little Sawyer water filter is one of my prized possessions now," said Grady. "Another week or two of this nonsense, and it will be worth more than your Mercedes."

"Do you mean the Mercedes that crashed into the ditch back there? I think that little filter thing already is!"

"So, it's a trade?" asked Grady, handing it out towards his friend. Rick paused, thinking about his response.

Grady started laughing. "I'm just messing with you. I've got more, and this one is yours to keep. The only thing your car is good for now is maybe a raccoon den. A couple of things, though. It's going to take a day or two to get home, unless we get lucky and hitch a ride with a running vehicle. We've got at least one night out here, and unless we find an empty car near our stopping point, we are going to have to make a shelter and fire to stay warm."

"Even with our sleeping bags?" asked Rick.

"Yep. Put those things directly on the ground and they will suck out your body heat faster than anything else. The question I have is where these people are," Grady commented, pointing to a car up ahead on the roadside.

They cautiously approached the opened driver's side door, looking in at papers strewn across the seats and the glove box open.

"Either someone just started walking, or this car has already been rifled through," said Rick. "There's bound to be more on this road."

"Can you imagine how many are on I-25 right now?" asked Grady.

"Thousands in between here and Denver, I bet. Where do they go, and how far from home are they?" asked Rick.

"What's that?" said Grady. "Did you hear that?"

"No, I didn..."

"Wait, there it is again. It's coming from the trunk! It sounds like clanking or banging. Do you think an animal got in there?" asked Grady.

"I don't know but hold on," replied Rick. "I'm going to pop the trunk. Just stay back, so you don't get a face full of vermin... Ready?"

"Yeah, go ahead," said Grady.

"One...two...three!" called out Rick, pulling the lever hard.

Clunk... the trunk released, slowly opening.

"Oh, God!" gasped Rick, bending over.

"What? What is it?" asked Grady, quickly coming around from the side of the vehicle.

Both men stood in silence, looking down at a young man lying face-up in the trunk, covered in blood. His throat had been slashed from ear to ear, and his right foot flopped from side to side, banging against the steel trunk sides. *Clunk...clunk...clunk.* The man tried to speak as he held one hand to his neck. His mouth moved, with no words escaping. It was his eyes Grady would think about later—glassy, terrified, and at the same time accepting of his fate.

"I'll grab my medical kit out of my pack," said Grady, fumbling quickly.

"No," replied Rick.

"What do you mean, no? He's dying!"

"He's gone," replied Rick quietly.

Grady looked back inside and saw the young man's hands lying motionless at his sides and no more kicking from his foot. They waited for another few minutes to be sure before closing the trunk.

"Who would do something like this?" asked Grady.

"A better question is, where is the person now who did this?" replied Rick. "He can't be far, and we haven't seen anybody from our way."

The men sat on the ground, not speaking after scanning both directions down the road with binoculars.

Grady said a silent prayer for the man in the trunk and one for his wife and boys; thankfully, they were all home together on his last phone call just before it happened.

"What is going on here?" asked Rick. "We came up to the mountains to get away from all of this. This isn't supposed to happen here."

* * * *

A shot, followed by a woman's scream, pierced the clear mountain air up the road towards Estes.

"Let's go," said Grady, needing help getting his pack on. "At least my shooting hand is still good," he added, "but let's be careful."

Another scream, followed by one more from the same direction, had Rick nervous about what he might see. He was known as a cut-throat attorney back in New York City and was even labeled ruthless by more than a few in the media. But that was only words and laws, not this. Today was real, and he was scared—maybe for the first time in his life.

"Let's just check it out," said Grady, straining his ears to hear another scream or anything else that never came.

Cresting a large hill, they had a sight advantage of more than a mile.

"There," pointed Grady, "past that car down there about another 50 yards. See that guy walking?"

"Let's get his attention," said Rick standing to yell out.

"No," said Grady, grabbing his arm and pulling him back with a groan as his other arm felt a sharp pain. "No. We don't know who he is, and I'm not sure I want to draw anyone's attention right now."

They waited ten more minutes as the figure looked back towards the car after every few steps and finally disappeared over the next hill, now more than a mile away.

"We need to find out where those screams came from," said Grady, fixed on the car below with his binoculars. The driver's side door was open, and something was on the ground underneath.

"Oh, no," said Rick, looking as well. "Is that a body on the ground?"

"I'm hoping it's just a pile of clothes, but I see what you're seeing. Let's be really careful going down there, and I want to keep an eye on that next hill. I'm not interested in getting ambushed right now."

* * * *

The steps down to the vehicle were the longest Rick had ever taken, and he wished he had never taken this drive. Stopping 20 yards out, it was clear that the body of a man lay on the ground just under the driver's side door. With pistols drawn, they slowly approached, calling out to see if there was a response. It was clear he had been shot in the head, with no chance of survival, from only five yards away. They approached the open door, gasping as they peered inside.

"There she is," said Grady. "The one we heard."

The middle-aged woman lay across the backseat with her dress pulled up over her chest and the same cut they had seen at the last vehicle. Her terrified eyes spoke volumes of the attack on both of them.

"I thought it couldn't get worse," said Rick. "I was wrong," he added, saying a prayer aloud now for all three. "So, we're out here on the road with a serial killer! That's probably the guy just over the next hill," he said, pointing up the road.

"Yeah, that sounds about right, and we're all headed back to town," replied Grady, clenching his teeth.

"I'm going to pull her dress back down," said Grady, reaching for the back-door handle.

"No, no. You can't do that," replied Rick. "We can't touch anything; this a crime scene. Sorry, ma'am... I truly am. Let's go, Grady."

* * * * * * *

Chapter Twenty-five Near Estes Park, Colorado

Thirty minutes later, they cautiously crested the next hill, with a vantage point of nearly three-quarters of a mile. A binocular sweep revealed only pavement.

"Where did he go?" asked Grady out loud, as they neared the halfway point of the valley.

"Over the next rise, I guess," replied Rick, "or into the woods."

"Closer than you think," called out a man sitting just outside their line of sight, behind a large rock and not more than 30 feet away.

Rick jumped back, and Grady raised his weapon towards the sound, only seeing two cowboy boots sticking out from behind the rock.

"Come on out," commanded Grady with a military authority and dropping his pack onto the cold pavement.

"Or what?" came the reply.

"I want to talk is all," said Grady, now feeling vulnerable in the line of fire.

"I'm guessing you boys want to talk about what you done saw back there. Am I right?"

"That's part of it," replied Grady.

"Well, I ain't the one who done it, if that's what you're thinking. I found 'em, just like you, and now you two are following me."

"No, we're just trying to get home," said Grady, getting a look from Rick.

"Home, you say—like as in Estes Park?"

This time Grady didn't answer.

"No mind... That's where I'm headed too."

"Where's your car?" asked Rick, as the man stepped out from behind the rock with a small backpack and a jacket stained dark red.

"Ain't got one—just hitchhiking across this great land is all."

"You're hitchhiking into the mountains in November?" asked Grady.

"There's no law against that, gentlemen—at least not that I'm aware of."

"Your jacket," said Rick, pointing to the man's chest. "What happened?"

"I believe you know what happened," he said, smiling a crooked cold smile that gave both men reason to pause.

"I think we do as well, but I want to hear it from you," said Rick, going over the options in his mind.

If we have a confessed serial killer headed back towards my town, he thought, *I want this done right now before he can hurt anyone else. I'm 90% sure he did it, but that leaves 10 percent for a jury—and that's only if I'm correct.*

He could see the headlines now. *Former New York hotshot attorney is sentenced to life in prison for the murder of an innocent transient, following a brief power outage near his home in the town of Estes Park, Colorado.*

"So, let's hear it," said Grady again, growing more concerned by the second.

"Got this here blood on me trying to help the man in the truck back there. He must have gotten busted up in the car crash and decided to rest in the trunk a bit."

"Did you help?" asked Grady, knowing the man was still alive briefly when they found him.

"Nope. He was dead already when I tried to revive him."

"What about the other man and woman?" asked Grady, not taking his hand off of the pistol.

"Well, I don't rightly know about that," replied the man, taking a step closer. "I must have walked right by them without seeing nothing."

"So you didn't see the driver's side door wide open and a man lying outside on the ground?"

"Nope, done told you that already," he answered as he took another step forward.

"You didn't see a woman inside with her dress halfway up, lying in a pool of blood?" added Grady, turning red with anger.

"The same one... That's close enough. Don't take another step!" said Grady, as he realized the man was now half the distance away from where he started. "The same woman," he continued, "that screamed out loud only minutes before we got down there?"

"I must have missed that too. Well, gentlemen, this has been educational, and that's a fact. But I'd better be moving along if I'm going to make it back to your town before dark. Lots of crazy things can happen when the sun goes down, especially out here," he added, smiling and waving his arm across the valley below. "Maybe I'll see you boys down there. I might even come on over to your place. What did you say your names were again?"

"We didn't," replied Rick, with a pit in his stomach.

"Well, everyone calls me Tex," he said, reaching out his hand, with no takers. "Be careful out there; there are all sorts of things that could get you in trouble. I'll see you boys down the road, then," he said, laughing as he walked away towards town and not once looking back.

"What do you think?" asked Grady.

"We can't shoot him in the back," replied Rick, "if that's what you're thinking. There are still laws in place for this type of thing. But I sure don't want him getting anywhere near my place. My wife can handle herself, but this guy is in a whole other league. I was in New York when the infamous white Bronco chase was all over the TV news. I studied the case because it's what I do, and if I had to bet my family fortune on whether or not the man was guilty…well, I was wrong, at least in the jury's eyes. Yes, this guy probably did these heinous crimes, but no, we can't take the law into our own hands. We can only hope there is nobody else stranded between here and town."

"We need to keep him in our sites, though," replied Grady.

* * * *

The two men walked in silence for a while, both hoping there were no more stranded motorists in front of them. "What about the kids?" asked Rick, finally breaking the tension.

"I think they will be all right as long as they keep their wits about them."

"How much food did they have?"

"About a week's worth," replied Grady. "Maybe a little longer if they have any idea of what happened and started rationing. I'll need to find a way to get up there soon, though, unless they get desperate and head down to town. I just hope Alex and Trey are getting along. Being locked up in a cabin for a week right after a major incident isn't the safest bet."

"They don't have any weapons, do they?" asked Rick.

"Yep, they do," sighed Grady, "but I'm hoping Alex has them both. He's a good kid, and he will do the right thing, I'm sure. I've got to stop for a few; my arm is killing me. Sorry, I know it's bad timing, but my pack is unlevel and I have to fix it."

"No worries, old friend. I could use a breather myself."

Ten minutes passed, and they lost sight of their new fellow traveler.

"There a hospital just above town," said Rick. "It's maybe a mile down from here; let's get you fixed up before we head out to my place."

The last hour was hard on Grady. His arm throbbed, and he held off on any pain pills, hoping for something stronger when they arrived.

"Down there, just ahead," called out Rick. "There's the hospital, and I know the head orthopedist pretty well. If he's there, we should have you fixed up quickly...

* * * *

"There is your guy!" said Rick, pointing to the man coming out the front door of the hospital with another man and woman.

"The name's Tex," they overheard, as he walked with a limping man and young woman. "Let's get something to eat, new friends," Tex continued.

"Hold on a second," called Grady to Trey and Beth. "I need a word with you kids."

"Screw you, both of you," said Trey, turning away and using his crutches.

"Please, just a moment?" asked Rick. "That's all we need."

"Nope," called back Beth, flipping the bird as they walked away.

"Where's Alex and the others?" called out Grady in a last-ditch effort to stop them.

"Headed home, for all we know," said Trey, not looking back.

"Watch out for that guy Tex," called Rick as they got further away. "He's bad news and dangerous."

Tex turned and gave his grin with his hands up in a "Whatever" pose.

* * * * * * *

Chapter Twenty-six Near Estes Park, Colorado

"I'll get you inside," Rick told Grady, "and see if I can talk to the Sheriff before this gets any worse."

"Can I help you, gentlemen? Oh! Hi, Mr. Holman," said the cheery woman at the desk, recognizing him immediately.

"Hi, Karen. How are things holding up here?"

"Good so far, sir," she said. Then, lowering her voice, she added, "We lost one in ICU when the power went out. It took ten hours to get one of the emergency generators working, and it is now hit or miss. We still have lights…well, sort of…" She smiled, pointing around to the emergency lights flashing throughout the lobby.

Now lowering his voice, Rick asked her, "Did you see the guy walk in here maybe 20 minutes ago with a backpack on?"

"The scruffy guy with the crazy smile?" she asked.

"Yes, that one. What did he want?"

"Same as every other drifter that runs through here—just pain meds. They all have a different story about an accident or surgery they had, and they ran out of pills."

"Did he seem agitated?" asked Grady.

"Sorry, Karen. This is my friend Grady; pardon my manners," said Rick.

"Oh, nonsense. A friend of yours is a friend of mine. Pleased to meet you, Mr. Grady. And yes, at first he seemed agitated, like they all do hearing the word 'No'—but only for a second until he saw a guy walking on crutches. I heard him asking what they gave for the pain. Then those two and a girl just walked out right away."

"If you see that man in here again, get hold of the Sheriff right away," said Rick.

"Uh, okay," Mr. Holman. "Now, I guess you're checking in your friend here for that arm. Is that right?"

"Yes, ma'am. I did the best I could to reduce the break, but I'm sure Dr. Thomas can do a better job."

"Have a seat, gentlemen, and I'll tell the doctor you're here."

"Should I have given the receptionist my health insurance card?" asked Grady, as they sat down.

"The good doctor and I go back a bit, and let's just say he feels like he owes me a favor. I never had a need to cash in on it, but fixing you up will at least make us even in his mind. Besides, he's the best ortho you're likely to find anywhere in the state... Hey, Doc!"

"Hi there, Rick. What's shakin'?"

"Just my buddy, Grady, here. He needs his arm looked at."

"What happened?"

"A car accident when the power ran out."

"We've had our fair share of those today. Come on back and we'll take a look," the doctor replied.

"So, you've got power here," said Rick, as a statement.

"Barely," replied the doctor. "But we have some emergency lights, a couple of X-ray units back up, and we got some ventilators working. We lost one, though, at the start," he added with a sigh.

"I heard," Rick was about to say, before replying, "That's a shame; sorry to hear that."

Removing the wrap from Grady's arm, the doctor pronounced it fairly straight.

"Looks pretty good—not too bad of a break."

"Well, it was worse, but I tried to set it," said Rick.

"I'll bet that hurt like crazy—huh, Grady?"

"Yes, doc, but it still looks better than when it happened."

"We'll shoot a quick X-ray series and see what else we can do...

"You snapped it at the radius—this bone right here," he pointed to the X-ray—"and the ulna, over here. You did a good job setting it, Rick...at least for being in the bush. We're going to have to do it one more time, but we'll get you numbed up first and it won't be hard to get it close. The swelling is minimal now and your body will do the rest. It should heal, good as new, in about six weeks once we cast it."

After his arm was set, Grady commented, "That wasn't bad at all, and I get to keep this bottle of pain pills?"

Grady told the doctor what he knew about EMPs and what he thought may have happened.

"That makes a lot of sense. Thank you," the doctor replied.

"What do I owe you?" asked Grady.

"This one's on the house, but we will need you back in six weeks to take the cast off."

"Thanks, buddy," said Rick. "Let's head to the house, Grady. I want to get there before dark."

* * * * * * *

Chapter Twenty-seven Estes Park, Colorado

They left the hospital, with Grady's arm feeling better.

"I just need to check on my office first," said Rick. "I'll grab the documents on Alex's case, just so I can review them, should it come up again. But I doubt that now."

"Hold on a second. Isn't that the Sheriff just across the street?" asked Grady.

"Yes, that's him," replied Rick, grabbing hold of Grady's shoulder as he started to cross. "Hold on, buddy. Let's just take a minute here."

"We have to tell him about the drifter and what we saw," said Grady, starting to move again.

"Let's go to my office first," suggested Rick. "We need to talk... Don't worry; he will be there when we're done." When Rick opened the door to his office, he replied, "The office looks just like I left it, except the lights don't turn on.

"How about a whiskey, friend, before we head to my place?"

"Probably not doctor's orders," said Grady, "but it's been one bear of a day, so why not?"

"Here's the problem," started Rick, handing his friend a half-full glass.

"There are three people we know for sure that saw the bodies. Us and that Tex guy, whatever his real name is. Each of us has our DNA on the bodies, or at least part of the vehicles. Things are different now, and that probably doesn't matter much if this power outage continues."

"Yeah, I see. So what's the problem?"

"The problem is the same—things are different now, and the power will shift from national and state governments to local ones. That falls on local police and the Mayor now; and to be honest, we're not on the best of terms. Do you see where I'm going with this?"

"Yeah, but I don't like it."

"There nothing to like—it's just the way it is, for now at least. There's no telling where Tex is now, and he will likely move through town and out the other side or stay hunkered up in one of the hundreds of cabins for the winter. Either way, it's a complicated business, and right now we can't prove it wasn't us that did those things."

"Okay, so we head straight to your place?"

"That's the plan. Just let me grab the file on your kid and we'll head out... Let's exit around this way and steer clear of the Sheriff for now."

* * * *

The men walked in silence up the road, past the Stanley Hotel. Other residents mulling about the downtown thinned to near zero as they traveled away from town.

"There she is," announced Rick, pointing down the long valley at his homestead. "Home sweet home... Wait a minute!" he added, looking through his binoculars. "The front gate is open!"

"So?" asked Grady.

"The front gate is never unlocked unless we're coming or going; and even then, for only a minute."

Rick scanned the driveway leading up to the house. "Oh, no!" he exclaimed, looking at the smashed window in the front living room. "No, that's not good at all!" he continued.

"I see it too," said Grady through his own set. "We need to think this through. We can't just go charging down the driveway, guns blazing."

"I know. Just give me a second to think. There's a drainage pipe big enough to crawl through, starting over in those trees," said Rick, pointing to the back of the property. "It dumps out right behind the garage in the back, maybe 50 yards from the house. We can go that way and hopefully get close, at least without being spotted."

They circled around the property and ducked into the trees.

"Here...over here," pointed out Rick. "That's the start of it. We're going to need to leave the packs here; it's too narrow to get them through. Sorry about your arm, but this is going to be a crawl unless you want to wait here."

"Not a chance. Your wife is there; let's get going."

With Rick in the lead, they headed into the large pipe.

"Get your flashlight ready," said Rick. "This thing dips down about 10 feet underground and sinks down in a few parts. I've been meaning to have it leveled out but thought it could wait until summer. Now I wish I had done it sooner," he added, shining his flashlight into the pool of water ahead of them.

"Keep weapons up," called out Grady, seeing the same thing, "and let's make this quick; I don't want to have come all this way just to die of hypothermia a quarter mile from your house."

"Ahh, the water's freezing!" said Rick, as he sloshed through the two-foot-deep ice-cold water, soaking his clothes.

"I'm right behind you, buddy," replied Grady, as he entered the water on his knees, struggling to keep his rifle and temporary cast dry.

"Almost there," called out Rick. "I can see the other side! Just keep moving."

At the end of the tunnel, they peered out, hoping to see something hopeful, something positive. *Crack! Crack! Crack!* The first bullet zinged over their head, with the second one hitting the hard ground, just to the left of the pipe opening.

"Get back!" called out Rick. "Get back!"

* * * *

I paused, not wanting to fire another shot until I could see something. Were they back for more? Was it the same men or looters looking to take advantage of a woman alone? I couldn't be sure and decided those three would be the only warning shots.

"You are sure you saw two men go into the pipe?" I asked Scott.

"Yeah. It was quick but I'm positive there were at least two," he replied.

"What do you want me to do?" I asked Judy.

"Let me think a minute, and I'll let you know," she replied.

* * * *

"What do we do?" asked Grady. "Maybe that was your wife shooting!"

"No, she has a shotgun. My other rifles are in the safe, and she never wanted to know the combination. I don't know who is shooting at us, but these are not shotgun blasts."

* * * *

"Alex, you cover Scott and me from here, and we'll approach the opening from the side and see if we can get a line on who's in there," said Judy.

"Are you sure you want to do that? I mean, you don't have to, Judy."

"Yes, I do. It's going to be dark soon and I can't have men 50 yards from the house, just waiting to find a way in. No. This needs to be settled right now, one way or the other."

"How are you going to get them to come out?" I asked.

"These," she said, holding up a wooden box and opening the lid, with the faintest of smiles.

I understood that she was scared to death on the one hand, and on the other, she was protecting her property and it had to feel good.

"Is that what I think it is?" asked Scott.

"Those are smoke bombs, right?" I added. "We used to play with those as kids."

"Not these," she replied. "These are special—the kind you can't buy in just any store. Grady gave them to my husband last year to smoke out gophers."

"Did it work?" I asked.

"Do you see any gophers around here?" she replied. "Let's get back down to business. Scott and I will approach from the side of the pipe, and you guys will both cover me while I sneak up over the top and throw a couple of these in the pipe. It will either drive them out the front or the back, but they will come out, one way or the other."

"Ma'am...I mean, Judy, let me do that part; you can cover me," I said.

"Thanks, Alex, but this is my property, and I'll be the one to defend it. I'm just glad you all are here to help. If you get a shot, take it, and we will ask questions later."

My stomach churned hearing her last words. Yes, I saw firsthand what the Mayor and his goons would do, and I wasn't about to let Judy get hurt and lose her ranch, or worse. It was the clarity of it all, like I was watching a movie where someone else, a highly paid actor no doubt, had to take the shot and end a man's life. A complete stranger may be just following orders and had a family to whom he may never return. This wasn't shooting a deer or catching a fish, but a man's life, and one I prayed I wouldn't have to take. I may have already taken one, shooting out from inside Judy's house, but that was different since I wasn't sure if anyone died or whose bullets hit them.

* * * *

Rick and Grady moved back into the pipe, not wanting to catch a bullet sneaking through the front.

"What do you want to do?" asked Grady.

"I don't know; they know we're here."

"Maybe we call out and say this is your place," offered Grady.

"No. If I thought it was my wife out there, I would do just that, but that fire was not her gun and I don't feel like getting shot today. With that being said, I'm also not going to be run off of my own property, especially with my wife inside. Let's just sit tight for a few and be ready to come out blazing if we have to."

* * * *

Judy exited the far-right side of the house, giving the shotgun to Scott to cover her. She put a finger to her mouth, gesturing for Scott to be quiet and not speak. They walked nearly 30 yards around before standing on top of the hard ground covering the pipe.

"I'm going to walk straight down the pipe," she whispered to him. "If we're quiet, they won't hear my footsteps. You walk beside me about five feet off the side of it."

"Then what?" he whispered back nervously.

"Then I drop two of these into the front, and you and Alex get ready for whatever comes out."

"Wait, so you want me to shoot them?"

"No, I hope we won't have to. There's a lot of brush in there from over the years, so I don't think they will backtrack. When they come out, they will be disoriented, and we have a good chance of keeping them on the ground with a show of force. But it has to be quick, and if they come out with weapons, it's them or us. No more talking; let's get this done."

I watched from the back patio through my rifle scope, with near nonstop barking from the dogs, only concentrating on their careful approach to the top of the pipe entrance. I held my breath, keeping my finger off of the trigger, hoping I wouldn't have to fire toward my friend and our new hostess.

She held up the first smoke bomb, lit the fuse, and waited until it burned down to the stub before holding her breath and saying a prayer. Reaching her good arm over the top of the opening, she swung down fast, tossing the bomb nearly five feet back into the pipe, landing just inches from Rick's face.

* * * *

"Back! Get back!" he called to Grady.

"I'm trying; I'm trying. I'm caught up in something," he yelled as they both started to cough. "I can't turn around. We have to go forward."

* * * *

"Get ready," Judy called over to Scott. "Here goes number two." She raised her lighter and lit the fuse. "Here's one more for you bastards," she yelled as her arm came back.

* * * *

"Wait!" called Rick, coughing hoarsely and sixty percent sure it was his wife's voice he heard coming from out of the pipe. "Please! No more!" he said, trying to look up through the smoke. "We can work this out."

* * * *

"Rick? Rick, honey...is that you?" called out Judy, almost sure now, seeing the back of his head facedown in the dirt.

Hearing her voice, he rolled over onto his back and gave Grady a hand.

"Oh my God! It's *you*!" she said, realizing the bomb in her hand had started to smoke.

Throwing it to her side, it bellowed thick green smoke into the air.

"Oh, honey. I'm so sorry."

"Are you trying to kill me?" he asked, coughing again.

"No. I just thought you guys were someone else. Are you okay, Grady?"

"Yeah, Judy. But man, I thought this was it for real."

"Are you mad?" she asked her husband.

"Give me just a minute to catch my breath?" he asked, before laughing deeply. "I thought I taught you well how to deal with hostiles, but it's clear you have something to teach me. Whose idea was this?"

"All hers," said Scott. "All hers."

"I guess you all made it back!" said Grady.

"Well, most of us," replied Scott. "We're missing Trey and Beth."

"Yeah, we ran into them earlier," replied Grady. "Where's Alex?"

"Up there," said Scott, pointing up to the deck. "You can thank him for the warning shots."

"Oh, I will."

"So, you're not mad...right, honey?" Judy asked.

"No, I'm cold and feel like I just smoked a carton of cigarettes, but you had the situation under control." Reaching to hug her, she turned and winced. "What's the matter, Judy?"

"I'll be all right."

"Did you get hit with glass? I saw the front window busted out."

"No, I just got shot in the shoulder."

"You what? Let me see! We have to get you to the hospital, right..."

"No, I'm good—for now, at least. The last thing we need to do is go riding around at night. Not at this point."

"Who did this to you?"

"Look, Grady's teeth are chattering," replied Judy. "Let's get you boys inside before you catch pneumonia, and I'll tell you everything."

"Yeah, okay," he conceded.

"The Mayor," she said, once they were inside. "He's the one responsible for all of this."

"Did he shoot you?" asked Rick, growing red in the face.

"I don't know. There were a bunch of them. It was scary, and I thought they would bust right through the door. It was the dogs, I think, that scared them off."

"That, and shooting back," I interjected, hoping I wasn't interrupting the moment.

"Dan came by right after and said he would be back with a couple of guys to board up the front window," she continued.

"Dan, huh?" asked Grady. He had heard about neighbor Dan more than a few times from his friend Rick.

The second I die, he will be trying to put his last name on my front gate, Rick would say.

* * * * * * *

CHAPTER TWENTY-EIGHT ESTES PARK, COLORADO

"We'll have this boarded up in just a few," said Dan, rounding the front of the house with his guys.

"That's a nice gesture," said Rick. "What do I owe you?"

"Nothing. You owe me nothing. It's just what neighbors do around here—help each other out. I'm sure you would do the same."

"Yeah, maybe so," Rick said under his breath.

"Alex, Shanan, Jo—how are you three holding up?" asked Grady after warming up a bit.

"Fine, sir," I said. "Well, at least we are alive, I mean, sir."

"For all of you," announced Grady, "you've earned my respect, so first names all around. Okay?"

"Yes, sir...I mean Grady. We can do that," I replied for us all.

"It looks like you found a friend, Shanan," remarked Rick, as she was followed only two steps behind by Scout wherever she walked.

"I just keep a little bacon in my jacket pocket," she joked. "It seems to work for Alex, too!" she quipped.

"Who doesn't love bacon?" I remarked, kissing her on the forehead. Grady gave me a nod.

"What was that?" she asked him, noticing the gesture.

"It's what's meant to be, is all," he replied. "You kids have come full circle, it looks like, and it took an Apocalypse to make it happen. I know your dad will be happy about it, Alex."

"Mine, too," added Shanan.

"Let's get a fire going for tonight," said Rick, "and we'll need to do two-person security shifts, at least for tonight. Judy and I will take the midnight to 4 a.m. shift, so you decide what you all want to do, and Grady can take one alone. Is that all right?"

"That's how I like it," replied Grady. "I'll take the 4 a.m. to 8 a.m. shift. So, the rest of you just work out the next few hours and then get a good night's sleep."

"We have a lot to discuss in the morning," said Rick.

* * * *

Shanan and I opted for the 10 p.m. to midnight shift, giving Scott and Jo the 8-10. In a flash, I wondered how Beth and Trey were holding up. I never did like him, and I was glad I broke it off with her, but that didn't mean I didn't care at least a little about what happened to them. Had I known about the killer on the loose who was last seen with those two, I would have lost some sleep tonight, for sure. But that information would be held in confidence between Rick and Grady until morning.

Perimeter shifts were inside only, with both Scout and Daizy following close behind each team. I checked the crude but effective window boarding and was happy to feel like we were all secure for a night. Everyone looked tired, dog-tired, like an adrenaline dump spread out over several days. The shootout from earlier would likely give me nightmares for the foreseeable future. There was one positive that came from it, though. Things were different now, and everybody knew it. The night was quiet, and the dogs only barked a few times. *Maybe a squirrel or rabbit*, I thought.

Shanan and I spent our shift quietly reminiscing about old times.

"Shanan...I..." I paused to find the words.

"You have already said that," she told me. "Now it's my turn to talk... I forgive you... I forgive you, Alex. The past is just that—gone, behind us, and has no bearing on tomorrow. Let's take things slowly, without expectations, and see where we end up. Okay?"

I sighed and spoke my last words about it. "I expected you to hammer me two days ago, yesterday, or today. I was expecting it and hoping it would happen, thinking you had to get it off your chest. But it was me; I was selfish."

"How's that?"

"If you gave me the hammer, maybe it would be done and I could stop feeling bad about it. Take my medicine, so to speak. But you won't. I know that it's not you, and I know you won't keep it bottled up inside either. I'm just not sure how you do it, and I love that about..."

"You what?"

"Sorry," I replied, feeling flushed. "We should get back to work."

* * * *

"Breakfast is served!" I heard, looking up at the bright morning light streaming through the bedroom window.

"This should be an interesting morning," I said to Shanan. "Like finding out all the secrets about Roswell or the Freemasons."

"I just want answers and a plan to get home," she replied.

"Me too," I told her. "Me too."

"Good morning, everyone," called out Judy. "Before you ask, my arm is feeling a little better. The glue job you did, Shanan, helped for sure.

"We're going to have breakfast from the propane grill—eggs, bacon, and anything else that comes out of the cooler. We have two freezers on the side of the house that are now powered by gas generators, but they will eventually need more gasoline than we have on hand. There's also camp-style coffee coming up, so we can take our time this morning and get a game plan on our future and yours. Sound good?"

"Great! Sure! Looking forward to it," we all replied.

"Okay. You start, Alex," said Grady, once we were settled.

I told him everything I could remember from the time he left until we showed up here. I intentionally left out the part about the Mayor and his thugs, opting to let Judy tell that story.

"So, you two locked Trey in the bear closet, huh?" said Grady, laughing. "Sorry. I know it wasn't funny at the time."

"No, it's fine," I replied. "The whole thing was one big mess, but I didn't get eaten by a mountain lion, and none of us got shot, so I call that good."

"Now it's our turn," said Grady. "And Judy, I'm not sure if you've heard all of it or not."

"She hasn't," Rick interjected—"at least not the bad part."

"What, honey?" she asked. "What happened that was so bad—Grady's arm?"

"I wish that was all," he sighed, gesturing to Grady to tell the story.

"Oh, no!" I said, when he was finished. "He's out there somewhere with Beth and Trey!"

"Yes, and that somewhere is around here," added Rick.

"What do we do?" asked Jo, as Shanan sat silent.

"About that, nothing," replied Grady. "We tried to warn them about Tex, but they wouldn't listen. Maybe we should have done more. I wasn't a fan of either one of them, but they don't deserve whatever that Tex guy may do to them."

"First things first," said Rick. "I'll get hold of the Sheriff somehow and give him a heads-up on the Tex fella without saying anything else we don't have to. Plus, I want him to know what happened here yesterday with that crooked Mayor, who was only elected because he ran unopposed."

* * * *

Scout and Daizy barked loudly, trying to see out of the boarded window that used to give a view of the front drive.

"Stay put, everybody," said Rick, motioning for Grady to go with him out the side door farthest from the front drive.

"You take this corner, and I'll go around back," he said to Grady.

"Nice and easy, unless it's the crooked Mayor again."

Grady cautiously slid across the outer wall, only hearing the dogs barking inside. "That's no squirrel out there," he said under his breath.

Staying low and peering around the corner, he could see a truck just outside the broken front gate. Grabbing his binoculars for another look, he saw the old blue truck, the same one I had described from up on the mountain.

As he zeroed in, he could see two men standing in front of the old truck. The sun beamed off of their badges.

"Stay there, Grady," Rick called from the other corner of the house, "but cover me."

"Will do. Be careful, buddy."

Rick walked slowly up the drive. His rifle pointed towards the ground. He half expected the Sheriff and his deputy to meet him halfway, but they didn't take a single step beyond his front gate.

"Hello, Sheriff. Nice truck."

"Good to see you, Rick," he said, extending his hand. "This old truck is one of the few running around here anymore. We had to confiscate it for official business. I hear you have something to tell me," he added, getting down to business.

What had he heard, thought Rick. *Did he find Tex?*

The Sheriff continued before he could answer.

"I heard you had some shooting up here yesterday afternoon."

"Yes, sir. That's true. I guess you know, then, who broke my gate and fired shots inside my home when my wife was inside."

"I've heard a few accounts of it, but let's hear yours."

Rick was careful and kept his mind one step in front of his mouth. Only a week ago, he would not have said a word, no matter how one-sided or justified it looked without council present, and even then only with a good reason. But now, things were different, and conversations just inside one's front gate on a chilly November morning were just as valid as one in a court of law in front of a judge and twelve jurors. He told the story his wife had told him, including the kids who were staying there. *The Sheriff met them all only a week ago, so there's no point in leaving that part out*, he thought.

"My wife and those kids were defending our property and were in fear for their lives. If you take a look, you'll see they never even came out of the house. This was a clear assault meant for me by the Mayor. I'm going to let you inside my house right now. Do you know why?"

"To clear this up, I guess. We could just take a quick look, and when the power is back up we'll figure this mess out."

"Really, Sheriff Bradley—when the power comes back up?"

"Yes, that what I said. Shouldn't be more than a few days, maybe a week tops."

"Okay, I'm going to ask my friend Grady to come up here. He's not a threat, but he knows more than I do about what's really going on with the power being out—the reason our cell phones don't work and most of our vehicles don't start. He's coming up now, okay?"

"Sure," replied Sheriff Bradley, waving his arm for Grady to approach, signaling to keep his rifle pointed to the ground.

* * * * * * *

CHAPTER TWENTY-NINE ESTES PARK, COLORADO

"Let me ask you, Sheriff Bradley. Who do you work for?" asked Rick.

"I work for the citizens of Estes Park, of course."

"I would agree with that. Now tell me who has the power to fire you."

"Well, that's different. The mayor thinks I work at the pleasure of the Mayor's Office."

"You dont, and why does he have more power over this town than you do?"

"It's just the way it works—government, I guess."

"What if it didn't, and you two were vying for the head position in this town, without all the government red tape? Who would do a better job, is what I'm asking?"

"Well, that's an easy one," interjected his deputy. "The Sheriff here is darn near a hero in this town—grew up here and everything."

"And the Mayor, Sheriff. What about him?" asked Rick, not concerned if he was bringing up a sore subject now.

"It's not my place to say, but I wish I were working with you, Rick. That new election can't get here soon enough, is how I see it. For the record, I don't want the mayor position, I'm fine right here," he added, tapping his Sheriff's badge.

"There's not going to be an election—at least not in the traditional sense," Rick continued.

"I'm not sure what you're talking about."

"This is my friend Grady, from Denver. This is Sheriff Bradley and his right-hand deputy, Jenkins. They are both good men, and we are proud to have them keeping our town safe."

Grady shook hands with both men.

"Now, Grady here knows more about what's happened than I do, so I'm going to check on my wife real quick while he fills you in. All right?"

"Sure, just don't be gone long. We have a few other matters to get to this morning."

* * * *

Rick walked back into the house and informed Judy that the Sheriff and his deputy would be coming inside.

"Are you just going to let them come in, Rick? A week ago, you would have made them get a warrant—even for something like this, defending ourselves."

"I know, honey, and the lawyer in me is screaming not to. But things are different, and they're not changing anytime soon. We can't afford to wait this out and let that scumbag Mayor and his thugs get another crack at us. Sheriff Bradley is a good man whose hands have been tied, and he needs to feed his family. But he cares more about this town than anyone I know. We need him on our side—not a week from now or even a few days. We need him with us today. I'll be back in a few," he added. "Just tell the truth about what happened, precisely as you told it to me."

* * * *

Walking back to the truck, he saw a different man—two, in fact, who were sitting on the truck's tailgate, staring off into the distance.

"Everything all right, Sheriff?"

"Yeah, Rick. It's just a lot to take in, is all. It's the first I've heard of this theory, but it's the only one that makes sense."

"I wish it were a theory," said Grady, "but it is the only thing that explains a power outage, fried electronics, and vehicles that won't start. We've either been hit by a coronal mass ejection or..."

"A Corona what? Sounds like a beer!" said his deputy.

"Well," continued Grady, "it's basically a power surge from the sun. It happens every day, but every 150 years or so, it hits Earth and causes problems. The more we depend on electronics, the more problems it causes. The second is a nuke detonated 300 miles up into the atmosphere. Either way, the result is the same. Months at best, to years most likely, living like we're back in the 1800s in a split second, without warning."

"So, to be clear," said Rick, returning to the front gate. "I'm asking you into my home because I believe 100% that the current Mayor has no more legal authority over you, and it will be the citizens of this town that decide who they want in leadership. Do you think, given a choice right now, they would pick him again?"

"Not a chance in Hades," the Sheriff replied, lowering his voice and looking around cautiously.

"It's just us out here, sir," said Rick, "and anything you say wouldn't leave this property. Now let me show you what they tried to do to my wife and our guests."

* * * *

"Hello, Sheriff...Deputy," said Judy.

"How do you do, ma'am. Mind if we take a look around and talk for just a few?"

"Sure. It's pretty easy to see," she replied. "They came in from the front and started shooting. We returned fire in the hope to save our lives, and eventually, by the grace of God, they just left, but not without the Mayor's warning to my husband, saying that he was 'on notice.' Now, I know he's your boss, but this isn't right."

"Judy, you know I've backed your husband when I could for this upcoming election, and I would like to see nothing more than that thief of a mayor we have now be unseated.

But you're right—he is still my boss, at least up until a few days ago. If I were to find out with reasonable certainty that he could no longer fire me...well, then that would be a different story entirely. I'd lock him up so fast he'd...well, he wouldn't be anyone's problem anymore."

"I think you will find that to be the case," interjected Grady.

"Well, until then, let me get all of the information from you, ma'am, so we can have some ammunition." Sheriff Bradley went through his list of standard questions typically saved for car accidents and minor disagreements, such as with the kids in the hotel last week. When he was finished he commented, "We will get this figured out. Until then, keep a low profile and watch your back. I'll be in town if you need me."

"Thank you, Sheriff. There's just one more thing..." said Rick.

* * * *

Sheriff Bradley and his deputy tore out of the ranch, kicking up dirt and rocks as they fishtailed out of the front gate.

"I wish you would have told me this first," the Sheriff had said.

"That's why I didn't," Rick told everyone after he was gone. "He would have never heard about what happened here if I did."

* * * * * * *

CHAPTER THIRTY SOUTH OF ESTES PARK, COLORADO

Sheriff Bradley sped down the winding highway, stopping briefly at each scene Rick had described. It was the first body he had ever seen that had not died in a car, or other type, accident.

"It's hard to wrap my mind around it," he said to his deputy. "I mean, they are in a car and obviously dead, but it wasn't an accident. And now we have a drifter named Tex somewhere in our town who could be held up in any one of hundreds of vacant summer homes. It could take most of the winter to find someone like that, if he's even still in town. Let's get the boys and do the best we can to preserve the scene and collect evidence. I want to stop by the hospital on the way and talk to the receptionist Rick told us about. At least if she can corroborate something about this Tex fella, I can be sure Rick is telling me the truth, or at least part of it."

Wrapping each car with yellow tape and shutting the doors and trunk, they made a quick stop at the hospital. Rick's story checked out with the receptionist and two additional employees, describing the same man Rick had. A drifter with a backpack, scruffy blonde beard, and long greasy hair, who got upset when he was told he wouldn't be getting pain killers, they all agreed.

"Good. Rick's story checks out," he told his deputy.

"Did you think it wouldn't, Sheriff?"

"I believed him. I didn't want to be the only one is all. Not a word about Rick or any of this. I don't want it getting back to the Mayor yet. He may just try and pin it on Rick and his buddy. Also, we need a sketch artist. In all the years I've been up here, I've never seen the need for one until now. Who do we know in the department that can do it?"

"I don't know anybody like that, boss—except the kid my boy hangs around with at school. He's not a sketch artist per se, but I've seen his drawings and he does a pretty good Morrison and Hendrix."

"Let's find him and hope he can do one without a picture."

* * * *

Picking up Rick from his home, they met the kid and staff members at the hospital.

"Okay, everybody. This is unusual, I know, but we need to talk with this man," he continued, without going into details of why. "Let's start by each of you going into the room one by one, with our artist, and describing the man you saw. We're confident that he goes by the name Tex."

"Can't we just all say what he looked like?" asked the receptionist. "It would go a lot faster, I'm sure."

"I wish we could, but we don't want one person second-guessing their description after hearing another version of it. Does that make sense?" asked the Sheriff.

"Yes, sir. I guess it does."

"Just start with the hair and work your way down the face and be as detailed as you can confidently remember. If we are lucky when we're done, we'll end up with a drawing everyone here can recognize," the Sheriff continued.

Three hours later, they had the sketch. Everyone agreed the kid did a good drawing, and the resemblance to the Tex they saw was spot-on.

"I would recognize him anywhere from that picture," said Rick, giving the young artist a high five.

* * * * * * *

CHAPTER THIRTY-ONE ABOVE ESTES PARK, COLORADO

T ex was surprised by the two black men following him down the road.

Now ain't this something. I'm out here trying to soak up some nature and start fresh, and I got two black guys following me, probably trying to take my cigarettes or necklace, or some crap, he thought.

Tex was not from the great state of Texas, but farther south. He grew up poor, as the oldest son in a five-child family. His childhood was a blur of insults and more than occasional beatings at the hand of his usually drunk father. His father was well known in the small southern town for drinking more than he was looking for work. He never held a job more than a week before arguing with the boss or scuffling with another employee. Yet somehow, it was always someone else's fault. Tex worked when his father didn't to support the family. It wasn't his choice, just what was expected of him.

His mother was a saint, if there was such a thing. She had always told him and his sisters that. She was usually sticking up for his dad and diligently told the same story he did about who was to blame. She buried herself in her volunteer work at the church, and most of the family meals came out through the chapel door.

Tex's dad didn't seem to mind being on the receiving end of it all, as long as there was enough money for a case of beer or a bottle of cheap malt whisky. He wasn't picky about the quality as long as it kept flowing. Whatever he drank was always in the same cup; it didn't matter if it was whisky, beer, water only on special occasions, or whatever else he could scrounge from the liquor cabinet.

"If you ever see this cup empty, boy," he would tell Tex, "it's either those African thugs down the road done stole it or I just finished my glass. Either way, it needs to be filled and back in my hand before anything else, including your mother. If she spent more time raising her kids than she does flirting with that pastor down at the church, I might just have time to work. You're one sorry son of a bitch, Terrance Xander," he would say. "You ain't goin' to amount to nothin', boy. That's the truth of it... You think you got it bad now? This place is going to look like a mansion when I kick your sorry ass out of here. I already got enough mouths to feed besides your sorry one."

"No, Dad. I believe it's Mom that feeds us..." He paused, watching his father's mouth contort as he slung his favorite glass, his only glass, towards the old stove, smashing it into a hundred pieces. Terrance paused as the scene played out in front of him in slow motion, like the only car wreck he had ever been in at the age of nine when his dad was drunk and slammed head-on into a pole. He remembered them ditching the car and walking home four or five miles through the woods, so his dad could sober up before talking to the police.

The large gash above Terrance's right eye wasn't as important to his dad as an alibi, he always knew, and by the time a doctor saw him it was too late to reduce the appearance of the nearly two-inch-long scar just above his eye. The kids teased him mercilessly, joking that his drunk dad must have fallen over on him, just trying to walk a straight line.

Terrance, aged thirteen, watched in disbelief as his father's glass shattered, with large shards exploding across the old wood floors. He instinctively ducked under the right-arm swing he knew was coming. He was faster than his dad today, but the left hand caught him just above the scar, knocking him to the floor. Crying, he lay on the floor with a lump forming, fast and large on his forehead.

"You always were a little sissy, Terrance. Ain't nothin' but a little girl. You remind me of your mother—weak," he said, disgusted as he turned around.

Terrance was a good boy, he thought. He'd done a few bad things to some animals over the years. "It don't really matter," he would tell his friends. "Animals ain't got feelings anyway."

He had lost most of those friends over the years, whose parents wouldn't let them play with him anymore. "Crazy animal lovers," he would call them. *Besides all that*, he thought, *he was a pretty good boy. He took care of his siblings and backed up his mother at every chance.*

Terrance lay on the ground, crying as his father ranted, throwing out more comparisons of him and anyone else his father hated.

"My name is Tex, you bastard! Everybody knows that," he said, feeling out of his body. He rose to his feet and seemed to float over to the side of the bar, grabbing hold of a half-full whiskey bottle and smashing it over the back of his father's head.

At first, he thought he had killed him and waited for the tears that never came. Seconds turned to minutes, as he watched his father slowly bleed out of the side of his head. A small pool collected on the scratched wood floor, with a small stream slowly moving across a larger crack in the wood. "You're headed straight to hell!" he said ten minutes later, turning around to walk out the front door.

"I may be," his dad said, raising as if he were playing along the entire time. "But you're going with me!"

* * * *

Tex remembered that line and nothing more, waking up in the pitch dark. His hands were bound behind him with a heavy chain on either side and leather straps digging into his wrists and ankles. He tasted the remnants of gasoline on the old shop rag his dad had stuffed into his mouth, and there was something over his eyes feeling sticky, like duct tape, wrapped around his entire head. His head was spinning and now had two spots that hurt; he guessed the second one was when he blacked out.

Whish! came the sound of the passing cars from out on the main road every few minutes, stopping every now and then for the first stoplight on the way into town.

Can they hear me? Could they hear me? he thought, with sweat pouring from his face and scalp. The July heat wrapped his small body like a heavy blanket. Hours later, or maybe only thirty minutes in his new time warp, he heard a large door open and footsteps, before hearing another door and a lock snapping open.

I'm in the barn, he thought. *But where?*

He and his siblings had played in his dad's old barn, set 50 yards from the house on the edge of their property. The front faced the house, and the back ran only a few feet from the county road most took into town when coming in from the big city. Never in his life had he seen his mom set foot near the barn, like there was some kind of curse over it. Even though she inherited the property after her parents were killed, and she grew up here, she never mentioned playing or ever stepping foot in the barn. It was as if it had never existed.

"Tex...think!" he said to himself. "You're in the barn," he said aloud, but where?

"In my special room, boy," came the sound of his father's voice, closer than he expected. Tex jumped and nearly choked on the rag in his mouth. His heavy breathing increased with each passing second, until the rag was yanked out, nearly pulling a tooth with it.

"You ran away from home, boy," his father said, before he could speak. "That's what I told your mom and your sisters, and it's all they will ever know."

"Daddy, I'm sorry about what I done. Truly I am."

"That's in the past, boy. No use dwelling on it now. So, like I said, you ran away. I'll feed you once, maybe even twice some days, and there's a hose in the back you can suck some water off of. I done put some hay over in the corner behind you, and if it were me in there, I would do my business over there," he said, with Tex still blindfolded.

"Over where? I can't see, Daddy." He could see a little but only with the small slit in his eye, and he kept that to himself.

"Along the far wall over there, where there's some more hay," his dad replied.

"I don't want this, Daddy. Can I please come home?"

"Nope, you done run away from home, like I done already said. Can't have your bad attitude spoiling your sisters now, can I?"

"I'll be good, Daddy. I promise!"

"I'm sure you will," he said, gagging him again and double-checking his tied hands before locking the door. "One more thing," he added from the other side of the door that sounded a mile away. "You call out, scream, yell, or try to find your way out, and I'll make sure you go to hell first."

Tex's nose and lungs burned from the gasoline. He played his father's speech over in his head—"You're in my special room." *The room*, he thought...surprised he hadn't figure it out yet. There was a room in the back of the barn with a solid wooden door. Not like a typical barn door but one specially designed to keep people out. Over the years, he and his sisters had disobeyed their father dozens of times and played in the barn when he was at work or passed out on the living room couch. They pretended to be treasure hunters, always trying to get to the secret stash they all knew to be behind that door.

There was a time only a few months back when they became so obsessed with it that he had secretly used money he had earned helping an old couple around the house with any chores needing to be done. He rode his bike there nearly twice a week and sometimes more, earning as much as five or six dollars for only a few hours of work. It didn't take him long to start hiding some of his earning in his sock, since his dad would take every penny from him when he got home. His dad would say that it's for the family as he would head to the liquor store and buy whatever he could with the day's wages.

Tex saved up twenty dollars over the course of about eight months and vowed to use it to find the treasure behind the door. His sisters agreed he would be reimbursed the full twenty before dividing up the rest of the loot evenly between them—everyone, that was, but Mary, his twin sister.

Mary had her own room in the small three-bedroom, one-bath, 1500-square-foot ranch house. She never came out except to pick up food and to go to the bathroom. One day, a year or so ago, she started acting strange. It was Tex who had his own room, and she shared with her sisters at that time. She wouldn't talk to anyone about it, and his dad gave her Tex's room one day without notice or any explanation at all. A week later, she stopped going to school and wouldn't talk to anyone, not even her twin brother. He remembered his father telling her "Congratulations. You've become a woman," and giving her Tex's room the next day.

Tex shared the other with his three younger sisters ever since, and his twin hadn't said more than a few words to him in almost a year.

He knew what was happening, seeing his father slip into her room sometimes late at night if he was up to use the bathroom. He knew they all did, but nobody ever dared say a word, not even his mother. Tex hated her for not standing up to him, not even raising her voice or even giving her own opinion on something...anything. He hated himself for covering for Mary at school when the teachers asked where she was. "Homeschooled" is all he would say and try not to answer any follow-up questions. Only his little sisters had no idea, and he feared they would be next.

He and his little sisters spent nearly two weeks together over the last summer while his father was in the longest job stint of his life, at just over three weeks long. He bought a used lock pick and an old stethoscope at the local pawn shop for $17 total, hoping to hear something through the walls or be so lucky as to pick the lock. Neither worked, and he inspected every inch of the room, from the front door and outside, facing the county road.

* * * * * * *

CHAPTER THIRTY-TWO THE BARN SOUTHERN UNITED STATES

Tex's remaining hard-earned $3 was used to buy a magnifying glass that he would hold up to the narrow cracks on the outer wall facing the road. He could just see in with small strips of light touching the room's far wall but couldn't make out anything useful inside.

"This place is locked up like Fort Knox," he told his sisters, even convincing the youngest one to innocently asked their mom what was inside the barn.

"There's nothing inside the barn," she snapped back, like none of the children had ever seen her. "You don't ever go near that God-awful place," she said. "And don't let your father hear you asking questions about it, neither. He'll tan your hide just for looking at it, and that's the truth. Now run along and find something else to play with."

* * * *

Tex had done as he was told and didn't make a sound. Hours later, he heard the door open, and his gag was removed from his mouth.

"Daddy, I'm sorry. Can I please come home?" he cried.

His father went to work without saying a word or even looking at his only son. He took off the tape over Tex's eyes, quickly ripping it without regard to the pain it caused, before cutting his hands loose. Tex screamed out initially but quieted down when his father struck him in the gut with his right fist, knocking the wind out of him.

He proceeded to take the left ankle shackle off and extend the one remaining chain length. Without looking at Tex, he held out a long stick with a grabbing hook at the end, turned, and left a small paper sack near the front door, walking out and locking the padlock behind him.

Tex pulled the gag from his mouth and threw it towards the sidewall with a silent scream, watching it flip end over end, landing on the single-wide mattress covered in rat feces. The same mattress with his older sister's pink teddy bear lying next to the pillow, its soulless eyes staring off into the darkness. Tears welled up in his eyes as he realized where his sister's abuse had started—"and now she has her own room," he said aloud, "because nobody cares if it continues."

"I hate you, Mother, for letting him prey on us. No wonder you spend every spare minute at the church," he said, crying. "You can't wash off that kind of sin with soap and water!"

The light shone through the cracks in the outer wall, and he took stock of the room. The chains and shackles were old, worn, and rusty. *How long have these been here?* he thought, realizing he had just enough chain to use the bathroom and get his bag of food with the grabber stick.

He could reach the mattress on the floor and lay on it if he put the restrained leg over the side. He checked the back wall facing the road and could get within a foot of it but no closer. He strained his eyes, turning his head, angling left and right to see something outside. "Mile Marker 6" read the pole on the highway, He could see that clearly but little else.

He used the bathroom, if one could call it that, with the upside-down arrow running down the wall, pointing to a small pile of hay. A large box, reading "Shop Rags," sat in the corner with one blue rag sticking out of the top, followed by another and another. The water hose ran alongside the same wall, with a small spicket and one arrow reading "On" and the other "Off."

Tex was able to hook the small paper bag with the grabber pole after several tries, pulling it closer before it slipped out. He steadied his shaking hand as much as he could for another pull. Opening the bag, he wasn't sure what to expect but found one medium red potato unwashed and two red grapes. The scared boy quickly ate the meal, brushing the grit of the potato with his dirty fingers. He drank deeply from the hose and brushed the rodent droppings off the bed and onto the floor. He listened intently, trying to hear the scurry of the rat who had been here before, without success.

"I hope you don't come back," he said aloud.

Laying his head on the sweltering pillow, he drifted off to sleep. Tex dreamed of his family, the one he used to have Christmases and Thanksgivings with—his mom and dad, sisters, and loyal dog. It played like a movie running on a wheel, only briefly interrupted by instinctively wiping the sweat off of his body but jumping right back in where he left off.

He awoke with a smile, fading quickly as he realized he never had that life. As far back as he could remember, his father drank his way through each week, and his mother spent more time with the church pastor than any other volunteer. Only his sisters could be counted on...well, at least the small ones. "Don't do it! Daddy, don't touch them!" he yelled.

* * * *

Tex would spend the next two years locked up in the barn, like a forgotten animal, locked away with only his thoughts, rage, dreams, and desires. He had just turned fifteen three weeks before it happened and he was able to escape. He ran as any scared young man may, and never looked back...

* * * * * * *

CHAPTER THIRTY-THREE ABOVE ESTES PARK, COLORADO

Tex knew he had a head start on his followers. How far, he couldn't be sure. Life as a drifter for the past 12 years, carrying a backpack everywhere he went, had built up his stamina and he was pretty sure he could outpace most seasoned hikers. Following the signs to the nearest hospital wasn't hard. He had learned to read quite well by the age of 13, and thankfully he thought he had never lost the passion for it. In fact, nearly half of his large backpack was filled with books he would borrow from those boxes some people have in front of their houses or businesses. It would say "Borrow a book and leave one." Over the years, he had borrowed plenty but never left even a single one.

He sat, watching the hospital for nearly ten minutes for anything unusual. Halfway in, he would see the Sheriff or law enforcement walking out and down the road. "That was close," he said aloud, not wanting to draw attention to the only guy backpacking into town in the month of November. He sat in silence for another five minutes, reminiscing over how many books he had accumulated over his lifetime, like a middle-aged person may count past lovers.

During his last book "exchange" in Texas, he opened the box to find nearly 20 books stacked in rows of 4. On the top of each stack lay a Bible, "one in every row," he said aloud. Tex pushed them to the side, only to find another, one to two books deep.

"Are you trying to tell me something, God?" he said, looking up to the sky. "Are you?!" he screamed at the sky...

* * * *

"Hey, you get out of here," yelled a woman, maybe 75 years old. "This is a quiet neighborhood."

He ignored her as he shook the pole supporting the glass-lined box, before giving it a roundhouse kick, shattering the glass. Books fell out, left and right, and he kicked those aside he couldn't bear to look at.

"That's enough!" called her husband of at least the same amount of years on this earth.

Tex ignored the advancing man, holding a shovel out in front of him.

"I know you're not going to try and hit me with that, old-timer," Tex said, not turning around.

The advancing man was angry and scared. Tex had seen both emotions from the men he killed over the years but most never fought back. This one was taking a stand about books, of all things, but it was more than most and he could respect him for that.

Tex looked him square in the eyes and asked him, "Do you want to die today?"

"No, I do not," the man replied. "How about you? Is today your day, above all others? We can do this, you and me, one of two ways," the old man continued.

Tex laughed out loud. Never in his life had he seen a man, any man, let alone an old-timer, stick up for himself like this. He debated killing the man where he stood with the simplicity of another man deciding between sandwiches—turkey or ham. Figuring he would have to kill them both for a chance to outrun the inevitable call to police, he raised his hand in a pistol-shooting gesture.

"Pow! old man," he said, adding, "I'm keeping this"—waiving the permanently borrowed book in the air and walking slowly down the road.

"Hmm," he said, looking at the book's tattered cover. *The Art of War*, he said aloud. "Sounds right up my street," he mumbled.

* * * *

Another mile up the road, he put out his thumb, not like a hitchhiker in the 1970s, expecting a ride any moment, but like any hitcher nowadays, not even turning around as vehicles were approaching from behind. In all his years bumming rides, he could count on two hands the number of times someone pulled over, and even less the ones that let him in. The ones who had all told the same story once he reached his desired destination. It was the last drive they would ever take. It wasn't that he enjoyed hurting people. He once told a stranger in a bar that it was just what he did, like brushing his teeth or matching socks. He neither took pleasure nor remorse in the deed. It was the planning that he thrived on.

Before the day when everything changed, Tex remembered how his twin sister would plan elaborate trips she would someday take, cutting pictures out of old magazines her mother brought home from church every few months. With the scantest of recourses, his twin would map out every detail so precisely, he thought she would make a great travel agent one day. He did the same with his victims. "After all, we're twins," he told the bar stranger before waiting to ambush him in the parking lot.

This day he wouldn't get a ride as he started up into the Rocky Mountains, heading for Estes Park and hopefully a new start where nobody knew him, at least for a little while. He sang his tune, one of the few he made up himself. "I'm a loner and a stoner and a part-time organ donor—not mine!" he would shout out at the end before doubling over in laughter.

Tex was past his normal stopping point for the day when it happened. He didn't carry a phone, watch, or anything else digital, and only had a clue when the bright light struck, like a thousand bolts of lightning in the darkening sky. By the next afternoon, he had taken his next victims, all stranded in their cars and easy pickings.

* * * * * *

Chapter Thirty-four Estes Park, Colorado

"**D**o you two know where someone can crash for the night or three?" a friendly sounding Tex asked Beth and Trey.

"We were wondering the same thing," she replied, with a flirt of a smile, thought Tex.

"I don't know much about this town," replied Tex, "but all of these sleepy winter places have dozens, if not hundreds, of vacant homes just sitting until next summer."

"My uncle has one just down the road that he says I can use anytime," said Trey. "It beats paying for a hotel, and especially now with the power out."

"Why, I bet we could find something suitable before it gets dark, and maybe even stay a while," replied Tex.

"That's okay, mister," said Trey, limping around on his crutches. "I think she and I will go our own way."

"Oh, sure thing. I get it," replied Tex casually, as if talking about whether he took cream or sugar in his coffee. "If it's the 'other guy thing' you're worried about, I'm gay and you're not my type—no offense, I hope, unless you don't like my kind in general..." Tex had used this line in the past, usually catching people off guard and going overboard not to appear insensitive.

"Oh no, no," replied Trey, caught off guard and falling face-first into the ruse. "What I mean is I don't have a problem with you, is all."

"I just think three is better than one or two, is all," said Tex. "We could pool our cash and get some supplies first," he suggested.

"I've got plenty of credit cards," replied Trey, "so we're good."

"It's cash-only now," replied Tex. "Look, it even says so on the door"—he pointed to the front of the grocery store.

Trey took Beth aside to discuss the options. "I've only got $10 in cash. What about you?"

"Let's see," she replied, rummaging through her purse. "I've got six, it looks like."

"Six hundred?" asked Trey, hopeful.

"Nope, just six."

"That's not enough to last a day, let alone weeks if it comes down to it," replied Trey, feeling nervous.

"We need to ask how much he has," she added, "before making a decision."

"We don't have a lot in cash," said Beth, coming right out and asking Tex how much he had.

"Somewhere north of $500," he said, without showing a single bill. He had swiped some bills off of his last victims stranded in their cars but hadn't counted it yet. No mind; he didn't plan on using any today. "Tell you what. As a gesture of good faith, you two keep your money and wait out here. If I come back with a cart full of groceries, then you can make your decision. Sound fair?"

"Sure," they both replied, each not wanting to bet on if he would come through.

Tex walked into the crowded store mindfully, adding items to his cart, the largest one he could find in the store, and the third one he had checked the wheels on.

"Can't have a free cart of food rolling on crap wheels," he said to himself, getting a kick out of his many musings. Starting at the far end of the store, he worked his way back towards the front. The fresh meat devoured the last bit of ice they sat upon, and he scooped up three large steaks with a handwritten plaque, reading "Must Sell Today. Thank you. —Management." Tex grabbed every canned good he could fit into the cart; the weight made him lean into the cart and mindfully push with his legs and not his back. Bending down beside the cart near the front of the store, now lit by sunlight and emergency lights haphazardly scattered across the aisles inside, he started his routine. Tex had done it more than a dozen times before, and so far, it had never failed. Pretending to check the cart wheels, he waited until the person working at the cash register asked if he needed any help.

"Uh, yes, ma'am," he said almost robotically. "I'd like to speak to the manager."

"Sure," she replied, "unless I can help you."

"No, thanks. I'll wait…"

* * * *

"Stan at your service, and I'm the store manager," the man said, walking up behind Tex. "How can I help you today, sir?"

"Stan, huh? Stan the man, the guy with the plan until he became frightened and ran, ran, ran. Came up with that on the fly," said Tex, snapping his fingers. "Let me ask you, Stan," he said, turning away from the register and line of sight of customers. "Now I understand the card machines don't work, with the power being out and all, so I've got this here check," he said, holding up an official-looking checkbook tucked neatly into a brown leather case dotted with specks of dried blood.

"Oh, no," said Stan. "Before you go any further, I'm not authorized to take anything but cash today."

"Hmm," replied Tex. "Not authorized…my new buddy Stan is not authorized," he said again, scratching his scruffy chin and lowering his voice. "I thought you were the manager, Stan. The big man with the keys to the store. Maybe you're just the assistant manager or a department manager. Why, I bet you manage the carrot and potatoes section—is that right?"

"No, sir. I manage the entire store, and someday I'll be a district manager. Take that to the bank."

Tex laughed aloud at that, finding it hilarious that this man, any man, would tell him what to do.

"You, Stan, have no idea what we're doing here," he replied, now stone-faced once again. "Let me make it simple. You're going to take this check. I'll make it out for $1,500, more than covering my cart full. Should you refuse, I'll walk right out the door. Yes, I will, only to meet you in the parking lot after your shift and slice you, ear to ear." He subtly deployed a 5-inch switchblade knife, smiling in case any customers saw. "If you believe me, smile and say 'That's really nice' out loud, but not too loud."

Stan paused for a moment before speaking. "That's real nice," he said aloud. "Carey," he called to the checkout girl, "I'll take this one," pointing to Tex.

"Right this way, sir," he said, showing him around the side and to the front of the store.

"You want to see my driver's license?" asked Tex. "Name's Jim," he added, pointing to the local in-town check he pulled off the victim he'd left in the trunk on the hike in.

Stan looked at the check of his friend—not the best one, and maybe an acquaintance would be a better description, but a local man that everyone around town knew and respected. Stan didn't know what happened or who this guy was, but he knew this wasn't Jim.

"Uh...uh no, sir. I don't need a driver's license," Stan stammered. "A local check is good as cash up here. This should more than cover it," he added, wanting the man out of his store.

"Keep this our little secret," whispered Tex, as he walked by. "True to my word," he announced, walking calmly out of the store.

Tex wasn't concerned about Stan trying to flag down a cop or the Sheriff. Even before, with cell phones and everything, nobody had ever called the authorities to report a Tex grocery store run. *Guess they all knew I would be back later, true to my word,* he thought.

Trey and Beth were pleasantly surprised. Tex had bought food for them on good faith, and they would have shelter and food on their first night in town.

"Steaks for tonight, manager's special," announced Tex. "I'm cooking."

"I don't eat meat," said Beth quickly.

"Where did you say you're from again, darlin'?" asked Tex.

"California," she replied, adding, "You can just call me Beth."

"Figures," he said, laughing aloud.

"It looks like it's just you and me then, Tracy."

"It's Trey."

"Sure thing, Trey; it's just you and me unless you're from over there too."

"I am, but I love steak."

"Hallelujah! We've got a winner!"

"Winner, winner, chicken…I mean *steak* dinner," said Tex. "Don't you worry, pretty lady. We'll find some rabbit food for ya."

Something about this man made her skin crawl, and if it weren't for Trey being right beside her, she would have bolted into the woods the first chance she got.

"This is it—the one on the right up here," announced Trey, deciding in a split second to almost bypass it altogether. It had been a while since he was up here, maybe five years, give or take, but the bright blue mailbox matching the gaudy front porch was unmistakable. His uncle's neighbors had pointed out the eyesore color of the otherwise quaint little cabin numerous times, always getting a "Maybe I'll change the color next year." He was from Pennsylvania, so it was unlikely he would be here this time of year.

The key was under the third stair from the top, just as always, in a small metal box screwed to the underside of the stair. It fascinated Trey, even up to age 12 or 13, how one could screw a box on the underside of a narrow stair—like those bottles with the ship inside you may find in touristy beach shops.

"I mean, how do you even get a screwdriver under there?" he finally asked.

"Easy," his uncle had replied. "I mounted the box before the stair went in, turning a two by four over in his hands. Trey felt dumb for not seeing the obvious, but then he was still just a kid.

"The barbecue is around back," Trey called out to Tex. "It's propane, so hopefully it's not empty."

"Great! How 'bout you get things situated inside, and me and Beth will get these groceries brought in. No use trying to limp around with all of our food," added Tex.

"It's okay. I can help you get situated," said Beth, grabbing Trey's arm.

"No, no. He's right, Beth. Let's drop our packs out here on the porch and get everything else inside. I'll get the barbecue going," he added.

"Well, now what have we got here?" said Tex, rummaging through Trey's pack while he was around the side of the house. "He's been holding out on us," he said, holding the half-finished whisky bottle up towards Beth. "Still enough to have a little fun, you and me. What say you?" he asked, winking a few times like a nervous tick.

"First thing, that's Trey's stuff, not yours," said Beth. "Second, you said you were gay."

"I say a lot of things, darlin'—always have."

"Well, it doesn't matter anyway because you're not my type."

"That is of little concern to me; trust me on that," he replied.

* * * *

"That guy creeps me out," said Beth, catching up with Trey, "and he stole your whisky."

"He what?" asked Trey, around turning angrily before displacing his weight-bearing crutch and falling to the floor with a thud, cursing as he held his ankle.

"I'm thinking we let him stay one night, and then we divide up the food into thirds and send him on his way," suggested Beth.

"Now that's not nice; we were just getting to know each other," whispered Tex to himself, overhearing her comments. *I was thinking more like sharing the winter up here,* he thought.

They got the steaks on the propane grill, with Trey holding his tongue about the bottle.

"I'll just get another one in town," Beth told him once he calmed down. "Let's not mess with this guy," she urged.

"Yeah, yeah…okay," replied Trey, kissing her on the forehead for the first time. She turned slightly to meet his mouth when she saw Tex across the room, arms folded across his skinny chest and shaking his head side to side.

"There will be none of that while I'm around," he stated coldly.

"This is my uncle's house," spat Trey, "and I can do what I want in here. Just because you bought some groceries doesn't give you any rights to this property or what happens here," he added, turning red.

Tex smiled a several-tooth-missing grin and held up the bottle.

* * * * * * *

Chapter Thirty-Five Uncle's Cabin Estes Park, Colorado

"How's about we start over?" Tex suggested, loosening the cap on the bottle. "Pass around or glasses?" he asked, holding out the bottle towards Beth. She looked at Trey, not sure how to answer.

"All right, I guess," said Trey. "At the very least, a few drinks should help my ankle pain."

"Glasses, then," announced Beth, heading into the kitchen.

"Steaks and grilled broccoli coming up," called out Trey, finally loosening up after only two drinks.

Finding an assortment of candles, they sat around, wrapped in blankets, with none wanting to attempt building a fire tonight.

"Monopoly by candlelight, and I'm the dog, scrappy woof woof..." announced Tex before trailing off and realizing he hadn't played since he was a kid with his sisters before the day. "Never forget how to play a game like this—no, you never forget," he added, shaking his head. "Whoo!" he yelled, "like using a megaphone!" catching Beth and Trey off guard.

"What the crap?" said Trey, instinctively scooting away from the game board.

"Just getting the demons out, is all," said Tex. "Let's play!"

Round after round and drink after drink, they played until Tex accused Trey, who was also the banker, of cheating, throwing the entire board across the room as houses and hotels clinked across the hardwood floors.

"That's perfect," said Trey, trying to stand. "Just great, really."

"I'm going for a walk," stated Tex, opening the front door. "See you two love birds later," he called back over his shoulder, stumbling onto the porch and down the seven front porch steps, landing with a thud at the bottom.

The silence lasted a full twenty seconds but seemed like an eternity for Beth, who couldn't decide if she wanted him to get back up.

"I'm okay," he finally announced, springing back up with childlike reflexes. "Thanks for checking on me, guys," he added, stumbling down the road.

"What do we do now?" asked Beth. "Should we stop him? I mean, he'll freeze out there; he's not even wearing a jacket."

"So," replied Trey, "he's a grown man. And I, for one, won't be missing any sleep if he doesn't come back. Besides, you're the one who said he gives you the creeps."

"Okay, I guess you're right," she conceded. "Just make sure you leave the door unlocked; I'm going to bed."

"Sure thing," Trey replied, quietly locking the front door and the back after she disappeared upstairs. "Thanks for the groceries, you freak," he said into the darkness, blowing out the candles and carrying the last lit one and heading upstairs.

* * * *

The front door handle shook back and forth. *Clank! Clank! Clank!*

Trey heard it straightaway, jolting up in bed maybe an hour later. He listened for Beth in the other room but heard nothing. The banging on the front door, and eventually the back, continued for several minutes, with pauses in between trips around the house, Trey guessed. He held the pistol retrieved earlier from his uncle's secret spot.

Trey and his siblings remembered it as kids, always in the same spot underneath the kitchen sink—tucked up and back—though they had promised to never touch it. *Yes!* he thought when he grabbed it first thing today, finding it loaded and ready to fire, minus the engaged safety. He tucked it deep into his pack. Tex, fortunately, missed it when he rifled through it, looking for booze. *That could have been really bad,* thought Trey.

Now he was walking slowly down the stairs, clutching it in one hand and with a tight grip on the rail with the other with no light, holding the weapon out in front of him.

"I'll shoot you, freak boy! Count on that if you try breaking in," he said, under his breath.

The front and back doors were solid, but the windows—even double pained for the climate—wouldn't stop a brick or large log hurled at them. The moon shone bright, and Trey could see shadows dancing across the windows, left to right and back again. It was the sound that made his blood run cold—a whooping war cry, like all the Indian movies he saw when he was young, right before an attack. Maybe just the Lone Ranger episodes he watched with his siblings, but it sounded the same, as a declaration of war. Trey strained his eyes and ears, not sure if he wanted to know what lay on the other side of the wall. He heard a thud towards the east side of the house, and then silence. Trey held his breath, straining to hear something...anything.

"What's going on down here?" called Beth, slurring her words and scaring the daylights out of him.

"You scared the crap out of me," he replied, before he saw it and tried to get the words out quicker. "Watch that first step," he got out but was too late.

Her right foot missed it and caught the top edge of the second, throwing her forward into the pitch dark of the staircase. Screaming, followed by thuds down the stairs, made Trey sick to his stomach. He reached out, only half catching her at the landing.

"Shanan! Shanan! Are you okay?" he asked. Finally, remembering he had the wrong name, he corrected himself. "Sorry, Beth. I forgot is all. Are you okay?"

She didn't respond and felt lifeless in his arms. He laid her down, fumbling for his flashlight he would dare to turn on. The knot on her forehead grew in front of his eyes, settling as a small chicken egg in size. Checking for a pulse and putting two fingers on her neck, he listened for breathing, finding both.

"Beth! Beth! Can you hear me?" he asked, afraid to shake her.

Everything looked straight, arms- and legs-wise, as he looked her over. The few cuts he could see bled, but none appeared life-threatening. Trey couldn't be sure if there were any internal injuries but was sure she had a bad concussion, at the very least.

"How will I get you to the hospital?" he said aloud. "I can't even get around by myself... No, I'm not going to go out looking for Tex," he said, answering his own thought out loud.

Trey half hopped, half hobbled over to the coat closet, retrieving several more blankets and two pillows. His uncle always planned for guests. "The more, the better," he would say.

"I guess we're down here for the night, beautiful," he said, arranging her in between two blankets.

Morning intruded on the sleeping pair, complete with bright light and songbirds.

"I'm glad someone is awake," remarked Trey, shuffling under the blankets.

Beth was moaning, or talking in her sleep maybe. Either way, she was alive, and Trey breathed a sigh of relief. A few gentle shakes and "Hey, are you okay?" got her eyes open and exclaiming about a headache and body aches.

"What happened last night?" she asked. "I remember coming down the stairs, and that's it," she said.

"Well, you came down the first stair but missed the second entirely," he explained, "ending up right here," pointing to the hardwood floor.

"What about Tex? Did he ever come back?" she asked, noticing the locked door. "You locked him out?"

"No, it's not like that at all. He went out and didn't come back. Right before you fell down the stairs, I went outside looking for him. I called out his name and everything, but he was gone...just gone," he added, with as much emotion as he could conjure up at the moment. "So I locked the door an hour later when he didn't return. He's a drifter, so you know he probably drifted, is all."

Beth half stumbled towards the front door, holding her ribs on the right side, with none obviously pointing out. Just the act of unlocking the front door caused her to scream out in pain. The bright light glowed off new snow, blinding to the naked eye. Holding her hand to her forehead, she scanned the area surrounding the cabin.

"Let's go back inside," he said, carefully scanning the area he had heard the thump from last night.

A boot belonging to the man called Tex stuck out from behind a large fallen log, faced downward towards the ground.

He must be dead, thought Trey—*froze overnight with nothing but jeans and a T-shirt on.*

Trey glanced in her direction subtly, hoping she hadn't seen the same.

"Let's go back inside," she announced. "It's cold out here. I guess our new friend has moved on," she stated bluntly.

"Let's get you back up to bed," suggested Trey. "We have plenty of time later to get settled in."

Trey tucked her back into bed, vowing to see about getting a fire going downstairs. According to the thermometer stuck on the side window, reading 36 degrees, the inside temperature seemed just as cold, near-freezing. But his first thought was to check on Tex, hoping he was frozen solid and not having to make the choice of trying to save him or not. It was something that lawyer guy had said outside the hospital that kept resurfacing in his mind, although he hadn't brought it up to Beth. "Watch out for that guy, Tex; he's bad news and dangerous."

Stepping out onto the first porch, Trey cautiously approached the downed man. Tex's feet were in the same place and seemingly had not moved an inch. Grabbing his uncle's walking stick—always on the front porch ever since he could remember as a kid, Trey held it out in front of him, watching it shake as if he were about to poke a hibernating bear.

"Tex? Hey, Tex," he called out, not expecting a response and not getting one. "Hey, Tex?" he asked again, with the end of the stick in reach and hearing his heartbeat in his ears. *Thump! Thump!*

Trey nearly chickened out, wanting desperately to run back inside and assume the worst—or the best, if he were honest.

"Here goes nothing," he announced, poking one of Tex's legs mid-calf.

The stick slid off of its target, like it may off a solid rock or frozen block of ice.

Okay, that's a good sign, he thought—*frozen through.*

He instinctively tried it again before his brain could say to move on; nothing more to see here. This time the stick pushed into the calf with ease, not tearing skin but what one might expect pushing into a plump abdomen with two fingers.

"What the..." said Trey out loud, struggling to understand what happened.

His breathing intensified, and when Tex grabbed the stick quick as lightning, Trey let out a scream, dropping his pistol to the ground and stumbling backward. In an instant, Tex was on him, pinning his arms to the ground with his knees like young boys may do, pretending to spit in another's face. But this was no joke or some bully trying to scare him. This was life and death, and Trey knew it. He struggled to free his arms, screaming to be let go.

"It's cold out here, huh?" asked Tex. "But you wouldn't know about that because you slept inside last night, right?"

"What do you want?" asked Trey hoping for an easy solution.

"Well, it's funny. You have three things I want. This here's one of them," he said, reaching for the pistol in the snow. "That was easy. Now it's just the two."

"What's that?" asked Trey, feeling both angry and scared.

"I want the house and the girl, of course. The problem is, I can't just let you go now."

"Why not?"

"You'll just hobble back into town, and the Sheriff will be out here before sunset, aiming to wreck our plans. No, that won't do. Not one bit," he added, pointing the pistol in Trey's face.

"No! No! Please, you don't have to do this," Trey begged. "Besides, anyone hearing a gunshot up here will come looking around, that's for sure."

"You have a point," Tex conceded casually, as if they were discussing dinner options. "Maybe something more subtle," he offered, pulling a Bowie knife from his hip inside his jeans, which Trey had not seen before.

"No. Listen, I'm sorry," stated Trey. "About last night, we thought you took off, and I locked the door so bears wouldn't wander in."

"Bears can be a nuisance, that's for sure," replied Tex, straight-faced. "But they are hibernating now, and my gut says you already knew that, Trey."

"Okay, okay," replied Trey, sighing loudly and not as scared as he would be, knowing Tex's past. "I locked you out of my uncle's house and planned on keeping the food. There now, it's out in the open, and you're just fine. Go ahead and take 1/3 of the food and go," he added, as if it had already been decided. "Go on now; we don't have all day."

Tex shook his head back and forth with a smile he couldn't hide.

"I have had conversations over the years with a lot of men like you, Trey—some weaker but most stronger than you. In all that time, only a few ever dared to speak to me carelessly like you are now, with the first being my father. It cost him his tongue and, days later, his very life, but that's a story for another time. Upstairs," he commanded, waving the pistol towards Trey and raising from his chest with an I'm-done attitude.

Tex followed him closely up the stairs.

"No, not that room," he said, as Trey reached for Beth's door handle. "The other one at the end of the hall," he motioned with the pistol.

Trey disappeared inside with the distinct sound of a locking door to follow.

"You have no idea," whispered Tex.

Ten minutes later, the banging started. Tex knew his way around construction sites, having been kicked off more than a dozen crews for fighting or threatening fellow workers. Still, the life kept him in food and various types of shelter over the years. It was the only work he knew how to do that didn't ask any questions about his past and, even better, skipped the background checks altogether. The money was good with most jobs while they lasted, and coupled with cash he swiped from his victims over the years, he gave much of it to his twin sister, Mary. His other sisters seemed to be doing fine from what he could tell at a distance, but she had always struggled, flip-flopping between shelters and rehab clinics, never once leaving the state. Still, he dropped off money whenever he could, not daring to show his face but leaving anonymous envelopes where she was sure to find them. Sometimes it was $30, and once over $1,000, but usually somewhere between $200 and $300 at a time. Since he was 15, he'd been on the run and wasn't interested in answering any questions from his family or anyone else.

Scrounging around in and outside his new house, Tex was certain Trey was too scared to come out of the room. Two by fours he found in the basement, layered with half-inch thick plywood sheets and scraps of rebar found in the back of the carport, and a hodge-podge of nails and screws would secure his prey and give Tex time to think. This wasn't his first rodeo locking an opponent, as he called them, inside a house, but it had always ended in a fiery mess before. This time, that wasn't a possibility, drawing too much attention in this tight-knit community. *Besides*, he thought, *I need somewhere to wait out the winter.*

"Wouldn't you know it!" he said aloud. "After all these years, I'm finally a homeowner!"

* * * * * * *

CHAPTER THIRTY-SIX SAFEWAY GROCERY STORE ESTES PARK, COLORADO

The Sheriff checked in with the only two printers in town. The hope was to get copies of the kid's sketch out around town, like Old West "Wanted—Dead or Alive" posters. He would have to talk with the Mayor about offering a reward for credible information or a sighting, but for now, he wanted to stay as far away as possible.

The first printer had the doors locked and a sign out front, reading "Sorry folks—the machines are all broken." He explained the situation to the second store owner, who told the same story. "Ever since the power went out," he said.

"I need to get these out, and I can't have the kid draw ten more of these things," he told the store owner.

"Check out the photography store down the street; they may have something," the man suggested.

"Yeah, okay, I'll try them. Thanks for the suggestion."

"Bingo," the Sheriff told his deputy, walking out of the store carrying a small box. "Every fancy camera in the place got zapped. But not this one," he added, holding up an old-fashioned-looking but actually brand-new Polaroid camera. "I've got twenty pictures in here," he told his deputy. "They're not real big but we'll put them out around town. Like that show with the guy John—what's his name? 'America's Most Wanted,' I think.

"The one with John Favreau, maybe," replied his deputy.

"Sounds right—something like that. If this Tex guy is still in town or tries to stay the winter, somebody is going to see him. I've got twenty shots in here."

"How is that thing working and nothing else?" asked the deputy.

"I don't know. Maybe no electric parts, or maybe we just got lucky. Either way, his ugly mug will be everywhere I can think of."

"And what if we do catch him—what then?" asked the deputy. "You can't just transfer him down to Supermax in Colorado Springs, not now."

That thought alone made the Sheriff shudder. He had been given a rare tour of the Supermax prison just a few years back.

"We've got the worst of the worst," the warden told him. "There's no such thing as probation or rehabilitation here. No sir, just a bunch of really bad men all looking for an opportunity to add to their list of heinous crimes that brought them here in the first place."

"I sure hope they have a good backup generator there," said the Sheriff. "I would hate to have all those degenerates walking out of their cells, only to end up somewhere like here. It sounds like the Tex guy would fit right in with them, though."

* * * *

The Sheriff showed the picture around, leaving one photograph at the hospital, another at the coffee shop, a third at the Stanley Hotel, and last of the day, the Safeway grocery store.

"I saw that man yesterday, or maybe it was a few days back; I'm not sure," said the cashier.

"What was he doing?"

"I don't know. He came up with a full cart of food and talked to the manager before just walking out the front door. I don't even think he got checked out... Hey, Stan," she called out, as the store manager tried ducking into his office. "Stan, hey Stan. These officers have some questions about that guy from the other day."

"I don't remember anything about that," he said, slowly walking towards them.

"Is this the man?" asked the Sheriff, showing him the original drawing he kept with him.

"Hard to tell," said Stan. "We get a lot of customers here, especially now, as you can imagine. We're almost cleaned out, though, unless we get another shipment in soon."

"Did he come in here or not?" asked the Sheriff, sensing the fear in the manager's voice.

"Yes, maybe. I mean, it's complicated," he replied, fumbling. "Can we talk in my office, just the three of us?"

"Okay, but it better be good. I've had enough of this today," added the Sheriff.

"How did he pay for the groceries?" asked the Sheriff, getting right to the point.

"A check, sir. He paid with a check."

"A check, you say. Hmm... It says right on the front door that you accept no out-of-town checks. So, you either made an exception or something else."

"Is it a crime to take a check now?" asked Stan, starting to sweat through his white polyester shirt. Dark rings staining under the arms worked their way south down each sleeve.

"No, but it is a crime to lie to a Sheriff during an investigation, especially when you're a person of interest."

"Me a person of what?"

"Interest, seeing as you may be the last person to see our suspect, and you appear to be covering for him. Isn't that right, deputy?"

"Oh, definitely. Stan is our guy," playing the bad cop, or was it the good? He wasn't always sure.

"Okay. Okay now. Wait just a minute," said a squeaky Stan. "I want to help."

"I need to see that check," said Sheriff Bradley.

"It's been deposited, sir. Sorry, I can't help you."

"The banks haven't been open since the power went out, so unless you deposited it overseas or maybe Canada, then you're lying to me. Cuff him," he told his deputy.

"No! Wait! Please just wait a minute," clambered Stan. He took in deep gulping breaths, falling back into his desk chair, fumbling in his drawer, and grasping an old wrinkled brown paper bag he had clearly used multiple times before. Shoving his thin face deep inside, Stan sucked and exhaled rapidly. *Woosh, crinkle, woosh, crinkle...*

At this point in the investigation, a quick reach into a drawer after an apprehension demand would have the Sheriff drawing his Glock in seconds. But Stan was harmless—a liar scared out of his mind maybe, but harmless nonetheless.

"The man threatened me with my life," said Stan, once he controlled his breathing. "He gave me this check," he said, handing it over.

"Do you know who this check belongs to?" asked the Sheriff.

Stan stared down at the floor, not responding.

"Do you know who this check belongs to?" asked the Sheriff again, this time grabbing Stan by the collar and shaking him.

"No! Yes...I mean maybe, but I didn't know what to do. I was so scared."

"And you didn't think about coming to me—two days ago, according to the date on this check?"

"I should have, I know. I'm sorry."

Stan told the Sheriff and his deputy everything he could remember about the man and what he said, citing he was in the store shopping alone.

* * * *

"Okay, he could be anywhere," the Sheriff commented when they left the store. "But unless he stole a car, he's hunkered up somewhere on this mountain and at least has some provisions. Is it enough to last the winter? I'm sure not, but there are a lot of summer homes up here stocked with food, and it's impossible to search them all."

"So, we wait until he kills again?" asked the deputy.

"No, but we also don't harass every good citizen in town while we're looking for this guy."

"Should we talk to the Mayor about it, boss?"

"No! And besides, I have an idea."

* * * * * * *

Chapter Thirty-seven Holman Residence Estes Park, Colorado

Shanan and I were settling in at the Holman compound, and I, for one, was concerned about overstaying our welcome. Having spoken with Scott about it, we agreed we should look for alternative housing sooner than later. We talked with our other, and I'm quite sure better, halves and all were on the same page. On the one hand, it would be easy for us to stay the winter and get moving again in spring, but it would also be presumptuous and just plain wrong to stay in another couple's home for months on end. We called an informal meeting with Rick and Judy to look at alternatives.

"I can buy us a house or two if we need it," said Scott, not in a snobby rich-kid way but in a matter-of-fact, let's-get-this-done kind of way.

"That's going to be a stretch," replied Grady from the kitchen. "Banks are closed, no doubt, and home sales are no more."

"How many homes up here are summer-only?" Scott asked Rick.

"Maybe half, I guess."

"Do you know of any ones specifically?"

"Yeah. A few we keep an eye on. Judy here checks on maybe ten or so every couple of weeks—during the winter, that is."

"Are you expecting the owners back anytime soon?" I asked.

"No, not until mid-May usually. And even then, who knows if they will ever be back," replied Judy.

Scott's mind was churning over the possibilities.

"Maybe we could rent one or two if you think they would be okay with it? I'm good for it, maybe not right now with the banks closed, but once everything gets straight again. I'll pay double the going rate around here."

"I know you're good for it," replied Rick, smiling. "You probably don't know this, Scott, but I did some work for your father and grandfather years ago—legal work, that is."

"No, I didn't know that, sir," replied Scott.

Well, the specifics aren't important, but I do know you have the means to afford it, so that's not my concern. We need to give this a little time, though, maybe a few days or weeks, to see if some do make it back up here before moving somewhere."

"That's fair," replied Scott, with the rest of us agreeing.

"I've got a couple of ideas not far from here, assuming they don't," replied Rick. "And when Grady's family makes it up here, they will need one as well."

"Are you trying to get rid of me already?" joked Grady.

"Well, you're eating up all my food! Nah, I'm just joking, Alex," said Rick, maybe noticing my *this-is-awkward* look. "Grady here is the reason we stockpiled in the first place; without him hounding us to do it, we would have been sheer out of luck already. And don't worry, there's plenty for all of us... Feel better now, Alex?"

"Yes, sir. Yes, I do."

"All right, Rick," said Mrs. Holman. "That's enough of the joking around; let's get dinner ready."

We all pitched in to help, with Shanan and me signing up for a "New World Appetizer"—canned Spam and deviled eggs. It was a hit, or maybe everyone was just polite. I had three, plus two servings of Mrs. Holman's near-famous ham and broccoli pie, swimming in cheddar cheese. A classic board game of Clue rounded out the night, with all looking forward to an early bedtime.

"What do you guys think happened to Trey and Beth?" asked Jo.

"I don't know," I replied, giving Shanan an awkward look apparently.

"What?" she asked.

"Nothing, it's just odd talking about them. Maybe they're still in town, or halfway back to California by now. It doesn't matter, I guess, but I do hope they make it home."

"Yes. Me too," said Shanan.

Grady was getting nervous about his family making it up here. They had always had a plan, but the days were ticking by with no sign of them. It wouldn't be long before the mountain roads were impassable, even on foot. His house in Denver was 64 miles from Estes Park and approximately a 24-hour walk that could reasonably be done in 3-4 days if all went well. The question was, did it all go well and had they even started yet?

He wished he and his wife had taken that ham radio class offered at the local community college. They were both on board but somehow never found the time to sign up. Now the choice was to wait and see, or decide if he would head there. While they had discussed meeting up here at the Holmans' place, they hadn't discussed a specific route if something happened and they were separated. By car, there were multiple ways to get here, and even more by foot. One side street, bathroom break, or cut across a parking lot and he could miss them entirely—and that's if they were even taking the same route, in the first place. The odds were bad either way, and he vowed to give them a few more days before heading down the mountain to search for them. He could ask Rick to go with him, and he would, but it wouldn't be fair to Mrs. Holman. No, trading one family for another wouldn't do at all.

* * * * * * *

CHAPTER THIRTY-EIGHT THE MAYOR'S OFFICE ESTES PARK, COLORADO

The town Mayor heard about the road killings as soon as his informant, a low-level deputy, returned from the scene. He was angry he had to find out this way.

"I run things around here!" he screamed at the deputy and the other men, local thugs before the day and now somehow on the official Town payroll.

He lost two men at the "Holman Compound," as he now called it, with another one coming away with non-life-threatening injuries. When asked about what happened at the hospital, the Mayor would only say this man brought a knife to a gunfight, but it won't happen again.

If he were honest, he felt Mr. Holman put up a good fight, and he didn't really care about the outcome. But now he had a story and, even better, a reason to bring him in. He also knew about the signature book left on the Holman's front gate and even attempted to intercept it, but his timing was off by mere minutes.

"No worries," he would tell his men. "A dead man, or at least one locked up, can't run for Mayor anyway."

A few of the Mayor's crew thought he would be angry when they first told him. Who wants to find out the town they lead all signed a document trying to force them out? He didn't care either way, not liking people in general as far back as he could remember. In fact, it was only the power and steady paycheck that made him run for office in the first place. *Of course, running unopposed to fill a dead man's seat is not all that hard*, he always thought. No matter, he had a job to do and a lot to lose if Rick Holman had his way.

"Go and find me the Sheriff," he barked at his informant.

"You're not going to tell him what I said, are you?" he questioned, looking sick.

"It's out now and I won't let him fire you. So go on, get him and bring him here."

* * * *

The informant and the least competent deputy, for good reason, found the Sheriff at the jailhouse. The jail had seen its share of renters over the years, most only a night after a drunken brawl or DUI charge. The few staying longer were eventually transferred to larger towns, awaiting a judge's decision on their future role in life. *Now thankfully*, thought Sheriff Bradley, *it sits empty, minus the deputies pretending to do paperwork, or maybe getting away from the family for a short bit.* Still, they were all good men—well most, that is.

"Sheriff," said the deputy, out of breath after running full out from the Mayor's office. "It's the Mayor, sir. He wants to see you in his office."

"So..." replied the Sheriff.

"So he said right now!"

"Did he now, and you came straight from his office to tell me?"

"Yes, sir," the deputy said. "I ran the whole... Wait a minute... I didn't say I was at his office."

"Yes, you just did. Now what were you doing there?"

"Just passing by, and he saw me out the window."

"Tell him I'll be by later," replied the Sheriff, not concerned with making his counterpart wait.

"But sir, he's really mad, and I don't want to get in trouble with him!"

"You didn't tell him about what we found out on the road, did you?"

"I uh...I didn't mean to... He just got it out of me, is all."

"That's what I thought," replied Sheriff Bradley, shaking his head side to side.

"I'll go tell him then, and I'll be right back."

"Yes, go. But don't come back."

"So I have the day off?" the former deputy asked nervously.

"Yep, and the next, and the one after that."

"You letting him go, boss?" asked his lead deputy.

"Are you saying we should keep him—a snitch?"

"No, just asking, is all."

* * * *

Sheriff Bradley took his time about heading downtown to the Mayor's office.

"I heard you were looking for me," he said confidently, walking in the front door and seeing his former deputy sitting in the far corner of the office.

"You heard right, and I expected you here two hours ago."

"I'm busy," said the Sheriff matter of factly. "Now, what can I do for you?"

"You can start by telling me about that mess out on the highway and why I see these pop up all over town," he added, holding up one of the Polaroid pictures in his hand.

"All right. I can do that, and you can tell me what you and your men were doing out at the Holman Ranch recently. You start."

"You heard about that," the Mayor said with a laugh. "Well, I was just there checking up on them when they started shooting at us for no good reason."

"Did they shoot at you from the house all the way to the front gate that's always locked?"

"Funny you should mention that; it was wide open when I got there."

"You mean *we*, like you and your ragtag crew here," the Sheriff said, pointing to a few troublemakers he had locked up in his jail numerous nights over the years for fighting, disorderly conduct, and minor vandalism.

"Sure, I have a right to defend myself, and it's a good thing I brought some backup the way they were shooting and all."

"You say they were shooting from inside the house out towards you?"

"That's what I said."

"I went inside; we both did," he said, gesturing to his deputy, the one still employed. "Can you guess what we found?"

"There is no way he let you inside his house without a warrant," argued the Mayor.

"But he did—maybe because he had nothing to hide. Two things we learned. One, there were sixty-three bullet holes inside the house. Some in the walls, the kitchen cabinets, not to mention the windows shattered, with glass on the inside. And two, Mr. Holman wasn't even home when you stopped by to 'check on them,' as you say."

"He was there! I saw him! We all did, right guys?" he said, sounding defensive for the first time today—*maybe ever*, thought the Sheriff.

"Now it's my turn," said the Mayor, flipping the table as fast as he could. "Why didn't you tell me about three bodies on the highway and a manhunt for a fugitive called Tex?"

"It's not an issue that concerns you; it's the official business of the Sheriff's office."

"Every issue in my town concerns me," spat the Mayor, growing red in the face. "And your office is an extension of mine, not the other way around. With that, I want you to arrest Rick Holman, Attorney at Law," with the title dragged out like a boxing announcer— "Attorney at Lawwwww."

"You mean Mr. Holman? Should I arrest him for defending his property? Wait, he wasn't even there. Maybe we arrest him for having a big house? Maybe his dogs barked too loud when you were shooting at his wife!" shouted Sheriff Bradley, putting his finger in the

Mayor's face, having an easy six inches in height and more than 50 pounds on the slight of a man if things went sideways. "For the record, my office is not an extension of yours, maybe down in Denver, but not here."

The Mayor's henchmen stood, instinctively reaching for their weapons.

"Hold on now, boys," said the Mayor. "We're still just talking here. Isn't that right, Sheriff?"

"No. That's where you're wrong. Let's go," he told his top deputy.

"If you don't arrest him, then I will!" the Mayor called out as they left the building.

"That didn't go well," said his deputy.

"Oh, I don't know," replied Sheriff Bradley. "It's about what I expected from that snake. We do need to warn them, though—the Holmans, that is."

* * * *

A quick trip to the Holman property offered the second meeting at the front gate in so many days.

"He's coming for me?" asked Rick. "He's coming for me?" he repeated.

"Only because I'm not," replied Sheriff Bradley. "I've got something for you, sir," he continued. "Give me a second," reaching inside his truck.

"A radio," said Rick. "Where's the other one?"

"I've got it. If the Mayor comes back here, you get hold of me."

"Will you break rank?" asked Rick.

"In a New York Second, sir."

"I appreciate that. We both do," said Rick, shaking both men's hands.

"I'm glad we're on the same side, gentlemen," added Judy.

"We are. But a fight is coming...I can feel it," said the Sheriff.

"Here?" she asked.

"I'm not sure about that, but I mean the Mayor and me. It seems he's been asking around the local watering holes for anyone willing to work Town Security. I've heard the pay isn't bad, and I'll bet you dollars to donuts it's coming out of the Town's general fund. I may run the only jail in town, but I have only so many deputies and a limited supply of weapons and ammunition. There is apparently zero budget for my department now, and I don't expect that to change anytime soon."

"What are you saying, exactly?" asked Judy.

"I'm saying, ma'am, that the future of our great town may come down to who has the most weapons. Last I checked, deputies don't work for zero pay, and the Mayor has the Town funds on lockdown. We need the citizens on our side sooner than later, and your husband is the one they want in charge. Are you ready if it happens soon, Rick?"

"An election... That's what you're referring to, right?"

"Yes, exactly."

"I'm your guy!" replied Rick.

* * * * * * *

CHAPTER THIRTY-NINE ESTES PARK, COLORADO

"**O**kay," said Sheriff Bradley. "Let's get started."

It was a bold move, either way. Stick it out under the command of a corrupt mayor who didn't like him anyway and gutted his department's funding, hoping he had a change of heart. The alternative was to arrest the Mayor on questionable charges and hold him long enough to execute an election five months before the one already on the books.

The Sheriff talked it over with his closest deputies, along with his wife, who rarely was asked about his work decisions. She had been so focused on an in vitro family for the past few years, after they had troubles conceiving children, that it was all she could think of. She would sing the praises of her fertility doctor in Denver—one of the best in the country, several girlfriends had told her. The two were expecting twins by mid-April, and that point alone weighed heavily in the decision process.

Sheriff Bradley wanted the best life possible life for his boys or girls, or maybe one of each. He and his wife had been to multiple doctor's appointments all the way down in Denver because of the higher-risk twins pregnancy but instructed their doctor not to reveal the genders and keep it a surprise.

"I don't know whether to get your kids trucks or dolls for a baby shower," said his deputy and, coincidently or not, his best friend.

"Well, then you're off the hook—unless you really want to come."

"You won't mind if I skip it?"

"If it were the other way around, we wouldn't even be having this conversation!"

* * * *

It was settled—almost, that is. The town elections would be moved up, and the Sheriff would need to make the first move.

Today was a Thursday, and one of the few things still ringing true in this crazy next-world was that people tried to save the weekends for family. Sheriff Bradley would act on Monday, and so far, his wife and best-friend deputy were all who knew.

* * * *

Rick and Grady spent the first part of the afternoon securing the front gate to Holman Ranch.

"We can't have people driving in any time they want," said Rick.

They stopped for a soda around 2 p.m., according to Rick's pocket watch his father had given him as a young boy. The last thing his dad ever did was give him the watch, saying, "Son, this watch was given to me by my father. Don't ever sell it." Minutes later, he passed in his hospital bed.

Cola was Rick's drink of choice, and he didn't even care what brand. He had shown Grady the supply as a joke, mostly, when he started preparing. Eight pallets stacked ten cases high of random brands, but all the cola was delivered to the Ranch on a random Tuesday, nearly six months ago.

"This must have cost a fortune!" said Grady, seeing it neatly stacked in the large house's basement.

"You told me to be prepared," joked Rick, who never in his life did anything small.

"Hits the spot," said Grady, only looking up when a flash caught his eye.

"A truck's coming up the valley," he said, subtly reaching for his rifle.

"I haven't seen too many of those lately," replied Rick. "It looks like he's going slow, so maybe ranchers, but I don't recognize it. They're headed this way, looks like, so we'll at least see who it is that's passing."

"Let me get my binoculars," said Grady, reaching into a small fanny pack his wife always teased him about. "I've had this thing since the mid '80s," he would tell her, "and it still looks brand new."

"Exactly!" she would tell him. "The mid-1980s, and you will never have to worry about anyone stealing it."

Grady got a visual track on the truck winding down the canyon road, occasionally losing sight with dips and turns.

"I can't see the driver clearly, but it looks like three up front in the cab and four or five riding in the bed," announced Grady.

"Can you see any weapons?" asked Rick, kicking himself for not bringing his own pair.

"Nope, but the guys in the back are wearing some type of masks, looks like. Maybe just because of the wind or maybe something else. Keep your rifle at the ready but low," said Grady to his old friend. "I'm not too sure this is just some passing farmer heading home."

The truck stopped 30 yards down the road but didn't park. Even with mild weather for the season, the 36 degrees showed steam from the exhaust—or was it just bad O-rings? Rick couldn't be sure. Either way, the truck idled and didn't move.

"What's the plan?" asked Grady.

"I don't know," replied Rick, feeling out of place as the man who always had a plan and was usually three steps ahead of everyone else around him. "If it's bad, we'll never make it back to the house at a run, and if we stay to fight, there's no protection. We're sitting ducks."

Nothing happened for two minutes, which felt like a hundred.

"Hold on," said Rick, remembering the radio Sheriff Bradley gave him. It was inside a small daypack he used for minor fence repairs around the ranch.

Turning it on, the Chanel said 11. "I hope it's set to the right one. Let's see if he knows anything about these guys."

"Sheriff! Sheriff Bradley, it's Rick Holman," he said.

"Over—you have to add 'Over' at the end, so he knows you're done talking," said Grady.

"I know that—everybody does," said Rick. "Do you hear anything, Grady?" He was hoping it would be different from what he was hearing.

"Only static..."

"Sheriff, this is Rick. Do you copy? Over."

"This is Deputy Jenkins. Sheriff Bradley is indisposed at the moment. What can I do for..."

He cut off, overcome by more static and a high-pitched sound neither man could make out.

"Hello, Deputy Jenkins, can you hear me? Over."

A series of jumbled words followed for the next two minutes, but they might as well have been in another language. He explained the situation in case they heard on their end but never could get confirmation.

"Well, so much for that," said Rick, turning off the radio entirely but securing it to his pants belt once the truck began to move again.

"Here they come," said Grady, with a glance back towards the house, not seeing anyone outside. "Nice and easy boys," he said aloud. "Just keep moving down the road."

The next time it stopped, it took no binoculars to see the Mayor driving and his crew raising rifles over the cab of the truck, counting five in all.

"Keep your rifle down," whispered Grady. "We can't win a shootout here."

The Mayor exited the driver's side cab slowly, like an old man may do getting out of a truck for the last time in this life.

"Rick Holman, Attorney at Law. I hereby place you under arrest. Put your weapon down real slow like, so my boys here don't make Swiss cheese out of you. You too, fella," he said, pointing at Grady.

Both men did as asked, not having much choice in the matter.

"That's good...that's real good," said the Mayor, as two men came out of the cab, rifles at the ready.

"Now you, what's your name?"

"Grady. I'm Grady."

"Is that a first name or the last one?"

"Does it matter?"

"No, I suppose not," he replied, spitting a large mouthful of chaw juice halfway across the highway, as if he were practicing for an upcoming local watermelon-seed spitting contest. "Anyway, you're free to go, for now. I don't have any charges on you just yet, but don't go far. Nothing gets my goat more than having to chase a man down," he concluded, looking at Rick.

"Now, Mr. Holman, slowly put your hands behind your back and turn around."

"What are the charges, and what gives you the authority to arrest me?"

"This here is a concerned citizen's arrest. As to the charges, well, let's see... How about firing a weapon at a public official, like happened here a couple of days back?"

Rick wasn't about to tell the Mayor he wasn't even home then, not wanting him to try and pin something on Judy or the kids.

"Is that it?!" he asked defiantly.

"It's more than I need, quite frankly, but I'm sure I can come up with a few more things, like trying to undermine an election's outcome by unduly influencing would-be voters."

"That's a stretch, for sure."

"Is it? What do you think, boys?" he asked. They all nodded their heads, some up and down and others back and forth.

"Figures," said the Mayor. "Got some real idiots working for me, but they shoot straight as long as they're sober and they know where their next meal is coming from. Can't ask for much more than that nowadays."

"Get hold of the Sheriff, even if you have to go into town," whispered Rick to Grady. "And tell Judy I'll be all right."

He was sure he was solid with the Sheriff but wondered where they were headed and if he knew. Rick complied, even now with things turned upside-down. There still had to be justice, and he was confident he would have his say in court, or wherever it was held now.

The short drive back to town had the Mayor indecisive. Should he parade his captive through the center of town for all to see or take him straight to the jailhouse for a quick lockup? He settled on the latter, with an option to do it later if he saw fit.

* * * *

"Just what in the world do you think you're doing?" asked Sheriff Bradley, as they pulled into the station's parking lot.

"I told you if you didn't pick him up, then I would. I've already got a slew of charges on him," the Mayor continued. "Now I'm adding resisting arrest."

"You want me to believe Mr. Holman, one of the top attorneys in the country, resisted arrest?"

"Yes, Sheriff. Happened just like I said. Isn't that right, boys?"

Half nodded up and down, and the others side to side.

"Do you see what I'm working with here? I got three idiots and the rest imbeciles. It's a wonder I can get anything done for this town with this kind of incompetence."

Just this morning, Mayor Haskins thought but would never say out loud to anyone how a group of men—known for fighting and who-knows-what, now all carrying guns— would let him or anyone else talk to them the way he does. *Any one of these men single-handedly could hurt me badly*, he thought, *but they just take it as long as the beer money is flowing*. He wouldn't hire anyone with a family but didn't care if they had a girlfriend.

He only had two rules for them to follow. "No day drinking and do what I tell you."

He made a point to pay them every two days, not much, but enough to drink at night and get something to eat each day.

He overheard a few talking about their money running out hours before the next paycheck, and he wouldn't want it any other way. *Just enough to come crawling back each day and do what I tell them.*

Sure, the Town Fund would run out eventually—but not today, tomorrow, or even next month, and cutting the other departments' budgets in half, or altogether, could buy him a year or more of protection.

"So that's it? You just want me to lock up this man?" asked the Sheriff.

"Yes, that's about the gist of it—at least until I can figure out what to do about him. We still have a few judges around, probably not a one worth a crap but we'll see if any have the stomach for the kinds of rulings a new world like this is going to need. I'll check back tomorrow. And Sheriff, don't you dare lose this man," he added. "Let's go, boys," the Mayor said, exiting the jailhouse.

* * * *

"They cuffed you and everything!" said Sheriff Bradley. "Sorry about that," he added, using his master key and unlocking them.

"Yeah, I wasn't expecting them to have cuffs," replied Rick.

"Oh, I'm pretty sure I know where they got them," replied the Sheriff, holding up the key. "I can't trust my boss, and even a few of my deputies. I'm sorry to say..."

"...that you have been eliminated from the race," joked Rick, using a classic line from the Amazing Race he and Judy had applied to participate in just last spring.

"Not exactly," smiled the Sheriff, getting the reference, "but you will have to stay here for a few days. I was planning on getting this situation turned around on Monday. I didn't count on him actually arresting you. Must have caught you off guard."

"Yeah. Grady and I were working on the front gate when they pulled up. No use in trying to get in a fight or run with that many guys all armed."

"We are agreed on that point," replied the Sheriff. "His new crew may not be the smartest bunch, but it doesn't take much in that department to fire a gun, and from what I can tell, he's paying all of them for protection."

"So, what's next?" asked Rick, resigned to stay for a few days.

"Well, seeing as you still have the radio on you—can't believe they didn't see it on your belt and confiscate it," he laughed. "Anyway, since you do, I'll need to let your wife know what's going on. You can't have her worrying about you or trying some sort of revenge plan against the Mayor and maybe getting hurt, or worse."

"We'll keep you fed, and my trusted deputies (who are supposed to be paid next Friday)" he added in a lower voice, "will switch off, so someone is always here with you. Who knows if that crooked Mayor will try something stupid in the meantime. One thing is certain," he said, lowering his voice so his two deputies in front wouldn't hear, "we've got until next Friday to turn this around. I've got a few good guys working for me, but I'll lose them for sure if they aren't paid on time. Everyone has to feed their families."

"I get that and wouldn't even mind picking up salaries for all of you for the next few rounds, but that just prolongs the inevitable, and it's the in-between that could go bad. So, what's next?"

"Deputies, can you make a quick Town sweep?" he asked, not wanting anyone else to hear the next part.

"Sure thing, boss," they said. "Be back in about an hour... Are you going to be all right here?" one added.

"Yep, all good."

* * * *

"Okay," Sheriff Bradley said, once they left. "This whole thing happens fast and timed like a Swiss watch. First, we need an opponent to run against you—someone kind of known around here but not well enough to divide the citizens."

"Who did you have in mind?" asked Rick, thinking maybe a local banker, business owner, or a longtime resident who most knew.

"I'm thinking the kid," said Sheriff Bradley.

"What kid?"

"Your client—the Alex kid."

"Alex? Are you serious? He would never do it!"

"He's perfect. Not super well-known, but most in town now know his name. He's articulate from what I can tell and not a real threat to win," added the Sheriff.

"Who would be a threat to win?" asked Rick.

"Only me. And even then, I don't want the position, and you'd probably still beat me anyway."

"I still don't think he would do it," said Rick. "He's only sticking around until spring, maybe, before heading back to Texas."

"That doesn't matter. And for the record, that's going to be a suicide trek, if you ask me. We just need someone to give our citizens a choice, is all. Once this is behind us, we (you and I) can make this town thrive again. I can feel it. What do you say?"

"Do I have a choice?"

"Of course—no, I'm just kidding; this is as good as it gets. The only other way out is defending yourself in front of the Mayor, and who knows if he would try to pay off a judge, maybe one from out of town, to rule on the case. The few up here are solid, but that doesn't mean he has to use one of them. Plus, you know what they say about a lawyer who represents himself at trial."

"Yeah, I've heard that one a few times," agreed Rick. "I am good, though..."

"So I've heard. I'll leave Deputy Jenkins here, and I'll shoot over to your place. He's a little off today on account of us having to clear the crime scene this morning out on the highway. The families haven't been notified yet. We've got the bodies in the county morgue and towed the vehicles back to town for a look-over. Your fingerprints aren't going to show up on the bodies or the vehicles, right?"

Rick rubbed his recently stubbled chin, the first one he'd had since right before law school.

"Where are they?" asked the Sheriff, sighing. "And I'm guessing your friend too? Man, I want to find this Tex guy sooner than later."

Rick told the Sheriff what he remembered, although it went against everything he stood for as a practicing attorney. Don't say anything to law enforcement and make them build a case. But it was Grady—his friend he trusted more than anyone in this world, after his wife—who was 100% sure this thing was long-term, and life would never play by the same rules again.

* * * *

Judy was the first up—behind Scout and Daizy, of course. The gate still wasn't fixed, but Sheriff Bradley stopped just outside of it. He exited the truck, hands out to the sides. Not up, like in every bank robbery movie he had ever seen, but palms forward, like one may do at church.

She recognized him straightaway and waved her arm for him to approach the house. We all watched through binoculars—and me through my (or more accurately, Grady's) rifle scope from behind the window, so as not to look like a gun was trained on him. I tried to give it back to Grady earlier but he told me to keep it for now.

Judy had the story, at least what Grady knew from the Mayor's encounter, but was both eager and nervous to hear the rest from the Sheriff.

"Judy, he's all right," was the first thing he said as she, Grady, Scott and I stepped out the front door.

"He's in my jailhouse, and we're taking good care of him."

"Well, that's a relief," replied Judy. "Why didn't you bring him home then?"

"Ma'am...it's complicated, is all," he started and went on to tell her what happened and the plan to fix it.

"That's where you come in, Alex," the Sheriff added.

"Me?" I asked. "Is this about the fight with Trey at the hotel? I thought that was a wash now with everything that's happened."

"No, not that. We need you to run against Rick Holman for Mayor of Estes Park."

"What?" asked Shanan, opening the front door but keeping the dogs inside.

"I couldn't run against my attorney," I told him. "The man whose house I'm staying in and whose food I'm eating? No way! Count me out," I said, shaking my head back and forth.

"You have to, Alex. It's the only way. Let me explain."

* * * *

Ten minutes later, it was Judy who spoke first for our side.

"It makes sense, Alex. This town needs this...Rick and I need this town. Will you do it?"

"Yes, ma'am," I said, "but I've been told I'm pretty charming. I'll try to tame it down a bit, but only for the election," I added, getting a shoulder punch from Shanan.

A wave of doubt hit me, as Judy had no expression and I thought I had said something wrong—like a joke at a funeral. Then, finally, she smiled.

"My Rick is all charm! Bring your best game, college boy!"

We all smiled—even Shanan.

"That's the spirit, everyone," said the Sheriff. "Now, between us, let's go over the timeline. I need a written statement, signed and witnessed by a notary—there are still some in town. I'll need it in my office by Monday morning.

"Also, Judy, write up exactly what happened here with the Mayor and his men. They shot first after trespassing on your property. Is that right?"

"Yes, sir, that's how it happened."

"That's enough for me and enough to arrest him initially—after that, we'll see. One of the Judges here is a good friend of mine and she has no tolerance for criminal behavior, no matter who's doing it. I'm hoping to get a trial delayed at least a week so we can move up the election. Worst case, he gets out early and puts his hat back in the ring against you, Alex, and Rick. The Mayor won't get two votes this time around, since the whole town knows what he's done.

"Last thing...and this stays here. Mayor Haskins not only cut my budget and many other Town departments, but he also cut the Judges' salaries by 75%!" This one got the Sheriff laughing so hard, he could hardly get it out and required a deep breath when he finally did.

"Talk about screwing over the wrong department!" added Scott.

"Exactly," replied the Sheriff, wiping the tears of laughter from his eyes with a red checkered bandana. "Sorry folks," he announced, "but I needed that."

"No worries, Sheriff. You're a good man, and it's been one heck of a week so far," replied Judy, hugging him. "Now, go check on my husband and then get home to your sweet wife and little ones hot on the way. I'll have your letter Monday morning, if not sooner, and tell Rick that Grady and I will be by tomorrow morning for a visit."

"Sure thing, ma'am. Stop by around ten tomorrow. I'll be there too. Thanks, everyone—I'll show my way out."

* * * *

The night was sad but hopeful.

Judy had just gotten Rick back, only to lose him again. Still, it was her calming the rest of us. Who would have ever imagined my attorney would be the one behind bars?

I slept well. We all did, considering the week ahead of us.

Shanan, Scott, Jo, and I didn't have anywhere to go or be—for now anyway—so I felt good that I could at least help the election process a bit. I vowed, with Shanan's help, to polish up on Town politics, so I didn't appear like a shill to the voters.

"I want to be someone who they would say, 'He could be a great Mayor in ten years or so, if Mayor Holman ever retires,'" I told Shanan.

She laughed, asking, "Why would anyone retire now? There's nothing to do—no Internet to surf, no binge-watching cable TV, no traveling across the world, and most of the new books were available mostly as e-books. No, I can't imagine anyone retiring, not anymore," she concluded.

"I miss my mom and dad," she continued, seemingly out of the blue since we hadn't talked much about family recently.

It's strange. I thought family was at the forefront of most people's minds at all times—well, at least for me. Yet I had barely mentioned my mother, father, or brother the past few days. I wondered many times a day if they were doing okay, had enough to eat, or were defending their homestead with guns, as Mrs. Holman had done. Was it just another day, minus power, in Dallas, or had my mother taken a bullet in the arm, as Judy had, or worse?

I vowed at this moment to do everything I could to protect the ones I cared about and figure out a way home for Shanan, Jo, and Scott—if it cost me everything.

The timing sucked. I mean, who goes into the Rocky Mountains with a pack in mid-November anyway?

Me...that would be me! I felt myself raising my hand to answer my own question.

It didn't matter now anyway. We were here and stuck for the foreseeable future.

Grady told me the best time to travel on foot here was between mid-spring and late summer. Of course, his family was hopefully doing it right now.

I resigned to do my best while we were here. I would participate in the election and welcome a new transition of Mr. Holman to office, hopefully, find our own house soon as a couple or shared with our friends, and be an asset to everyone around me until spring. Then we would be homeward bound—hopeful, homeless, and scared to death of the in-between.

"Lord," I said aloud in the empty upstairs bedroom, "this is new territory for all of us. Tell me what to do—I'm lost."

* * * *

Scout and Daizy barked the typical "someone-is-at-the-front-gate" scenario, getting us all downstairs and ready for a fight.

"It's a girl," said Grady, peering through his binoculars, "and she appears to be alone."

"What's a girl doing up here all alone?" asked Judy, not putting eyes on her yet. "Unless she's one of yours, Grady?"

"Oh, no. She looks sweet, but she's as white as Alex."

"Hey, now...I heard that," I said, looking through my own binos.

"I want to talk to her," said Judy, "but I'm not sure. It could be some kind of trap."

"I'll go," I said, with Shanan trying to hold me back.

"No, you can't," she said. "What if it's a setup from the Mayor?"

"He has nothing on me, and I see a young girl at the end of the driveway, probably lost and cold."

"If it is some kind of trick, then they got me," I added, leaving my rifle inside and asking Judy, Grady, and Scott to cover me.

I slowly opened the front door, keeping the dogs back, and walked up the drive.

She was 13, maybe 14, with brown hair and eyes to match, sitting on her banana-yellow bicycle, one foot ready to push the pedal.

I sized her up, as she did me.

She looked sad, not the "I had a bad day" or "I lost my favorite scarf" sad, but the kind reserved for pets' or close family and friends' funerals. Her pink down jacket seemed appropriate for the climate, in my estimation, not having ever lived here, and it hung half unzipped.

We stared at each other for what seemed like hours, but maybe seconds or a long minute at most.

"You are not the lawyer I'm looking for," she said flatly. "You're just a kid."

It caught me off guard. I had been called a lot of things lately by more than a few people, but "a kid" was not one of them. I defended myself with a juvenile response, even in my mind, blurting out, "I'm not a kid but a partly educated college boy."

"Yeah, that's what I said," she reiterated—"a kid."

I couldn't tell if I was being patronized but gave her some leeway.

"I'm guessing you were looking for Mr. Holman, the attorney," I said.

"Yes, that's right," she replied. "Somebody killed my parents, and I want justice!"

"Oh my, I'm so sorry," I said, realizing she must be talking about the couple Rick and Grady found out on the highway.

"How did you hear? I mean, how did you know that?" I asked.

"It's a small town. Everyone knows everything, and I want the man they called Tex to pay. I'm going to sue him for a million dollars before he gets life in prison, or worse."

I didn't know what to say, a near first for me, having always been knee-deep in any conversation, whether talking with one person or fifty.

"How did you know Mr. Holman lives here?"

"Like I said already, it's a small town. When someone builds a house this big up here, everybody knows who owns it."

"Not a lot of secrets up here, I guess," I mumbled.

"Oh, we have those too, but the owner of this house is not one."

"Who's taking care of you now?" I asked, seeing her face contort.

"I am. It's just me now; our other family is a long way from up here. In case you're wondering what I want, it's justice—and food for me and my dog, I guess."

"Where is he now?" I asked.

"*She!* Her name is Mama and she is back at the house, where I should be soon. Now, where's the lawyer?"

"He's not here at the moment, but let's start over real quick, if that's okay," I suggested. "My name is Alex, and yours is...?"

"Does it matter?"

"To me, yes. Yes, it does."

"Oh, all right. My name is Jenny. Not Jennifer or Jen, Jenni with an 'i,' or Jenna. Just Jenny—J-E- N- N-Y. Jenny. Got it?"

"Yes, Jenny. I think so. Mine is short for Alexander."

"Of course it is," she said, matter-of-factly.

* * * *

"I have some friends down at the house who would like to meet you."

"Nah. I may be on my own now, but I'm not stupid. I think I'll stay right here," she replied.

I heard the front door close and saw Shanan walking towards us, hands to her sides.

"Who's that?" asked Jenny.

"That's Shanan, my ex-girlfriend...I mean, the current one, I think."

"Well, which is it?" she asked. "Because I'll bet she's going to want an answer either way, and it looks like you have about one minute to get it right."

"I only need a second," I responded. "She's both my ex and current girlfriend," I blurted out, feeling on the losing end of a battle of wits.

Jenny smiled as Shanan came into view.

"Good call, college boy. She's cute and way above your pay grade."

"Wait...what?" I asked.

A slight smile came over her face, as she admitted she was kidding. "It's what I do now—play tough and joke around a bit, so I don't have to think about my mom and dad never coming home again."

She burst into tears, taking me off guard from her demeanor only moments before. I froze, not knowing what to do next. Do I hug her, let her stand there and cry, or something else?

"I have this," said Shanan, rescuing me, or probably Jenny is more accurate, holding her for several minutes as she wailed.

"You're not alone," Shanan said towards the end.

"Yes, I am," Jenny replied. "Nobody is coming for me. It's just Mama and me now, and I'm so scared."

"Shanan," I said, lightly touching her shoulder. "It's cold out here. Let's get her inside and figure out what to do."

"Grab her bicycle and bring it inside the gate," she told me.

After several more minutes, Jenny agreed to come inside for a little while with Shanan before returning to her beloved dog.

* * * *

"Good job, kid. Looks like you had that situation under control," Grady whispered to me.

"Looks can be and are quite deceiving when it comes to...well...that," I said, pointing to the road where we stood minutes before.

I filled Grady and Scott in on the little I knew while the ladies talked more with Jenny in the other room.

"This day just keeps getting crazier," said Scott. "I can only imagine a full day six months from now."

"That day will be on the road," I added—"somewhere between here and Texas."

It wasn't that I didn't like the town, the Holmans, or Grady. I just needed to get home, like Shanan, Scott, and Jo. If it were spring or summer now, we would have been on our way already.

Shanan, Jo, and Judy talked with Jenny for maybe an extra hour.

"Her dog will be okay for tonight," said Shanan. "We will get her home tomorrow. Besides, Judy wants to go to town in the morning to see her husband."

"Will you go with us?" Judy asked.

"Sure," I said. "Are we walking?"

"You may be, but the rest of us will ride in the golf cart!"

"Oh, I see," I said, smiling and feeling bad for Jenny at the same time.

It was strange that I could have so many different feelings on the same day now. Before the day, a spilled coffee first thing could ruin many people's day, and now one might get shot at and an hour later be joking and laughing. In a sense, things moved slower and at the same time with lightning speed.

Shanan shared a room with Jenny, and to me the house was quiet...too quiet. Back home, I was the guy who always had a fan blowing, summer or winter, and usually just for the benefit of noise—any noise to not hear every creak and crack, or a canine shuffling to a more comfortable position. Tonight was especially quiet on my own, under four pounds of blankets. It doesn't take too many days without electricity and heat to truly appreciate the luxury we all took for granted our entire lives, or at least mine.

* * * *

After a quick breakfast, we headed to town, leaving Grady, Jo, and Scott to hold down the fort. Grady wanted to come and see his friend, but Judy wouldn't have it.

"We can't risk both of you ending up in there," she insisted.

The golf cart was quicker than I had imagined, and the short few miles to town seemed like mere minutes to maneuver. We arrived earlier than the Sheriff wanted by more than an hour and stopped at Jenny's house first.

It was a neat three-bedroom home with a Cape-Cod style that looked out of place up here. Not glaringly like an orange in a bowl full of apples, but just different somehow. Jenny explained her mom was from Maine and took the ocean with her wherever she went. Inside was more of the same and could have doubled as a shell-and-sign shop. "Life Is Better at the Beach" said one, with another reading "My Other House Is on the Water."

Of course, we met Mama straightaway. She was a medium-sized brown and white older dog with piercing blue eyes.

"Nice Husky," I said, only to be corrected by everyone simultaneously.

"She's an Alaskan Malamute," they all agreed.

"Yeah, that's what I said—a Husky...Malamute—same thing. Like a sweet potato and the other one, the kind they bake with the butter and sour crea..." I trailed off.

I was joking a bit before seeing Jenny walking the house she grew up in with her parents and loyal dog, now empty by half. The feeling was sobering at the very least, and I vowed to pay more attention to the situation at hand. We were here to gather her things for the last time and pay a visit to a great man in jail for a crime he did not commit. Nothing about any of this was funny or lighthearted.

"It's okay," said Shanan, quietly having picked up on my revelation. "We all forget sometimes," she added, although I was pretty sure she never made that kind of mistake.

"Yep, there it is," said Grady in my head. "Reason Number 1203: why you need her in your life." I smiled for a second before getting serious again.

Jenny stuck to Shanan. Although they had only known each other for a day, they could have been sisters, or mother-daughter if they weren't so close in age.

"She's going to need someone, a family, now," Shanan whispered to me. "We can talk about it later."

"Now the hard part," I whispered back. "Does she want to stay here in this house or come with us to another?"

My question was answered as Jenny walked deliberately around the house with a large sports-style duffle bag sporting the Estes Park High School's logo, "The Bobcats," reminding me of the Jacksonville Jaguars' professional football team's logo, only in purple.

Meticulously she crept through the house, carefully placing fragile pictures, a flowered vase, a photo album scrapbook, and the rest from her room. She wasn't coming back, and it was clear to us all.

"I'm ready," she told Judy.

"Are you sure, sweetie? We can always make another trip or two; this is your whole life here."

"I don't want to come back here," she said, tearing up again—"not ever. Come on, Mama," she added, patting her hip and walking out the front door.

"Let me get that duffle bag for you," I said, reaching for it.

"I have it," she replied in a matter-of-fact way that was also respectful.

"Do you want to lock the front door?" I asked.

"No. Someone may need it. I left the food. I hope that's okay?" she asked Judy. "It wasn't much anyway."

"Sure, sweetie. It's just fine by me. It may mean everything to somebody else down the road."

I wasn't surprised, I guess, overhearing the conversation after getting to know Judy, but leaving food that someone may or may not ever eat still made me anxious.

* * * *

We were early to the jailhouse by fifteen minutes, arriving before the Sheriff. His deputy let us in straightaway and even opened Rick's cell so he could talk with his wife privately.

"You look like MLK inside here. Arrested on some trumped-up charge just to make some kind of point," she told him.

"It's just me," replied Rick, "but they are taking great care of me and even leave the cell door open most of the time."

"Sheriff Bradley and I played cards most all of yesterday, only pausing for the Mayor's inspection of my incarceration. Once he left, the cell door swung back open, and we resumed the game."

"I don't like this, not any of it," she said.

"There's nothing to like. We are playing a game of chess, and it's not a quick ending. Who's the girl?" he asked, pointing over towards the rest of us.

"You know the husband and wife you and Grady found out on the highway?"

"Yes... Oh, no," he replied, shaking his head and realizing he never thought about collateral damage. "Does she have siblings or family up here?" he asked.

"No, and she's our responsibility now, although she seems to have taken quite a shine to Shanan. She just showed up at the house yesterday afternoon, looking for you."

"For me? Why?" he asked.

"She wants to sue the Tex man for a million dollars and needs a good lawyer."

"Oh, I see," he replied. "She won't get that but hopefully will get justice soon."

"Alex," he called to me. "Come here for a minute."

"Yes, sir," I replied, walking over to him.

"The Sheriff told you what we need from you, right?"

"Yes, he did, and you can count on me to take it seriously."

"That means campaigning," added Rick. "The real deal, getting to know the citizens of this town."

"Yes, sir."

"Is all that necessary?" asked Judy, once I was out of earshot.

"It is if he's going to be my Deputy Mayor," said Rick, smiling. "Besides, he's up here for the winter anyway. I could use some help, especially at the beginning, and Grady hates politics."

"You're a good man, Rick Holman," she said, giving him a kiss.

"Yes, I am... Supported by an even better woman!" he added.

"Don't you forget it!" she said, playfully.

Sunday was another card day for the Sheriff and Rick, at least the first half. At lunchtime, Rick kicked him out of his own jailhouse, ordering the Sheriff to spend some quality time with his family. "Next week is going to be a grind, starting tomorrow," he pointed out, with Sheriff Bradley agreeing.

* * * *

Judy asked around Saturday afternoon after seeing her husband but could not find a notary on the weekend to sign the complaint.

One she ran into while out walking with her family was a banker Judy knew from town. She and Rick banked there since they had first arrived in town, and when one checking account has a balance with two commas, word gets around the office.

"Sure, Judy, I can take care of that for you, but it will have to be Monday. Banks are all closed Saturdays now. It should be closed every day, but I still go and they are still paying me, only in cash now."

Judy thought that was about to come to an end soon but kept her mouth shut.

"Thank you," she replied. "I'll stop by, say, 9 a.m. on Monday?"

"That's when we open. See you there," said the assistant bank manager.

Sunday was slow at the Holman Ranch. Mama fit right in with Daizy and Scout, and Jenny kept mostly to herself, asking for some alone time. Shanan helped me practice a few short speeches and had me brush up on interpersonal communication, touting my need for a refresher.

"Ouch! Is that a dig?" I asked.

"Nope. Just an observation, and I'm not even getting paid to be your campaign adviser."

"Good point," I replied.

* * * *

Each of us took turns in pairs walking outside but close to the house, paying attention to our surroundings. Judy's neighbor came by with a question for Rick, but Shanan pointed out later to Jo and Scott that it looked like an excuse just to stop by, and I agreed.

"He seems nice enough, but something is off about him. I can't put my finger on it, though," said Shanan.

The neighbor I noticed, as we all did, except for Judy, seemed overly concerned about Mr. Holman's incarceration. Not that he shouldn't care, like any good upstanding rancher who nearly shared a fence with the Holmans, but it was forced somehow—like a fake crier or a soccer player rolling on the ground for the penalty after a mild altercation on the field.

Judy, though, ate it up, which seemed completely out of character for a woman who had everything together.

"Should I say something to her?" I asked Shanan in confidence.

"Don't you dare!" she said, holding up a finger.

"Was that a shush? Did you just shush me?" I asked.

"What do you mean...?" she began to ask, before bursting into laughter.

"I totally shushed you; I'm sorry. Am I turning into my mother?"

Her voice trailed off, and I knew right away what happened. The crazy thing about the world now is that a single word like *Mom, Dad, brother,* or *sister* brought up a ton of memories and what-ifs, not knowing if they were okay and not being able to talk to them.

My own family was the same, and I wished we had all learned how to use a ham radio. But really, who thought we would ever need them?

"I know," I told her, as her bottom lip trembled. "You miss your mom. Your dad is going to make sure she's okay. You know that, right?"

"Yes, I know... It's just Jenny over there," she whispered, pointing across the room to the curled-up ball under the blankets on the couch most of the day. "She is not an adult and is 100% sure she will never see either of her parents today, tomorrow, or ever. It's not fair, and I'm over here crying over my own, who both have a good chance of coming through this unharmed. I feel guilty and privileged, is all."

"Things happen... Terrible things happen to good and innocent people, like Jenny, every day now and before all of this started. It doesn't mean you should feel privileged or bad about your parents being alive. It just means you and I need to step up for Jenny and not make her Judy and Rick's responsibility."

"Do you mean to take her in, like our own?" she asked.

"Yes, that's exactly what I mean—and her dog, the last family she has left, at least up here," I added.

* * * *

Monday morning came early, and it was decided that Grady would accompany Judy to have her document—handwritten neater than any I had ever seen—notarized at the bank before meeting Sheriff Bradley at the jailhouse.

When arriving at the jailhouse, Judy was given a few minutes to speak with her husband privately, or as much as a jailhouse allowed.

"The timing of today's happenings is essential," the Sheriff stated to everyone there, including the four trusted deputies he had left.

"Three of you"—he pointed to everyone except Deputy Jenkins—"and I will arrest the Mayor with this evidence in hand," holding up the signed document. "We have eyes on the Mayor's office and are good to roll, although we will check again before doing so. Also, he's likely to have a few of his goon squad with him, unless the drunkards are still sleeping off last night's hangovers. Either way, it could go down easy, or harder than you expect. Once we leave this building, Deputy Jenkins will release Mr. Holman, and you all will go straight home, right?"

"Yes, Sheriff, that is correct," replied Judy. "I'll take him home straightaway."

"Okay. Then wait for my arrival—maybe tomorrow or the next day—to see how this all plays out. The goal is an election this coming Saturday for Mayor, but I'm not sure we can pull it off so quickly. Get the kid ready and keep your radio on you. When I signal he's in custody, get out and campaign, the both of you."

* * * * * * *

CHAPTER FORTY ESTES PARK, COLORADO

S heriff Bradley and his deputies put on their bulletproof vests for only the second time since he was sworn into office. The first was three years ago when a criminal escaped the Supermax prison in Colorado Springs—not from the inside out, the warden made clear to everyone who would listen, but when his transport vehicle was t-boned by an ambulance moving fast, with sirens blazing. The result was a mess, the Sheriff heard firsthand a few weeks later, but two convicts escaped and were thought to be headed up into the mountains. They were apprehended a week later, or at least the one who was still alive. The other escapee boasted one more kill under his belt before being locked up in a plexiglass cage forever.

Now the vests were a little tighter! "Suck in that gut, boys," the Sheriff called out. "Don't let good living get you killed today!" Sheriff Bradley was joking, of course, but this whole business had him nervous. *I had better get it right the first time*, he thought, *and bring everyone back safe or I will never hear the end of it!*

"All right, gentlemen. We have eyes on him. He's inside, is all we know. No firing of any weapons unless it's self-defense. If he's got any of those barfly boys inside, use the tasers first. I don't need any of us losing our weapons in there.

"Huddle up for a quick prayer... Lord, we are called to bring in a bad man today. Now, I know he's one of yours, like we all are, but he's lost his bearings, I guess. Anyway, keep us safe on all sides, Lord. Amen.

"Let's get this done!"

The four men headed down the street towards the Mayor's office, inside the courthouse. The outside doors were unlocked, and they did their best to walk quietly up the creaking wooden staircase. The two shudder-type doors were shut, with a sign reading "Meeting in Session" taped near the top of the door. Music—some metal band the Sheriff hadn't heard before—wafted under the hundred-year-old doors, with laughing and the sound of pool balls broken up in the initial strike.

"You boys looking for the Mayor?"

Sheriff Bradley jumped, turning sharply around and relaxing just as quickly. "Oh, hi Martha," he said, trying to keep his voice lowered.

"Hello, Sheriff. You don't have to lower your voice around here!" she nearly yelled up from downstairs. That SOB never stops playing that racket up there. Sometimes I wonder what this town is paying him for."

"Me too, Martha," he replied, asking her to wait outside for ten minutes or so.

"Well, okay. I'll get a smoke or two. Just let me get my jacket, then you boys can talk. And tell him to keep the office clean. I'm tired of cleaning up after those ungrateful men—or boys, whatever they are."

"Yes, ma'am. Will do."

He waited a minute until he heard her walk out the front door.

"Sorry about the door, Martha," he said aloud, giving it a solid kick in the middle. Fifty years ago, he likely would have broken his foot on the solid door but add other fifty, plus rusty hinges, and it burst open with a bang. He was right about the pool, just realizing the table was absent last time he was here, two weeks back. The Mayor nearly dropped his cue before holding it up in a defensive stance.

"Mayor Haskins, you are under arrest for aggravated assault with a deadly weapon and trespassing. Raise your hands slowly and turn around."

Click! Click! came the unmistakable sound of several goons racking slides on semi-automatic pistols. The Sheriff's men responded in kind, shotguns at the ready.

"You can't take us all!" said the Mayor defiantly.

"Well, you're right about that, sir. We're just here for you. Unless, of course, your boys give us any trouble."

Truth was, they were probably all involved, but to take them all in now would surely end in a fight. The Sheriff planned to take each of his goons, one by one, over the next week, hoping to ensure safety to all involved.

"Here's the deal, gentlemen," he said aloud. "You can put up a fight right now and risk your life to try and save your new boss here, or you can walk out of here and be down at the bar in ten minutes."

Nobody said a word, with eyes on both sides darting across the room nervously. The Sheriff counted down from ten in silence, not sure which way this thing would go.

"Let's get out of here, guys," said one, maybe a leader of the degenerates, thought the Sheriff—certainly not a core sample of the town's population. "This should cover our pay for the next couple of weeks," he said, snatching what looked to the deputies like two hundred dollars in 20s off the Mayor's desk.

"Hey, you can't take that," said a deputy.

"Let them go," said the Sheriff, happy to be rid of them for now.

The four men stomped down the stairs to the complaining of Martha, talking about being quiet in a government building.

"It looks like it's just us, Mayor. Let's get going; I have other matters to attend to."

"You let me go right this minute, or I'll have your job!" the Mayor screamed, struggling against the deputy who was trying to zip-tie his hands behind his back.

"Can't do that, sir. You've got some splainin' to do," the Sheriff added in his best Ricky Ricardo accent.

His deputy looked confused.

"You've never seen Ricky Ricardo, the bandleader on 'I Love Lucy'? You know, Lucy's husband—the guy? No? You guys are missing out on some classic TV comedy. Okay, Mayor, let's go."

* * * *

A slamming door, followed by a scream and ending with a demand, echoed from downstairs.

"Keep an eye on him," Sheriff Bradley told a deputy. "Jenkins, come with me."

Three men had apparently taken door number one, with $200 to spend at the bar, and the fourth was clearly not so smart.

Martha was scared. Her usually hard and straight-line view of the world was no more. Here before Sheriff Bradley's eyes was a scared little girl in an 80-year-old body.

"Hold on, Martha," he said, slowly walking down the stairs with both his and Jenkins' shotguns pointed in the same direction.

"Son, let's just take a step back here and talk."

"Talk about what?" the goon asked. "Looks like I'm the one who will do the talking now," he added, with his left arm wrapped tightly around Martha's neck and using her body as a shield.

She began to gasp.

"Let her go now, and we can figure this thing out."

"I can't do that."

"At least loosen your grip. She can't breathe!"

The man looked down at his captive, struggling to take in a breath, and loosened his grip as she sobbed.

"Okay, that's a start," said the Sheriff. "Now, what's your name, and why are you back here?"

"I want the money. Oh, and my name is William."

"You guys got the money already, William," pointed out the Sheriff.

"No. We got some money, but not all of it—not by a long shot. If you lock up the Mayor, I'm out of a job, and that cash will be gone by tomorrow. I want the rest of it."

"What rest of it?" asked the Sheriff.

"The seventy large in the safe up there, that's what I want," he replied, as if he had just watched a mobster series on cable television.

"Shut up, you idiot," the Mayor yelled from his office.

"Where do you suppose the Mayor got seventy grand?" asked Sheriff Bradley, only half surprised by the confession.

"From the bank the day after the lights went out. It was nearly $85,000 a week ago, but he can't stop spending it."

"That's a lot of money for a Mayor to have in the bank, don't you think?" asked the Sheriff.

"Wasn't even his; it's from the Town Fund and would have been more if the bank had it on hand. I don't give a crap where it's from or if it's supposed to be feeding orphans. I want it now."

"Or what?"

"Or Martha here has spent her last day in this building…and stop pointing those shotguns at me."

"Tell you what, William. I'm going to lower my shotgun, but my deputy here has to keep his up. It's a start, okay?"

"Yeah, okay. But it don't change nothin'."

"How about you let her go, and I'll give you another $200 from the safe you're talking about. I'm sure we can't get the Mayor to open it up. Right, Mr. Mayor?"

"Go to hell, the both of you!" came the response.

"Let me talk to him and see if I can change his mind real quick," said the Sheriff, asking if Martha was okay and getting an affirmative nod without a sound.

"Make it $500...no, $600. Yeah, $600, and you have a deal. Scout's honor."

Oh, I highly doubt that, the Sheriff thought. "Everyone just stay put, nice and easy."

The Mayor wanted no part of his money division, but he was already gagged, and this meeting was merely a distraction anyway.

"One, two, three...draw. One, two, three...draw," the Sheriff said under his breath, re-membering weekends off in the Academy with his buddies, when they practiced drawing a pistol from a police-issued holster and shooting accurately in seconds, only to do it again. It's all muscle memory, his father would tell him, like how you can drive a car and space out, not remembering the drive but making it home safe. He pretended to be in negotiations with the Mayor while undoing the strap on his holster.

"Okay," he said to Deputy Jenkins. "They are working on the safe as we speak. It shouldn't be too long."

"You're lying!" the Mayor's man said, tightening the grip on poor Martha. But something was different now; her eyes weren't those of a scared little girl but the eyes of a lioness—and a mature one at that.

Sheriff Bradley's hand rested on the butt of his service weapon, and he felt ready for whatever may happen next. But he wasn't. Martha winked, clear as day, followed by stomping her right stiletto heel through her captor's tennis shoe with blood exiting, bright red. He screamed out, loosening his grip enough for her to latch on with her teeth to his fleshy forearm. Another scream followed as he pulled his forearm from her mouth, teeth and all!

Sheriff Bradley drew his pistol like he had done hundreds of times practicing over the years, but this time was different, "real and for keeps," he would say when asked later. The man threw her down to the side, and Martha landed awkwardly, with a crunch, but didn't scream out.

The Sheriff instinctively fired three shots towards the man, although he had never done so before. The first catching him mid-chest with a thump, knocking him backward, the second missing entirely, and the third just above the right eye as he fell.

"Cover me," he said to Jenkins, although it was pretty clear the downed man would not draw another breath. "Martha, are you hurt?" he asked, the question sounding dumb to him before he could take the words back.

"I think so...but I think I broke a bone, maybe two," she said.

"Is it your hip?" he asked.

"My hip? My hip?" she asked again. "I'm not that old, sonny boy," she replied calmly, as if she hadn't just been assaulted and the man lay three feet from her, now silent. "No, it's my ankle, and I don't think I can stand by myself."

She dragged her body across the old wooden floor to her former captor. "These belong to me," she mumbled, grabbing her false teeth from his arm before popping them back in her mouth.

"Did she just...?" the Sheriff asked his deputy.

"Yeah, boss. That's what I saw too."

"Call 911," he said, quickly correcting himself. "I mean, run and get a couple of guys from the hospital now!" he told a deputy. "On second thought, grab the truck and take her there."

"I'm sorry things ended up like this," Sheriff Bradley told Martha. "I never meant to have you involved."

"If it means I don't have to listen to that racket they call music every day, then it's worth a few bumps and bruises."

"Well, that is what it means—if I can hold the Mayor long enough, that is. But it's up to our fine judges now."

* * * *

A 95-pound Martha was easily transported to the Sheriff's truck and then to the hospital down the road. She insisted on riding in the bed, citing a need for some fresh air.

"Do you know," she told the deputies, "that when I was a little girl, my brothers and I all rode to town in the bed of my daddy's truck? Now you can't even have a pet back there!"

They dropped her at the hospital, with the promise by the front desk girl that they would take great care of her.

* * * *

"Okay, guys," Sheriff Bradley told his deputies. "Let's have a little fun. I saw in a movie once where they dragged a safe behind a truck down the highway, and after bouncing around a bit, it popped right open."

The Mayor, gagged and cuffed, could hear the safe containing his future pay and negotiations revenue bouncing down the pavement at 30 miles per hour. *Clunk! Clunk!*...and then a pause as it was tossed into the air before another *Clunk!* The two-mile trip to the jailhouse didn't do it, so the scenic route was employed. It was quick when it came open, like a raw egg cracked into a pan, with the contents strewn across the highway for 50 yards. Back in the day, there may have been a cash money grab on the street, but cleanup today would be easy, minus a few bills here and there swept up by the mountain breeze.

* * * *

"That's my money!" spat the Mayor, once inside his cell and able to speak. "It was supposed to get me through the next year in office, and I want it back."

"First, it's Town money, not yours," replied the Sheriff. "Second, seventy grand won't pay for all of your protection for very long, certainly not a year. And what about the other offices, Courts, Judges, Councils, and my office, just to start? You can't pay everyone."

"I wasn't going to," he said, keeping nothing back. "Let me out of here, and maybe I'll consider your salary as a priority."

"No need, sir. We are moving on as a town and without you. I'll need approval from the City Council, and maybe even the Judges here, but there will be an election for Mayor by week's end if all goes to plan."

"How am I going to campaign if I'm in here, and who's the guy dumb enough to run against me? Wait, don't tell me...it's that hotshot-Not Attorney Rick Holman—where is he, anyway?" he asked, looking around as if he had just thought of it.

"He's gone home," said the Sheriff, almost grinning. "In fact, you're in his old cell. But don't worry, he left it meticulously clean. I can only hope you will be as cordial as he was to my deputies and me."

"Screw you! When I'm out of here, I'll have your job and your head. That goes for every one of you!" he added, pointing to the deputies. "This is *my* town!" he screamed.

"Not anymore," replied the Sheriff, walking out of the building.

"Take the night off," he told Deputy Jenkins. "He'll be all right. And the less you guys talk to him, the better. I've got an election to plan for. I'll be by tomorrow to check in."

* * * *

Rick was glad to be home and grateful his brief incarceration wasn't any longer.

"Alex, let's make a plan," he told me after dinner. "You will start campaigning tomorrow. The Sheriff told me the printers in town are down, so we'll do it the old-fashioned way—good conversation and handshakes. You'll start at one end of town and I will begin at the other. Do you have a campaign slogan?" he asked.

"Well, uh, I was talking with Shanan, and we came up with 'Vote for Alex Kade—the Estes Park Crusade.'"

"Sounds biblical," replied Rick.

"And a bit cheesy," I admitted. "Okay, so what's yours, sir?"

"Well, mine doesn't rhyme, but back in my practice they called me the 'Iron Fist' for the way I hammered cases. So it's something like 'Vote Rick Holman—the Estes Park Iron Fist.'"

"I like Alex's better," said Judy, razzing her husband a bit.

"Yeah, yeah. Okay, it's just a formality anyway," he reminded her. "The citizens are scared and anxious. They all want to know when this will be over and how they can eat until it is. No slogan, good or bad, will change that."

"Oh, now Rick. I'm just kidding around a bit. Lord knows we could use a little humor now and then," she added.

"I know, honey. We've got a big day ahead of us. Alex, remember it's cold outside, so a lot of this will be knocking on doors. If you run into a guy called Tex or your two former travelers, be careful."

"Will do, sir," I said, wondering how many doors I would make it to before I froze to death.

* * * *

The number was 27, give or take a few. I tried my best to keep the conversations short at 10 minutes or less. A few made it easy, slamming the door in my face, and some of the old-timers kept me for nearly half an hour, talking about the old days of the town when run by a competent Mayor with the stones to make the right decisions.

"We're hoping to get that back," is all I could think of to say.

* * * *

"At least I didn't die," I told Shanan at supper.

Scout, Daizy, and Mama made a chorus out of continuous barking at the front door.

"Get in positions," called out Rick, with each of us scrambling to strategically located areas, practiced only yesterday.

Shanan and I had the upstairs, with a clear shot at the front door, with Jenny tucked safely away in an upstairs bedroom. Rick blew out the candles and both lanterns, leaving us all in the dark as I strained my ears to listen above the noise of barking, but I couldn't hear a thing. Someone—Grady, I think—got the dogs in a downstairs room, and the sound was muffled at least. We all strained our eyes to adjust to the dark, and I, for one, expected more gunshots or smashed windows. A flash of light came outside the front window from the end of the drive.

"The light is from up at the gate," called out Rick. "Get ready, everyone, and stay low."

One flash, followed by three, with a four-one-thousand pause, and then two more.

"That's me!" called out Grady excitedly, waiting for the second round to be sure. "They made it! They're here—my family!"

He ran to the front door and swung it open, calling out "Cover me!" just in case, as he made his way towards the front gate.

Grady and his wife were prepared people, his neighbors would say, but he much more than her. She quietly sat back, letting him indulge to a point, and didn't get involved until his second gun safe arrived by truck, maybe six months ago. He talked her out of returning it but had to give full account of his preps, number, and cost.

"Shouldn't I get to spend some money on preps and her on shoes without asking each other?" he asked Rick before it all happened.

The half plan turned out painful for them both, but they did get a basic get-out-of-Dodge plan together, a code phrase if they ever needed to hear the absolute truth next, and a flashlight code with a flash followed by three before the four-second pause and then two more.

"Grady," she called loudly. "Are you here? Rick, Judy, it's us! Can you hear me?"

"Yes, I'm here," said Grady, hearing her voice, shining his flashlight up on his face as a camper might do telling a scary story. Her voice was not the carefree voice he left a week ago, kissing her good-bye in the kitchen at home, but a tired voice—the voice of triumph, exhaustion, despair, and sadness all neatly layered like a sushi roll at a fine Japanese restaurant.

"You made it!" he said, shining his flashlight to the front gate.

"One, two, three, four," he counted. "One, two, three, four," again.

They were a family of six, so there should be five at the gate. He was at a full run now, panicked.

"I'm coming," he yelled, relieved as he approached the gate and counted five heads.

He missed his two-year-old son, Thomas, somehow relaxing seeing his wife holding him in her arms, wrapped in a blanket.

"You made it!" he said, smiling with an audible sigh of relief.

They didn't respond, not one.

Their faces, the faces he had seen since birth and his wife's since high school, were dirty and empty of joy.

"Honey, I know you all must be exhausted, but you're safe now. We're together again. I'll take my sleeping boy," he continued, climbing on and reaching over the gate.

Nobody moved.

"What's the matter, everyone? I'm sorry I couldn't come down the mountain; I would have missed you for sure. This was the plan all along, to be up here with Rick and Judy. Please, can I hold my son?"

She slowly reached out, handing him the boy wrapped tightly in a light blue blanket.

"Hey little man, I've been missing yo..."

Grady paused, seeing his son's face. His eyes were closed, skin pale and cold. "Thomas, son, can you hear me? Can you hear me?" he asked again, his smile gone and replaced by a face no one should ever see on a father—contorted, confused, unbelieving, and scared. "Thomas, no!" he said, pressing his face to his boy's. "Oh, no! Oh God, no!" he screamed, as his wife kneeled onto the cold pavement.

He held his son tight, with seconds of silence before Rick made it up there.

"What's wrong, Grady?" he asked, not getting an answer.

The faces of the Grady family said it all.

"When?" asked Grady.

"Two days ago," his wife replied softly.

"Where?"

"Halfway up the mountain."

"How?"

"I don't know. He just didn't wake up one morning. I kept him warm right on me the whole night, but it was freezing cold and the gear we started with was too heavy. It was just too heavy, and we dropped some on the way...too much, I guess..."

She wasn't crying now; it was clear she had cried herself empty. They all had over the last two days.

"Is everything okay?" I asked, running up to the gate. I didn't get an answer either but quickly understood it was a family matter, and I wasn't family.

* * * *

The Holmans went quickly from a house full of adults to kids aged early 20's and under. The Grady family insisted on sharing one bedroom this night, and we were not properly introduced until the following morning.

Little Thomas would be laid to rest the following morning, and Rick told me in all his years as a lawyer he never saw a man as sad as Grady. I overheard them talking late the first night after everyone had gone to bed. I wasn't trying to listen, honest...but the room we slept in had a vent that picked up the conversation like it was in the same room.

Grady blamed himself for his son's death by not going down the mountain to try and meet them. Rick's response was rational about the odds of running into them, given all of the possible routes they could have taken. Grady replied, "I'm the one who is supposed to be prepared. I should have planned an exact route here, but I didn't...and now my baby boy is dead."

I plugged my ears after that, my heart aching for his family. To be so close to freedom and lose a child, who would never know it, was impossible to understand.

"Can you even imagine losing a child?" Shanan asked me that night. "I don't know what's worse—losing parents, like Jenny did, or a child."

"I don't know," I replied. "But losing a child would be the hardest, I think, because they never get to experience things. Grady's son will never know a childhood friend, who is still around thirty years later; will never know a first kiss or girlfriend. Thomas will miss playing games and sports, graduations, birthdays, family trips; but most of all, he will miss out on his family...this one and the one he could have had of his own. Parents and siblings will miss him growing up alongside them. Finally, the guilt parents must feel if anything leading up to it could have been different somehow. It's so easy, too easy, to look back after something horrible has happened and come up with a hundred things that may have changed the outcome."

I could only imagine how many nights his parents would dream he was still alive, only to wake up to the realization that nothing had changed. "I couldn't," is all I said, suddenly feeling like the guy in college who goes over to a buddy's house, sleeps on the couch, and never leaves.

We gave up our room to Grady's family, as did Jo and Scott, without being asked. The four of us unanimously decided we would ask for another home sooner than later, even if we had to swap out a few times, as homeowners returned by foot. Unlikely but possible, we all agreed.

* * * *

Morning brought piercing sunlight through the half-open shutters downstairs. We camped out in the living room for the night, and I woke up once, disoriented and thinking we were still in the cabin, or maybe my dorm room from college.

I saw Grady first thing, and if I had forgotten what happened, the look on his face snapped me back to reality. I wanted to say something, anything that might make this day a little easier for him. But what? "I'm sorry for your loss?" A greeting card? Maybe "I wish it never happened" or "The good Lord needed him back sooner than expected."

If he were ninety-two instead of only two, any of those might have seemed appropriate, including a Celebration of Life gathering. But I settled on what I did know. Bad things happen, and only God knows why. Grady's little boy is home now, where we all hope to be eventually, carefree and unafraid.

I held out my hand to him awkwardly, and he shook his head back and forth before embracing me. He sobbed nearly uncontrollably, the military man "tough as steel" my father would tell me when talking about his Army days. I knew then and would never forget one thing that can bring any man to his knees, and I prayed I would never feel such pain.

The sprawling mountain home suddenly felt like a two-bedroom apartment shared by 11 people and 3 dogs. Shanan, Scott, Jo, and I needed a place of our own and quick, but I knew Grady's family needed one more. It's one thing to grieve in front of friends and family but quite another with near-strangers around every corner. Thankfully, Judy was on it, having scouted out three houses that would fit the bill. Our gang made her job easier, deciding we four friends would rather share one house.

* * * *

The move was easy and would only take two days since everything we owned fit snugly into a backpack.

"Hey, at least the houses are fully furnished," said Scott, with an excitement I hadn't seen for a few days.

Grady's family took the larger house, also closest to the Holman Ranch. Ours was only half a mile up the road—not bad for spacious Colorado. Jenny had a choice of where to stay and chose Shanan, or us. I should clarify, however, that I was pretty sure I was growing on her, not like a dad but more like an older brother.

From the moment we stepped into the new old house, I never saw her openly grieve her parents again. I know she may have in private; anyone would. But she stepped through the front door and was all business.

* * * *

Back at the Holman Ranch, Jenny said, "Alex, you have the campaign to run, and I'm your manager. Now let's get to work!"

I looked at Shanan, and she put her hands in the air in a "Well, what are you looking at me for?" pose.

"You heard the young lady," Shanan told me. "Now get to work," she said, keeping a straight face, almost until the end.

"So that's how it's going to be?" I asked playfully.

"It sounds like it," said Scott and Jo together, as if they planned it—both laughing.

"Are you *grown*-ups done joking around and ready to get to work?" asked a stone-faced Jenny.

"Yes, ma'am," we all replied, even Shanan.

"Good because you all are going to have a job in this campaign," she added.

"Great! I'm barely in my 20s and already have a sassy teenager in the house," I whispered to Shanan.

"It's okay," she whispered back. "She needs this right now; it's exactly the opposite of grieving. Don't worry. She will settle somewhere in the middle soon."

"I hope so," I replied. "But she is right. We need to get to work, so Mr. Holman gets a fair shot at the position."

"It's kind of already in the bag, though—right?" asked Scott.

"I get it," I responded. "I'm the guy put in to have the illusion of a fair election and a choice for the citizens, but it's more than that. I saw this writeup about a running race where a Kenyan was in the lead with an American, a few paces behind. At the finish line, the Kenyan is confused, thinking he had crossed the finish line, and stopped running a few yards too soon. The American, clearly in second place, yells to him to keep going across the line. The Kenyan doesn't understand English and fails to comply. At this point, the American pushed him across the finish line for the win. When asked later by a reporter why he didn't just cross in front of the Kenyan, the American replied, saying that the victory would not be earned, with a first-place medal meaning nothing and asking what his mother would think if he took it. So, I'm saying I need to give this my all. Nobody knows me, and they all love Mr. Holman, so I'm not worried about rocking the boat. But Rick needs me to give it my all, so it means something to him and Judy and this town."

"Okay, now I get it," replied Scott. "Let's do this thing!"

I pointed to Jenny, asking, "What's next?"

"I'm so glad you asked that," she retorted, pulling out a spiral-bound notebook I hadn't seen before and flipping between several pages, filled with notes. "Fliers. We need fliers, and lots of them. I'm going to need a Mission Statement and a headshot of you, Alex. Not you *now*, of course, but clean-shaven and recently bathed."

Scott couldn't contain himself, laughing out loud. He almost cried.

"You're not off the hook either, rich boy. I need you cleaned up too."

"Rich boy?" he asked.

"That's right. I know the watch you're wearing and the clothes. You probably have a Ferrari parked in the garage back home."

"No, but he does have a Bugatti!" I said, trading laughs with him.

"I'm not sure what that is," she replied. "But it sounds expensive."

"Yeah, like seven Ferraris expensive!" I got out, before gasping for air.

"Okay now, boys," said Jo, with Shanan and Jenny apparently in agreement. "Let's get serious here," she added, tossing a razor in the air to each of us.

"Don't drop it!" she called out, as I wasn't sure if I should try to catch it or not. I mean, whose first instinct is to catch a blade mid-air? I did. We both did and felt foolish seeing the cap on. "You'll have to use soap," she added. "There is no cream to be found."

"Great, just what I need," I told Scott. "A thousand blade cuts on my face."

* * * *

An hour later, only because we took outdoor showers under the rain bucket, we were good as new.

"That's what we call a Navy shower, boy," my grandfather used to say. And besides conserving water, I was now convinced it worked well in the cold.

"You clean up pretty good, Alex," said Shanan, with a wink. "I may just have to keep you around."

The smart-ass in me would have said, "That's a good idea," but I didn't. Maybe I was becoming more mature with all this election talk and sobering loss of life.

Up until this day, I had never known someone personally whose parents were murdered, or even someone who lost a child. Was this how it was going to be from now on? Was this the big change? I thought the power being out was hard; maybe that was just the beginning—the match strike that eventually torched a country, my country, all of ours. For the first time since it happened, I was depressed. I'd never felt it before, although I would have told a school counselor I was. I got depressed when I lost a girlfriend or bombed a test or if the snow was crappy on my paid-for luxury ski trips.

"That's not depression," Shanan reminded me. "It's life."

"What about missing my family I may never see again? Aching for Jenny and Grady, whose worst nightmares became reality? How about what may happen to Beth and Trey or the feeling none of us will survive the next year?"

"Yes," she agreed. "That's depression. We all have some of that now, although it's never even," she added subtly, nodding towards Jenny, who was furiously writing in her notebook.

"More to-dos for the campaign, I guess," I said quietly.

"Maybe," replied Shanan. "Either way, it's occupying her mind. And right now, that's a great thing."

* * * *

"Agreed," I said, going to look for Rick and Judy. "Let me know what we can do around here. We want to carry our weight," I said, getting an "Okay" from Rick.

"Us too," said Scott, Jo, and Shanan, coming up behind us.

"Follow me," Rick said, without expression, heading towards the garage.

"It doesn't have to be big, but I want it deep," he said, handing a pickaxe to me and shovels to each of the others. "The ground is hard, so the sooner you get started, the better. I want it right over there under that big pine." He pointed halfway across the property.

"Yes, sir. We will start right now," I told him.

He was right, and I had never dug into Colorado earth in November—or any other month, for that matter. We got it done, taking turns and smoothing the edges. I hoped we could do the same for Jenny's parents, and Rick vowed to check on them first thing in the morning.

Jenny was the only one who didn't attend Grady's boy's funeral, and nobody made her feel uncomfortable about it. I didn't think I would be joking around again for a while.

* * * *

In the morning, we headed into town—Rick, Scott, me and my new campaign manager—all meeting on the Courthouse steps. Rick excused himself to check on Jenny's parents, I assumed, just saying he would be back in about an hour.

"Are we ready to go?" I called out to Jenny, who was fixated on a street pole.

"Hey Jenny, are we read...."

I saw it as I walked up to her, staring into the eyes of the man who killed her parents. It wasn't him, but a sketch posted all over town now with "Have you seen this man? He goes by 'Tex' and is considered armed and dangerous. Please report to the Sheriff's office if you have any information about his whereabouts. A reward for his capture may be offered," it said in smaller print, handwritten like the rest of it.

"Jenny," I called out, with no response.

"Jenny!" I said again, louder, snapping her back to focus.

Her eyes, no longer sad or fearful, but filled with rage, changed in a second with her announcing, "Let's get to work."

"We will start here," she pointed, walking up to a roughly 6x8-foot map of the town that one may find in a shopping mall—well before the day, that is. "Then we head here, here, and finally here," she added. "Any questions?"

"No, ma'am," I replied. "Lead the way."

It was cold today but not bad mountain-wise, I guessed, because there was a lot of foot traffic on the street. Talking to people was easy, as apparently everyone knew Jenny. Only a few expressed condolences for her parents, leading me to believe that the word hadn't gotten out yet, at least on a large scale.

"Good morning," she would say. "I'd like you to meet my good friend, Alexander Kade, the Estes Park Crusade, who is running for Town Mayor."

The first few times it sounded so corny I could barely keep a straight face.

"I guess she's using my whole first name," I said to Scott after the first one.

He was about to say something back, a joke probably, when she continued. "And this is Scotland MacNaughton III, running for Deputy Mayor."

"We don't even have one of those now—no offense, Mr. Scotland," said an older man. "What kind of a first name is that, anyway?"

"Well, we should have a Deputy Mayor now, and we will soon," Jenny exclaimed, not addressing his name concern.

"What about you, Jenny?" I asked her. "What will you do when this election is over?"

"I'll run for Town Treasurer."

"Aren't you a bit young for that?" I asked.

"Not anymore," she said. "Besides, the current one gave all the Town money to that crooked mayor."

"Then there's probably no money left," I stated.

"Maybe not, but there will be."

"How?" I asked, suddenly realizing I wasn't talking to a 13-year-old girl but a full-on young adult who had apparently thought about this more than I had.

"Have you ever killed a deer, Alexander?"

"No, but I have killed an elk."

"You skinned it and processed the meat, right?"

"Well, no. Somebody else did that."

"But you like to eat it, right?"

"Yes," I agreed.

"Okay, what would you trade for, let's say, five pounds of the meat?" she asked. "How about that watch?" she said, pointing to the one Scott had given me.

"No way! It's worth a lot more than that."

"How much more?" she pressured.

"I don't know, maybe a few deer at least, now."

"How about your boots, or maybe a fishing pole? Can you fix things or sew?"

I paused, shuffling, "I don't know."

"Don't you? Everything is worth something to another. For the hunter who has an entire deer, five pounds may be worth a pair of boots, or a belt, or a fifth of whiskey."

I raised my brow.

"Oh, don't look at me like that, Alexander. I may only be 13, but I know things. The point is, everyone has something someone else wants or needs, and most people have a few talents that they can bargain with. If I'm elected, I'll have Estes Park trading in a week, and everyone will benefit, including the Town."

"Okay, Jenny, who knows things. Please call me Alex, will you?"

"Sure thing, when we're not campaigning. Now, let's go, Alexander. You too, Scotland. We're behind schedule now."

"Maybe she should be running for Mayor?" I whispered to Scott.

"At least we're just the fall guys," he replied. Rick will win in a landslide, no offense, and we can go home. Who is his Deputy Mayor anyway?" he continued.

"Grady, I'm sure," I replied. "He doesn't really need him campaigning, though."

* * * *

"The Sheriff is going to drop her parents off at the Ranch tomorrow," said Rick, quickly approaching us from behind.

"Thank you. I'll let her know."

"Thanks, but I'll do it," replied Rick. "I know the whole story now, and I'm sure she will have some questions. Most of them won't be answers a 13-year-old girl should ever know, so I'll keep it brief."

We walked the sleepy little town streets, just Scott, me, and our sassy manager.

"It's hard to picture," I told Scott, "but they get somewhere around four million people through here in only five months during the summer season."

"Are you sure? Four million people sounds crazy!"

"I know it's something like that—well over a million, for sure, because the streets are packed with sightseers, saltwater-taffy eaters, and those apples with the caramel."

"Candy apples," said Jenny, overhearing. "Do you see any of those, Alexander?"

"No, I don't."

"Good, then we can get back to work? Grab that guy up there," she pointed. "The old guy, I know him."

This grab-and-go strategy went on for several hours, until most of our exposed parts were numb.

"Good job, boys," she concluded. "A few more days and we just might win this thing!"

* * * *

I kept my mouth shut until I saw Rick.

"I don't think Jenny knows that Scott and I are just playing a role here," I told him.

"Why would she? I didn't tell her."

"Oh, okay. That makes sense, I guess. She's pretty good, though. You may want to borrow her for a day or two."

"Welcome to parenthood, Alex. You are looking to be the proud papa of a feisty teenager."

"So, I'm guessing Grady will be your Deputy Mayor."

"We will see," he replied, walking ahead.

"Let's go home. It's starting to get chilly around here," I announced.

"Starting to?" Scott asked me in a low voice. "I've been freezing for hours."

"Where's that Scottish blood?" I asked, shivering myself.

"I must have left it in Dallas!"

* * * * * * *

CHAPTER FORTY-ONE ESTES PARK, COLORADO

S heriff Bradley planned with his deputies to bring in the Mayor's goon squad one at a time, picked up outside local watering holes or passed out drunk at home. Either way, it was to be done in a week. He went through most angles and possible problems, as he always did before arresting anyone, although it was usually for drunken and disorderly conduct or trespassing on an abandoned property, aggravated by general mischief. It was the deputy he forgot about, the Mayor's new friend who, although now fired, had never returned his jailhouse keys and, more importantly, the cell keys.

Mayor Haskins was fed for the night and left alone until morning, or at least that was the plan. The breakout was quick and uneventful, at just after midnight while the small-town citizens slept, most not even hearing about the Mayor's arrest.

* * * *

Sheriff Bradley was second to arrive at work the following morning.

"Jenkins, what happened?" he asked, shaking his head and looking down the hall at the wide-open cell door.

"Well, boss, from the looks of it he broke out or was let out sometime in the night."

"I would say that's an obvious statement!" the Sheriff snapped, feeling frustrated.

"It wasn't me, sir! You don't think I had something to do with it! I just got here a few minutes before you this morning. You told me to go home last night and that he would be all right here by himself."

"Yeah, I did. Sorry to snap at you... Son of a..." he swore, glancing at the keys on his desk. They held down a note, signed by his former deputy, with the words "I Kwit!" written in red crayon.

"No," he said out loud. "You didn't K-w-i-t! I *fired* you—F-i-r-e-d!" He spelled out each letter, as if his former deputy were standing in front of him. "I didn't get his keys. I should have but I didn't."

"It's okay, boss. We'll just pick him up again; I'm ready when you are."

"Yeah, let's hold up a minute. We need to go in with backup. I don't want another person like Martha getting hurt. I stopped by the hospital on my way home last night, and she's doing good, by the way. I'm pretty sure she won't sue our department."

"How can you know, sir?"

"The best lawyer in town is on our side, and I'm sure that business is done now anyway. Let's round up the others," he added, grabbing his hat and locking the extra set of keys in his desk drawer.

"Let me just close the cell door," called out the deputy, walking down the hall.

"I'm going to kill that SOB!" Deputy Jenkins called from down the hall.

"What's wrong?" called the Sheriff, headed that way.

"All I saw before was an empty cell with the door open. But this," he pointed to the cot— "that just ain't right. Who craps on the bed when there is a perfectly good toilet right next to it?"

"The Mayor—that's who. He's sending a message... Let's go."

* * * *

They walked out of the building, leaving the mess for later. "Sheriff Bradley," said the man walking up to the front door and reaching to shake his hand.

"How are you, Judge Thomas? It's been a while," the Sheriff replied. "What brings you to our side of the tracks?"

It was kind of a joke, and nobody could pinpoint why it was still referenced, but apparently there were railroad tracks here in the early 1900s.

"Well, Sheriff, it's the business with you and the Mayor. I would prefer to talk with you both inside. I hear you have him locked up."

"That's right, sir. I did lock him up, but he seems to have disappeared overnight."

"Like a magician?"

"No. More like a jailbreak by a former deputy with a set of keys I forgot to take back."

The Judge of easily sixty-five years laughed. "Whenever I hear of something like that happening, I always picture it like in those old cowboy movies where they tie the rope to the window, and the horse pulls it right off. Nobody ever expects the obvious. With that being said, what's the play here?"

"What play?"

"What are you hoping to accomplish?" asked Judge Thomas.

"Mayor Haskins and his hired band of outlaws, paid with Town funds, no less, shot up the Holman place a few days back. He admitted to stealing Town funds and was adamant about not paying any Town's elected offices, including mine and yours."

"That's interesting; I hadn't heard that part. Do you have any witnesses to that account?"

"Yes, sir. Mrs. Holman and the kids up from Texas, for their part, staying at her Ranch. Plus, my deputies and Martha from the courthouse will corroborate the rest. I aim to call a new election this coming Saturday for the Mayor of this town."

"We have one coming up soon. Can't it wait?" asked the Judge.

"No, sir. I don't believe it can."

"We still have laws and protocols here, and that decision needs to be made in the courts."

"Can I apply for an emergency session, Your Honor?"

"Let me talk with the others, and I'll try to have an answer for you later today or tomorrow. Is it still just Mayor Haskins and Rick Holman running?"

"There's another one, a kid named Alexander from Texas, I think. One of the boys staying at the Holmans now."

"From Texas, huh? So not a resident, I'm guessing."

"Yeah, that's right. But he's here now and stuck, like the rest of us."

"If you two are headed out to bring him in again, hold off a bit, will you? Let's get this thing figured out first. Would you do that for me, Sheriff?"

"All right, Judge. But if he pulls any other stunts, it's game on!"

"Fair enough. I'll get back to you soon."

* * * * * * *

CHAPTER FORTY-TWO ESTES PARK, COLORADO

Mayor Haskins rounded up the usual crew, minus one awaiting an unnecessary autopsy in the town morgue. The rest had left the Courthouse scene before hearing about the stolen money, and now lack of it.

He needed them for a few more days at least and enacted a poorly thought-out backup plan. Scouring his home and a few summer ones on his street, he came up with 14 various unopened hard liquor bottles. If he could pay them with that and keep them playing pool in his office, maybe...just maybe...it would see his sinister plan to fruition.

* * * *

Tex headed back downstairs, pacing from room to room. He had only been cooped up a couple of days, but a wanderer by nature, he was already getting cabin fever.

Still half-dazed from her fall, Beth slept right through his rifling of Trey's pack, yielding $86.

A shave—his first in years and Lloyd Christmas self-haircut, taking 12 inches off the back, added with Trey's uncle's winter clothes, made him look like he fit in up here...well, almost. The base makeup he found in the medicine cabinet was certainly a first for him but the only thing that would even come close to hiding the two-inch scar above his right eye.

It wasn't perfect, and his Southern accent was here to stay, but to say he now looked like his "Wanted" poster would be a stretch.

His story was simple. His name was Trey, and he came up to his uncle's place late summer, following the tragic loss of his wife by some kind of car accident he couldn't talk about. He stayed close to home and didn't make any friends.

His plan was mostly on the go, but he would admit never putting this much effort into a disguise.

A quick conversation, or lecture maybe, with Beth about what would happen if she tried to scream out or get away, and another to Trey through a closed door, with no response, and he was almost ready to hit the town. He let Beth use the bathroom before handcuffing her to the bed, promising he would be back in a few hours.

Just a man out on the town, he hummed, walking out the door and towards town.

I got eighty bucks burning a hole, going to get me some whisky and maybe a roll, he continued, not caring if it made sense or if it rhymed.

The bar was just up from the Safeway store, and he wondered if his old friend Stan, the manager, would recognize him now.

"Maybe I'll pay him a visit just to see," he said aloud.

Back and forth he went on whether to find out, with the final decision stolen from him, as the note on the Supermarket door read "Out of stock—closed until further notice. —Management."

On to better things, Tex, he mumbled, almost forgetting his name was "Trey" now.

The man they used to call Tex was locked away in the barn with an old mattress, garden hose, and scraps of a meal here and there. He was gone—as good as gone—off of this earth, with only a fading memory of what people used to see.

"What can I get you, stranger?" asked the bartender.

"A bourbon, Scotch, and maybe a beer," he said, with a laugh. "Have you heard that one before, barkeep?"

"Nope," he replied, "but then again, I don't listen to a lot of music from Delaware."

"Huh?" Tex replied, not getting the reference. "The well on all those. I'm working on a budget here."

"Of course, sir. I'll have it right up."

The bar was maybe half full, near as Tex could tell, with a few guys just over his right shoulder talking in a near whisper. With no jukebox, radio, or cars outside to muffle the sound, it didn't take a lot for him to overhear the conversation, picking up a few pieces at first, and then a lot more as a dim-witted crew—and maybe one smart one, he thought—were no doubt on their third or more round already.

What started out as a lot of "sirs" turned into "Sure, Mayor" a few times over the next ten minutes. The gist of it, if he was correct, was that the Mayor fellow wanted to hire someone to kill a rival. The offer started at $100 and now stood at $850 cash, with half up front and the other due at job completion.

"That's my final offer, gentlemen," Tex heard. Moments later, the table companions left the bar to shouts of "Cowards!" and "Traitors!" from the Mayor, leaving one man picking up the tab.

* * * *

"Excuse me, mister," said Tex, walking over to Mayor Haskin's table. "I couldn't help overhearing your conversation, or maybe I could and chose to listen anyway... Name's Trey," he added, reaching out his hand.

"Haskins...Mayor Haskins," he replied, shaking his hand and immediately pulling away like he had been buzzed by one of those children's gag gifts.

"That talk you may or may not have heard was just talk. I'm writing a book, a thriller probably, and looking for some information that sounds realistic. You understand, right?"

"Ain't nobody sitting here but you and me now, Haskins, Mayor, sir. You have a problem I may be able to help with."

"How about you buy me another drink?" he continued, as the bartender put three in front of him, "and we'll talk."

"I'm listening," replied the Mayor, "but that's all."

"Oh, sure. Let me set your mind at rest."

"You mean at peace?"

"Yeah, that's what I done said. Now I heard something about an election and another runner-up."

"You mean candidate?"

"Yep. Runner-up...you follow?"

"Okay. Like I said, I need it for my book."

Tex looked around casually before opening his blade and setting it on the table, closer to the Mayor than himself.

"We can do two things here. One, you can stop talking in tongues and tell me about the real job. Or two, you can reach for this here knife. You cut me first, and I'll walk right out the door. But if you're slow, I'll take a finger—maybe two, if I'm lucky."

There was no answer from the Mayor, only shaking his head back and forth.

"Have it your way. On the count of three: one...two..."

"No, no! Wait! What are we doing here? We just met, and now you're threatening me?" the Mayor added, still keeping his voice low but clearly concerned.

"We're just negotiating here," replied Tex. "You need a job done, and I need the money. That's it. It don't get no simpler than that right there."

"I haven't seen you around before, in *my* town."

"Because I haven't been around—just been staying at my uncle's place since the summer."

"Oh yeah? Where's his place?"

"Don't matter. Are you going to grab the knife or give me the job? I'll need an answer by the time I finish my drinks," he added, shooting the first two and chugging the canned beer, with a belch at the end.

"Here you go, sir," said the bartender. "This one is on the house," handing him another beer. This one was a 16-ounce.

"You're not wearing some kind of a wire or some crap, are you?" the Mayor asked Tex.

"You tell me," said Tex, completely removing his jacket and shirt over his head in one motion.

The Mayor jumped back, transfixed on the long scars across his chest.

"Put your shirt back on, man; you look like you've been tortured."

"Oh, but I have," Tex replied, drinking half of his new beer in a single swig. "Now, let's cut the crap and get down to business."

"This guy you need to be gone. What does he look like, and where can I find him?"

"He's black, about 6 feet tall, always wears a tie, and lives up on the mountain."

"No, no. A picture. Do you have a recent picture of him?"

"Well, no, I don't think... Wait a minute. I'll be right back," he said, talking to the bartender and returning with a newspaper. "Here," he pointed to page one. "This is the guy—Rick Holman. He's an attorney."

Tex smiled, never forgetting a face but not saying a word.

Maybe I'll do a two-for-one special with his friend, the other hiker, he thought.

"Okay. Where can he be found?"

"He has a house a few miles up the road. But it's more of a compound, and I think he has a few people staying with him now."

"All right. Where else does he go? A coffee shop maybe? Does he jog? Things like that."

"Oh, I don't know, but he does campaign around town. One of my guys saw him just today, walking right up the main street of town."

"Do you want it to look like an accident, an execution, or what?" asked Tex.

"I don't know about an accident. Maybe. But then you have to leave town right away. And I need an alibi, a good one—like being here or at a restaurant maybe."

"Who's higher up than you in the town?" asked Tex.

"Only the judges, I guess."

"Okay. When it's time, you get seen with one of them, and we're good. Comprende compadre?"

"Yeah, I guess that would work. I can't think of anything better."

"Now for the why," said Tex. "Why do you want him gone?"

"He's going to take my job, that's why."

"Fair enough. I'll take the upfront money now."

The exchange made Tex a man with means, at least for now.

Maybe I should get my own place, he thought. *Out with the old and a new start in life.* He had no intention of leaving town when his business was done.

* * * *

"Hey! Hey, Mayor!" he called out, catching him out on the street. "One more thing. I heard there are a lot of vacant houses up here, with the owners gone now. My place is getting old, and who knows if something could happen to it. Anyway, if I need something down the road, could you find me one?"

"Sure, I guess, but just until this is done," he replied, with no intentions of putting any energy into the project.

"Where can I find you, Mayor?"

"At my office," he called out over his shoulder.

* * * *

Tex returned home, singing most of the way, with a stumble and foggy head he had repeated hundreds of times in the past.

"Honey, I'm home!" he declared, walking through the front door.

To be continued...

ABOUT THE AUTHOR

About the Author

Lance K. Ewing lives with his wife, three boys (Hudson, Jax and Hendrix), Ringo, Mini and Bobo (dogs and a cat) in McKinney, Texas. When he is not at work, he can always be found with his family, preferably outdoors.

Lance grew up in the foothills of the Colorado Rocky Mountains, with the Rockies quite literally in his backyard.

Long Road Home is the first book in his second series.

Follow the link to the next book in the series, The Plan, now available @ https://www.ama zon.com/dp/B09SD1MNS1

lancekewingauthor@gmail.com.

lancekewingauthor@gmail.com. Look for his other series, *Families First*, on Amazon @ https://www.amazon.com/dp/B07QP9W4Y3Visit the Facebook page: *Families First* https://www.facebook.com/groups/447305392509202

BOOKS BY LANCE K EWING

Books by Lance K Ewing

Families First ~ A Post-Apocalyptic Next-World Series ~ A Complete 7 volume series (PG-13)

Volumes 1-7 (EMP)

Volume 1: Families First

Volume 2: The Road

Volume 3: Second Wind

Volume 4: Hard Roads

Volume 5: Homecoming

Volume 6: Battle Grounds

Volume 7: The Change

Long Road Home ~ A Post-Apocalyptic Next-World Series (EMP) (PG-13)

Book 1: Long Road Home

Book 2: The Plan

Book 3: Turning Point (In Production)

Coming of Age under my pen name Kendall Ewing

Bonze (Bo-nes) (On Presale)

Fragile (In Production)

Children's Picture books (ages 3-8)

The Great Toy Revolt (Lost Toys Series)

The Super Great Adventures of Rico the Monkey-Tailed Skink

Nonfiction Health/Medical

(Chronic Pain Quick-Read Series)

The 30 Days to a Better Back Challenge

Printed in Great Britain
by Amazon

47774986R00152